Finch Books by Dionie McNair:

The Abrasaxon's Daughter
The Scorpion's Heart

I0663220

The Abrasaxon's Daughter

THE SCORPION'S HEART

DIONIE MCNAIR

The Scorpion's Heart
ISBN # 978-1-78651-884-2
©Copyright Dionie McNair 2016
Cover Art by Posh Gosh ©Copyright March 2016
Interior text design by Claire Siemaszkiewicz
Finch Books

Published in 2016 by Finch Books Newland House, The Point, Weaver Road, Lincoln, LN6 3QN, United Kingdom.

Finch Books is an imprint of Totally Entwined Group Limited.

THE
SCORPION'S
HEART

Dedication

This book is dedicated to all my family and friends, for without their ongoing love and unwavering support my dream of being an author may never have been realized.

Special thanks to my parents, Doris and Sandy, and my children Joanna, James and Georgia.

And

Also my gratitude to the amazing members of Eyre Writers Inc. for sharing their skills, providing guidance, constructive criticism and unconditional support.

Chapter One

Brianna paused at the top of the steep track scarcely long enough to catch her breath and check that the anjoa fruit had survived her hurried climb intact. A sense of pride flashed through her as she lifted the concealing cloth. The two oval fruit were the biggest and most beautiful specimens she had ever seen. The green skin of both was smooth and shiny—not a blemish in sight. They would be her offering for the Luna Goddess' table in the temple tomorrow night.

With reverent care, Brianna covered them again, and clutching the wicker basket close to her chest, she hurried through the orchard.

A sharp slice of stinging pain cut across her ankle. Her foot jerked out from under her and she toppled forward, the basket flying out of her grip. Her face slammed into the dirt. The air in her lungs rushed out with the impact.

"Oww," she croaked as she lifted her head and gasped for air.

Her basket rested on its side only inches in front of her, but both of her anjoa fruit had rolled away. "No," she cried and pushed herself to her knees as the biggest wobbled across the last inches of grass and slammed into the rock cairn marking the border of the orchard. It split open, the sweet red flesh torn into ragged chunks, juice and black seeds splattering the grass in a wide circle.

"My offering, oh my beautiful offering," Brianna howled as tears blurred her vision.

Somebody snickered. She turned toward the sound. Conal stood legs apart, arms crossed. At his feet lay the second anjoa fruit, still intact. Behind him waited the four boys who made up his bevy — the rich kids, Tobin, Kedem, Fabron and Rayan.

"Bit clumsy, Brianna," Conal said, a smirk twisting his mouth.

She climbed to her feet. One ankle was entangled in a grubby piece of rope. Unease stabbed through her.

"Well, I still have one," she replied, stepping forward to retrieve the fruit.

Conal rested his foot on it, very gently. "No you don't."

"Yes I do, Conal. Give it to me."

"Why should I?"

"Because it's mine. I brought them all the way from the forest," Brianna replied.

Conal scowled in the direction of the smashed fruit. "But you didn't take care of your gift for the Luna Godess, did you?"

"I would have, if you hadn't tripped me," she shouted, flinging the rope in his direction.

"Ha ha, don't blame me for your big clumsy peasant feet."

Rage burned a fiery path through her veins, melting her self-control into stinging sparks inside her gut. She glared at Conal. "Give it back," she said.

"I don't think so, peasant. The boys and I will take the surviving anjoa to the temple. Clearly you can't be trusted with the task," Conal scoffed.

A searing pain wrenched inside her, as if something had broken. She winced but kept her gaze on Conal, trying desperately to hold down the tight pressure threatening to overcome her. "Give it back," she bit out between clenched teeth. Something was wrong. A writhing, spiny ball of wrath twisted her stomach and she could hardly breathe.

Conal slowly bent down and scooped up the anjoa fruit. He cradled it in his arms and stared at her. "You appear mighty mad and all red in the face, Brianna. But you can't make me give it back."

His taunt stoked her rage. Brianna gasped at the painful implosion as her gut twisted, her lungs compacted and her hands sizzled and flexed with lives of their own. She trembled in a desperate attempt to hold the seething fury inside, but it was too big for her, rampaging with uncontrolled violence. Oh raving hojaks, what was happening to her? The power built until without warning it spurted from her clenched fists in a shimmering, pulsing stream that sprayed directly at the jeering boy.

The translucent force hit Conal in the chest, lifted him off the ground, threw him backward then dumped him on his knees in the dust. The anjoa fruit jumped out of his grip and floated in the air, twisting and turning several times before it landed with a soft plop by Brianna's shoes.

The four boys gaped as Conal very cautiously climbed to his feet and dusted himself off. The energy drained out of Brianna as she stared aghast at Conal. Oh moonbeams, had she done that?

"Run. Everyone run. Brianna's bedeviled by a Tyban. Run for your lives," Conal yelled.

The five boys fled, their screams piercing the air in terror-stricken gashes.

Brianna stood frozen, uncertainty swept over her in undulating waves and she swallowed hard on the surge of nausea that swirled in her stomach. She sagged onto a tree stump and covered her face with her hands. Oh fiery moonlight, moonbeams and luna darkness. What was wrong with her? Bedeviled? Oh dear Luna Goddess, no. Tremors raged through her. Her teeth clattered and she was so cold. The anjoa fruit she had fought to recover sat forgotten at her feet as she hunched protectively in on herself.

A light touch on her shoulder was enough to manifest her terror. She screeched and spun around, ready to defend herself.

"Mam," she cried. "Thank the moons."

"Come away into the house, daughter. There has been enough spectacle today to set tongues wagging from here to Okiyarra."

"I'm not bedeviled, am I, Mam? Is it a Tyban?"

Her mother's grip on her shoulders, urging her toward the house, was forceful.

"No, Brianna, it's not a Tyban."

"But something happened... I felled Conal. I was so angry and it just happened."

"I know."

"But how...? What?" Brianna wailed.

Her mother guided her through the doorway and slammed the door shut. "I know, Brianna, because I've been expecting it."

Brianna pushed away from her mother and looked up into her eyes. What she saw reflected there ballooned her uneasiness into real terror. "Expecting what?"

"Sit, Brianna, and I will explain."

"You're scaring me," Brianna whimpered as she sagged into the nearest chair.

Her mother's expression was grim, her face unusually pale as she wrung her hands in the folds of her apron. "I hadn't expected to be doing this alone and I'm scared too, my dear daughter. There are things you do not know and you should have been told well before this happened, and I've been afraid this would happen. If only your father had come."

"Then wait for Da to come."

Tears glistened in her mother's eyes before spilling onto her pale cheeks. "I didn't mean Lek, but your life-force father."

Brianna jerked back, her mother's words like a sharp slap to her cheek. "Life-force father? But you have never said…"

"No, I was forbidden, and now this…"

"This?" Brianna echoed.

"You're coming into your gift—one I'd hoped you would not inherit."

Brianna leaped out of the chair. "No. Don't say it, Mam. Do not say I'm Abrasaxon."

"I'm sorry, my daughter, but you are—well, half anyway. Your father is Abrasaxon, and I loved him very much."

"You loved him, but what about me—left to deal with a half-breed life, not one or the other? The Abrasaxon won't want me and the mortals will be terrified. What do I do now?" Brianna snarled.

"You can calm yourself for a start," her mother admonished. "Being part Abrasaxon is not a tragedy."

Brianna glared at her mother, infuriated by her unsympathetic response. "I don't want to be Abrasaxon, Mam, and why didn't you tell me before? You waited until something happened, that's not fair."

"No, Brianna, it's not fair, but... Well, I had hoped you would not inherit your father's skills because then no explanation would've been necessary."

"Really? You were going to let me simply go on living in ignorance of who I really am? And what of my precious life-force father, where is he in all this deception?"

Her mother frowned. "There is much to explain, but first I must get permission."

"Permission from whom? Whose business is this? Only yours and mine surely?" Brianna said.

"Yes, Brianna, it is about you, but not *just* you. There are others involved here — to some extent the whole village."

"Send the village to the moons for all I care," Brianna cried. "How're you going to fix this for me, *Mother*?"

They both flinched at the loud peremptory rap on the door. As they turned toward the sound, the door crashed open.

"Katrina, you are summoned to the temple. Bring your daughter with you. Tennille seeks an audience immediately," the tall, black-haired woman announced.

Katrina bowed her head in acquiescence. "I knew she would, Alicia. We will come now. It is time to get this over with."

"I don't want to go to the temple. You're the one who owes me an explanation, Mother. It has nothing to do with the priestesses."

Alicia frowned. "You should've taught your daughter more discipline, Katrina, for she will need it now."

Katrina sighed. "She's confused, Alicia. Angry and rightly so. She should have been told."

"Tennille only did what was best, Katrina. Besides, it's too late now. Come, they're waiting." Alicia indicated the open door.

"Not before I get an explanation," Brianna protested, desperate for reassurance as her secure world disintegrated around her.

Her mother shook her head. "Don't argue, Brianna, just obey. We need to go to the temple. This matter is now out of my hands."

Buffeted by apprehension but refusing to crumple, Brianna drew on her anger. She glared at her mother, then over her shoulder at the dark-haired priestess.

"What has it got to do with Tennille, or any of them?"

Alicia's frown deepened. "It concerns us because your presence in this village leaves everyone at risk. Now obey the head priestess' summons," she snapped, waving her hand in the direction of the open door.

Chills flickered through Brianna. *I'm endangering the whole village. Surely they don't blame me for my unfortunate parentage.* She flashed one more savage glance at her mother before she stomped outside, crossed the now deserted square and began the slow climb up the path to the temple, acutely aware of the two women trudging silently behind her.

Nobody spoke until they entered the temple.

"Wait by the altar, Brianna, until you're called. You're forbidden to leave the temple," Alicia instructed with an impatient sternness. "Come, Katrina," she said and walked away.

Without another word Brianna's mother followed Alicia to the priestesses' dressing room.

Brianna sank onto a small stool at the side of the altar. She clenched and unclenched her hands, trying to ignore their trembling and the swish of nervous fear in her stomach. Did her da know she was a half-breed? He was the only father she had ever known and she shivered at the thought of his rejection. Weighed down by pitiful thoughts, she didn't lift her head until she heard the dressing room door open.

The air was thick with secrecy and expectation as the five priestesses filed past the temple altar, their heads bowed and hands concealed in the flowing sleeves of their red robes. Only one spared her a glance — her mother. A furtive, anguished glance that speared dread and uncertainty right into Brianna's heart. For the first time in her life, she felt very alone and afraid for her future.

The impulse to flee was strong, but there was nowhere to go and no one to go to, so she forced herself to be still around the turmoil roiling inside her — to wait with some semblance of obedience.

The oppressive, cloying stillness of the temple wrapped around her as she surveyed the offerings to the Luna Goddess, all the time her ears attuned to any sound from the rear of the temple. Bored with waiting, she amused herself by arranging, and rearranging, the offerings, but as the distraction waned she slumped back on the stool, not moving until she heard hurried footsteps and the rustle of heavy robes coming toward her. She stood in fearful anticipation.

Her mother emerged from the gloom. "A decision has been made, Brianna. Please join us in the preparation room."

"What decision, Mam?"

Her mother shook her head, her expression frozen into a gray mask of resignation. "Come, daughter."

Brianna grabbed her mother's arm. "Mam, please?"

Her mother patted her hand. "I'm sorry, Brianna," she said, and turned to lead the way down the dark, narrow passage to the priestesses' preparation room.

Brianna's heart beat a frantic tattoo. She was acutely aware that the woman walking in front of her, at this moment, was a priestess, not her mother. A sense of abandonment ran coldly through her, over her heart and deep into her soul as the comprehension materialized — her mother could not, or would not, save her from what was to come.

The five priestesses sat behind a huge curved table that dominated the space. Her mother took her place beside the women. Brianna stood alone in the middle of the room, abandoned by the one person she trusted to protect her, and felt powerless to ward off whatever decision these influential women had made.

"Brianna, daughter of Katrina, it has been decided that after the ceremony tomorrow night you will be inducted into the Circle of Fledglings. Your training as an initiate priestess will begin immediately." Tennille's voice rang with a sharp edge of authority.

The world spun. The gloom closed in. She dragged in a deep breath and stared straight at her mother. Brianna saw the anguish in her eyes, but was still shocked when her mother made no move to dispute the head priestess's, Tennille's, mandate.

Brianna sighed then contemplated the head priestess. "I should have two full cycle rotations yet before I'm inducted... You are stealing my childhood and ignoring my plans to join the Watchers for one rotation — to benefit society."

"Brianna, daughter of Katrina, it has been decided. The matter is closed," Tennille snapped.

"No! It is an unfair decision that will have serious consequences for me. I am entitled to know why such a decision has been made. Is it because I'm not a true mortal? Is this why you intend to punish me?" Brianna wailed.

The six women glanced at one another. Brianna stared directly at her mother. Her mother lowered her eyes, but despite her averted gaze Brianna could see the tears that clung to her cheeks.

"You are not entitled to anything, Brianna, but for the sake of future goodwill, I will enlighten you. Unless, Katrina, you wish to?" Tennille did not even glance toward the woman as she spoke.

Her mother peered down at her hands clenched in her lap. It was the slightest of movements but it effectively abdicated her responsibility to her daughter.

Anger sparked to life. Fury fed by confusion and a raw sense of betrayal. "Mam, what is going on here? Tell me, please. Surely for such extremes it must be more than the fact that I'm a half-breed?"

"I can't..." her mother whispered. Her voice cracked into tiny inhuman sounds as she fought to control her sobs.

"Brianna, this decision has been made with your wellbeing in mind, and you needn't give me the evil eye, young lady," the head priestess scolded.

Brianna continued to glare openly at Tennille, despite the priestess's admonishment.

Tennille held up her hands as if to ward off an attack. "We are all aware, Brianna, of the training in weaponry and hand-to-hand combat you have procured for yourself from those who would give it, and we are all aware that your intention was to join the Watchers.

Unfortunately this is not an option for you. Your parentage makes you vulnerable, and the only way we see to protect you is to enclose you in the priestesses' retreat until your father's return."

"You're going to lock me up because by chance my father was some stray Abrasaxon? As far as I'm concerned I have one father—Lek of Tash. Not a true life-force one maybe, but the only one I'll acknowledge." Seething with resentment, Brianna turned again to her mother, but she had covered her face with her hands and the rise and fall of her shoulders told Brianna she was sobbing.

"You do have a life-force father, Brianna, and he is not merely any Abrasaxon. Your mother wanted to tell you about your father as soon as you were of an age to understand, but we forbade it." Tennille's voice had softened a little.

"You forbade it?" Brianna retorted in hostile disbelief.

"We felt it was safer. If you didn't know the truth you couldn't accidentally reveal it to those who would've kidnapped you or taken your life because of your connections." Tennille sat forward, her hands held out in a placating gesture.

"And my life-force father is?"

"Your father is Hakon, the Grand Archon of Okana," Tennille said softly.

Brianna's whole body trembled and her legs turned to mush. She hit the floor with a thud. For a moment a hazy gray fog enveloped her mind, cushioning it from the brutal shock of Tennille's revelation. She struggled to stay in the now even as she felt the hard floor give way to gentle hands helping her to rise, and slip into a chair before cool water was forced between her lips.

"No, this cannot be true," she muttered. "I am only me, Brianna, daughter of Katrina and stepdaughter of

Lek. Mother? Mam, tell me it's not true. Tell me I'm not the daughter of the Grand Archon. Tell me I'm just ordinary, just an ordinary half-breed of no importance."

Even as she asked, she could see her mother's tear-stained face shaking from side to side in denial — denial that her daughter was merely an ordinary half-breed of no importance.

An irate ball of emotion exploded inside her — rage, terror, self-loathing, fear and pain. She slapped at the women around her. The container of water flew across the room and the women retreated when Brianna began to yell.

"Did you make covenant with this Abrasaxon? Am I blessed?"

Her mother nodded. "We made covenant before you were born and we unbound before he left. You were but a babe."

"Get away from me. Leave me alone. It's a lie. It must be a lie." She jumped out of the chair, barged through the temple and outside.

Three steps down the path she crashed headlong into a burly body. Unnerved and angry, she shoved away and kicked out. "Let go of me. I won't. I won't," she screeched.

"Shhh, Anna, love. It's me, your da," her stepfather said and enclosed her in a tight embrace with his muscular arms.

Suddenly she was sobbing — huge, loud, choking sobs. Sobs for her, her mother and even for the whole rotten mess.

He eased her from him. "They told me in the village what happened. It didn't go well then?"

She squinted up into the darkness of his gray eyes and saw sympathy lurking in the depths. "I'm not mortal, Da. I'm not me anymore."

"Don't you fret yourself, Anna, love. This doesn't change who you are or how much we all love you."

"But it's not fair," she wailed as she buried her face in her stepfather's shirtfront. "I don't want to be half mortal, half Abrasaxon…and an Archon's daughter."

"Shh. Don't fret yourself like this. It's not so bad having a drop of magic blood in your veins," her stepfather soothed as he gently stroked her hair with his large, callused hands.

She gazed up at him.

He nodded and a faint smile curled his wide mouth. "Believe me. It's not so bad."

"But they want to lock me away! Can you save me, Da? Can you?"

"Lock you away?" he roared. "Where? How?"

"In the retreat as an initiate…"

"Stupid women! To think that is going to solve the problem. Come, Anna, I will sort this." Her stepfather laid his hand on her shoulder and urged her back into the temple.

"No, Da, you cannot go in there. Males are forbidden," Brianna moaned as she stumbled down the corridor, propelled ahead of him by his anger.

"Forbidden or not, I will be heard on this matter," he stated.

"But, Da, Mam agrees with them."

He stopped so suddenly Brianna was almost jerked off her feet. His grip tightened on her shoulder. "No, Anna. Your mother would never willingly agree to that. They have given her no choice. Fear is a powerful motivator."

Brianna shook her head. "She was crying, but she didn't protest."

"So I will, where she can't," he replied, pushing the door to the preparation room open.

"Halt. There is no invitation to enter." Tennille's voice was sharp and authoritative.

Ignoring the command, her stepfather stepped across the threshold and strode into the middle of the room before he stopped. Brianna stood beside him, trembling with trepidation. These women were powerful. One did not challenge them and expect to escape without censure.

"Halt, I said. Lek of Tash, you have no right to be here. Be gone," Tennille said, rising from her seat and pointing at the door.

Brianna watched her mother. She half rose from her seat, her mouth open as if to say something, her white features accentuated starkly by her red robes. Then with a thump she sat back down.

"I have come to speak on behalf of my daughter, Brianna, whom you intend to punish unfairly because of her birthright," Lek announced.

"She is not your daughter, Lek, for if she were, this situation would never have arisen."

Lek nodded. "True, but this situation is unprecedented. No Abrasaxon has ever failed to return to a child at the manifestation of their gift. Hakon would never break such a promise or fail in his obligation. Something is amiss."

"I agree, Lek, hence our move to protect the village and Brianna herself. It is the ideal solution."

"Moonlight and madness, Tennille. Your efforts are futile. You think the Tyban cannot smell Abrasaxon magic from across the ravine? If they do not know of her existence yet, they soon will now that her gift is manifest."

"But we can shield her."

A sharp bark of laughter burst out of her stepfather. "You think your puny skills can shield the powerful magic that runs through her veins? Even I, as part Abrasaxon, and Hakon's cousin, would not make such a claim."

"Then what do you suggest?"

"We need to find her father. Hakon is the only one who can fix this. Until then we will combine our skills to shield her as best we can. But she shall not be initiated."

"Katrina, what say you? This is of your making. You were so sure he would be here. You assured us when we gave permission for your union to an Abrasaxon."

Brianna's mother struggled to stand. She held the edge of the table for support. "Things were different then. He was a younger son. He was never meant to be called to serve," she muttered then peeped under her lashes at her partner. "Can we shield her, Lek, or would she be safer in the retreat?"

Lek frowned. "She is not safe anywhere, Katrina, but imprisoning her in the retreat will not help."

Anger seethed beneath Brianna's quiet exterior, and as the words flew back and forth and no resolution seemed possible, the tension inside her snapped.

"No! I won't have it," she proclaimed. "Enough, all of you. This is my life you've messed up and can't fix."

In the ensuing shocked silence she pulled away from her stepfather and blundered out of the temple, slamming the door behind her with a satisfying thud.

Desperate to escape from the self-righteous adults determined to organize her life, she hurtled down the street, her golden plaits slapping against her back.

Without pausing, she climbed the fence at the edge of the common land and pushed her way through the newly harvested weepers crop, oblivious to the fine dusting of golden pollen that rose from the stubble and settled on her skin, luminous as moon dust.

It was still and shady in the forest clearing, and with practiced ease Brianna scrambled up to her secret hideaway, a rough platform nailed to the widest branch of the old gark tree. From here she could survey most of the valley as it spread out before her like a patchwork quilt, green and yellow in the sleepy warmth of the afternoon sun. She tucked her skirt up to her knees and settled back against the trunk with her legs crossed beneath her. On a sudden wave of pain and frustration, hot, salty tears filled her eyes and fell unchecked down her flushed cheeks.

A battle raged inside her — to rebel against those who had lied to her, and the unwanted new knowledge that she was half Abrasaxon with uncontrolled magic skills, or capitulate to their demands and the fear that drove them. Bitter resentment toward her mother's deception and her failure to protest the priestess's ultimatum threatened to choke her. *My whole life is a blatant lie. I, Brianna, died today.* The self-pitying thought cut deep.

The shocking revelation of her father's identity had changed everything, turned her world upside down, and if the priestesses had any say, it would be the end of her freedom. There would be no adventures, no journeys to unknown places, no hanging out with friends — solely duty, servitude and ritual.

Surely her father would have wanted more for her than that. Why hadn't he come? Fresh anger boiled inside her, but it was mixed with pain. Even if he didn't love her, surely he owed her the guidance required to master her gift. It was his fault she had the gift, and now it was his fault she didn't know how to use it. Her thoughts tumbled round and round, but no answers were forthcoming. Imprisonment in the priestesses' retreat seemed inevitable.

Unless she ran away... No, that would be foolish and reckless, but... She could go and find Hakon, Grand Archon, and demand that he fulfill his duty as an Abrasaxon father.

Her mind danced away from the thought then back again. It was a bold plan because a journey of that magnitude would be fraught with difficulties. She rolled the idea around in her mind, contemplating the possibilities, and quickly convinced herself it would be better to do something, anything, than be trapped here in flimsy protection waiting for a Tyban to 'smell' her magic. *Besides, if I have Da by my side, I'll be safe.* Yes—it felt right. Calmed by the development of her plan, she rested her head back against the tree trunk as she watched for her parents to return from the temple.

Farther out on the branch a zeppler chittered, his bushy red tail and droopy mustache twitching in delight above overlarge teeth as he plucked a nut from the branch and carried it away to a hollow in a neighboring tree. A couple of branches away a blue-and-white shandina desperately flapped tiny wings in a determined effort to protect the fledgling chicks in the nearby nest from Brianna's invasion of her nesting space. Overhead, the soft green sky glowed with the last of the reaping cycle's late heat. The emotional upheaval had drained Brianna of her energy and as she relaxed, her eyes closed...

* * * *

She shivered and opened her eyes with a start as cool air whispered across her skin. It was cold now and a deep-green gloom had settled over the clearing. "Oh, dear moonlight, I must have slept for ages." She eased the kinks out of her body then climbed down the smooth, thick trunk, dusted herself off and headed toward home at a brisk walk, keen to present her plan to her parents.

It was almost dark and the six moons were rising together above the mountains when she stormed into the cottage. "Mam, Da, I've decided..." Her words died in her throat as she faced the empty room. *Surely they're not still at the temple?* A sizzling burn of apprehension curled in her stomach. Would Tennille hold them for ransom to enforce her edict? Brianna cringed in answer to her silent question. No, not even Tennille would go that far.

She dragged on a coat and snatched up her crossbow, slung it over her shoulder and left the cottage. As she hurried up the path toward the temple, stumbling on unseen rocks and hollows, her dress flapping at her legs, her determination to find her father firmed in her mind. *I will not just acquiesce to their demands, because I have other plans.*

Hoping to slip unannounced into the preparation room, she crept through the side door and tiptoed up the corridor. The door to the preparation room was wide open, but the room was dark and silent. The two white candles on the curved assembly table had burned down to guttering stubs. A tight grip of trepidation wrapped itself around her chest. *This is so wrong.*

"Hello. Anyone here?" she called. Silence engulfed her. Fear rose like bile in her throat and threatened to choke her. She forced it down and took a few slow breaths.

Her eyes adjusted to the darkness as she moved cautiously through the silent building and out of the front door. The six moons were now high in the translucent green of the evening sky. She hesitated in the darker shadow of the portico and peered into the evening gloom. There was no sign of life anywhere. The only things that moved were the breeze through the trees and the undulating shadows of the leaves on the grass.

Fear tingled down her spine and she shivered as if someone's hand had lightly brushed her shoulder. Where were her parents? The priestesses? *Searching for me, maybe. Oh, moonbeams, now I'll be in even more trouble. Better let them know I'm back...and take the consequences for my defiance.* The thought of punishment didn't worry her, but their possible refusal to listen to her plan did.

Nimbly she climbed the wooden ladder to the bell tower. From here she could survey the whole valley, and a peal of the three bells would carry all the way across to the forest, summoning them back to hear her plan.

A small movement in the meadow on the edge of the forest caught her attention as she lifted the clanger to whack the bell, but as she swung it down the clouds swept away from the moons and she could see clearly. The movement was not her parents or the priestesses. She gaped, twisted her arm and brought the clanger to a silent stop in the tangle of her skirts. Horror seeped through her as she studied the shuffling huddle of people moving slowly across the meadow behind the temple. Her hands trembled and the clanger fell with a soft thud at her feet.

"Tyban." The word whistled quietly out before her breath died in her throat and she dropped into a low crouch behind the bell tower balustrade, every inch of her body trembling with disbelief and horror. Tyban, here in Kenon. *Oh, dark moons, a Tyban has taken the whole village.* That word, the name of the dreaded creatures from across the ravine, echoed around and around in her head. Gagging on the sickness that rose in her throat, and struggling to control her limbs effectively, Brianna climbed to her knees and peeped over the top of the stone wall.

In the silver luminescence of the moons she could see a black-robed figure astride an alien-looking whituka with black scaly skin, elongated, saliva-covered fangs and a wide, flat snout with nostrils that snorted smoke. The Tyban's face was hidden in the all-encompassing cowl while skeletal fingers clutched the reins. Jerky movements of other, smaller creatures caught her attention. Hideous pug-nosed beasts with weeping yellow skin herded the villagers, pushing and shoving them to hurry their shambling pace up the rough path. There was no resistance from the captured mortals. She dismissed the repulsive guards as underlings and turned her attention back to the rider.

Brianna felt sick. The stinging burn of apprehension in her stomach turned into the fiery acid of terror. Her da had feared evil, and if this was what he'd feared then she was to blame – she, who had been defiant and rebellious. Her scent had brought the Tyban. Now it was her duty to save her people.

Hidden under the doffer brambles, she moved cautiously through the darkest shadows, determined to get ahead of the slow-moving column. She was panting by the time she reached her chosen vantage point directly before the gorge. From her elevated position above the path she had clear sight to fire upon the Tyban from behind the shielding boulders. Tremors battered through her as she squatted in the dark, watching and waiting. Brianna could make out individuals in the group now, and a putrid stench wafted up on the breeze, filling her nostrils and burning the back of her throat. As she gagged and choked on the bile that rose unbidden, she covered her mouth to stifle the sound, her gaze riveted on the horrible spectacle moving toward her.

Brianna gripped the rock in front of her so tightly her hands trembled with the effort as she forced herself to remain concealed instead of jumping up and hurtling down the slope to smash that creature into a million pieces. Slumped across the shoulders of the whituka, eyes closed, face pale in the moonlight, was her mother, and being dragged behind on the end of a chain was her stepfather, his face bruised and bloodied. Beside him, also chained, was Tennille, her gown torn and blood on her exposed shoulder. With desperate force, Brianna held her cries deep inside as she bit hard on her knuckles in a struggle to bring her terror under shaky control. *How dare this creature, this Tyban, come and mess with my people?* There was no time to think, or to plan. She had to act now or it would be too late. *Oh, Luna Goddess, help me.* And with the silent prayer still echoing in her mind, she fixed a bolt into her crossbow and rose to her feet in one fluid movement. The bolt was aimed directly at the Tyban on the scaly whituka.

"Release them," she ordered.

The column swayed to an untidy halt.

The Tyban glowered up at her. Malevolence emanated from the embers that marked its eyes. It made no move to obey her command.

Her da peered in her direction and shook his head. "No! Run!" His voice was no more than a harsh groan echoed in the narrow cut through and up the cliff.

Brianna wavered between obedience and vengeance then ignored his instruction and steadied herself, feet planted wide. "Release them or die," she declared. Her nerves jumped and twitched as she waited for a response.

The Tyban threw back its head and laughed. The eerie cackle shivered up her spine and made the hairs on her neck stand up. Fury and fear washed over her but the burning tide quickly drained away to cold resolve. She released the bolt. Her aim was straight and true. With a soft *psst* it struck the Tyban in the middle of where its chest would have been. Triumph energized her for a fraction of a second then, in an instant, turned to cold horror as the bolt passed right through the entity and thudded into the dirt embankment behind the creature. The end quivered slightly with the impact.

The Tyban cackled loudly again, but this time the sound turned into a soft whistle that filled the air, hypnotic, irresistible. Brianna felt herself drawn forward. Her feet moved of their own volition. The sound coming from the Tyban tickled her ears and whispered through her mind before the unknown entity raised a clawed finger. "Daughter of Hakon, you will come," it said.

Brianna's innate stubbornness and newly fired up rebellious streak flared at the order. She hardened her mind against the pull, determined to resist the call of the Tyban. Over and over she recited the steady beat of familiar temple chants, and after what seemed like an eternity her own words sharpened and rattled above the whistle. With awkward, shaky steps, she moved backward gradually, all the way to the crest of the gorge. Brianna shuddered with revulsion and consciously repelled the pulsing evil that emanated from below. As she reached the summit, the spine-chilling sound died into a pregnant silence.

Brianna paused for a moment to catch her breath and saw two of the revolting guards moving through the doffer brambles, scrabbling up the slope on their stumpy legs. They were coming for her. Two red fires sparked in the black hollow of the Tyban's face as it pointed at her with a claw-like finger. She turned and ran. Fear and rage pumped her tired limbs into extraordinary efforts. Her lungs burned with the sheer effort of filling them with huge gasps of damp, cold air as she pushed her body past the limit of normal functioning. A stitch in her side almost dragged her to the ground as she fled through the darkness. It was imperative to remain free, for she was the only hope of rescue for her family and friends.

The thump of her pursuers' big, clumsy feet close behind her spurred her forward, but she couldn't seem to get far enough ahead to turn and fire her bow as they chased her down. With erratic leaps and bounds, Brianna crisscrossed the rough terrain on the slope above the village. Her breath wheezed in and out of her constricted throat and laboring lungs. There seemed no solution to her dilemma, and they were closing in fast.

Then she saw it, rising above the horizon in a sharp, angular silhouette—the unfinished soldiers' welcome home monument. She hurtled toward it, stumbling and gasping the last few steps. As her hands touched the cold, hewn rock, she immediately found handholds in the crevices and began to climb.

Something went splat on the rock behind her, then again. Brianna continued to climb. A wet glob landed in the middle of her back. She cringed and tried to shake it off, but it clung to her dress, the wetness burning her skin like acid. The top of the memorial stone was a crumbling platform of rock and mortar barely big enough for her feet. Balanced precariously, she swung one leg over and sat astride the stone tower. A terrible stench wafted around her and she could hear the slap of the creatures' footsteps and snuffling and growling as they circled the base of her refuge.

After blindly scratching around, Brianna found a couple of clefts in the rock and jammed her boots into them. She clenched her thighs tightly against the rock and gingerly slipped her bow off her shoulder, nocked the bolt, dragged the lever back, and waited until the first of her pursuers was highlighted by the moonlight. With a light, controlled pressure, she let the bolt loose. The creature screeched as it crumpled. *Yes! One down, one to go.* She reloaded and waited. It was silent below. *I'm going to make you dust, you rotten little moon rocks. Just show yourself, why don't you?*

It was now obvious to Brianna that they must have some level of intelligence, despite their appearance, and that the second creature was smart enough to keep out of sight. She peered through the darkness, terrified it was going to climb up and get her. The squelching sound from below was barely a whisper, but it was enough. Brianna aimed and released the bolt. It whistled, then thudded into flesh. The creature screeched, and Brianna heard the plop as it hit the ground.

Reluctant to give up her safety, Brianna clung to her unsteady perch for quite a while, but all below remained still and silent. Trembling now with a combination of shock, cold and fear, she slowly climbed down the uneven rock face. A quick inspection confirmed both creatures were dead. Barely able to stay upright on stiff, aching legs, and sagging under a heavy blanket of fatigue and disbelief, Brianna stumbled back home. Afraid of being accosted, she peered into the darkness and jumped at the tiniest sound, but no more creatures confronted her.

The cottage was cold and dark, the fire barely warm embers. Knowing the Tyban would hunt for her, Brianna immediately abandoned any thought of sleeping there. She'd gather some food and go across the stream to the hideout the children of the village had used for years to keep out of sight of demanding parents. It would be warm, dry and well hidden from the intruders.

By the feeble light of a candle, Brianna quickly stripped off her smelly dress and pulled on a pair her stepfather's trousers, a shirt and a vest. They swamped her small frame, but were eminently more practical than a skirt. She gathered up some bread, cheese, fruit, a couple of candles, a flint and two blankets. The eerie emptiness of the cottage played havoc with her senses — every flicker of movement, every whisper of breeze seemed to have a monstrous life of its own. Brianna shivered as she took one more lingering look around, willing with all her being for things to return to normal.

She retrieved her sword from the box under her bed and strapped it around her waist, using the belt to hold her pants up. The metal felt cool and strong in her sweaty hands. Her grandfather, Kassio, had inspired her love of swordplay at the start of the Yabix War, and after he'd passed, she had continued honing her skills with the blacksmith, a retired soldier. Combined with her crossbow, and the dagger she always carried tucked in her boot, the sword gave her a sense of security, somewhat shaky, but something she could cling to when all else had dissolved into a bad nightmare.

Chapter Two

Brianna moved slowly, burdened by her pack and the instinctive need to keep hidden. She didn't delude herself for a moment that their flimsy concealment would protect her from the Tyban, but nevertheless she felt exposed and vulnerable when she left the protection of the trees and climbed down the bank of the stream and scrambled through the reeds.

The small, round stones on the streambed were loose and slippery underfoot. Despite her primeval need to reach sanctuary she waded with deliberate steps, finding her balance and a secure footing before moving forward. All around, the trees loomed, their huge trunks silhouetted by the moonlight, making the almost naked branches appear like grotesque grasping hands in the fractured shadows. Nothing moved. Not even the night hoots were hunting for their supper in the meadow. Only the water whispered softly as it dragged at her tired legs and filled her boots.

Brianna paused a moment before she climbed up to the cave, scanning the valley behind her, studying every movement. Finally reassured she'd not been followed, Brianna pushed the branches aside and scrabbled up to the well-concealed entrance of the hideout. With shaky fingers, she carefully locked a bolt into her crossbow before she slipped into the cavern.

Dense blackness enveloped her and the dank smell of stale air filled her nostrils. A tiny whisper of sound from deep in the cave ignited every nerve ending into a searing frenzy. She froze, poised for flight. Seconds later a stone crashed into her forehead.

"Eeek!" she yelped as she staggered backward. Her finger jerked against the trigger and sent the bolt whistling across the cavern to clatter against the rock wall. Another rock crashed into her shoulder.

"Ouch. Stop that! Who's there?" she yelled as she retreated.

The hairs on her neck spiked with awareness. Her muscles contracted, ready to carry her away, but she held steady, ready to fight. The next missile landed at her feet.

She reloaded the bow and pulled back the lever, her senses beginning to steady, a possible target area lined up. No foul scent assailed her and rocks were pathetic weapons. "Who's there? Come out, or I'll put a bolt in your guts!"

Something scuttled in the corner. "Brianna! Don't shoot! It's me, Conal."

"Light a candle so I can see you," she ordered, recognizing his characteristic whine but determined not to be tricked.

The scratch of a flint sounded loud in the cavern, then the flickering glow of a single wavering candle flame drove the darkness to the corners of the cave and highlighted Conal's thick mop of shocking blond hair and pale, sulky face. It was tear streaked and grubby. Brianna lowered the crossbow and a sliver of sympathy mixed with irritation washed over her. Her forehead still smarted and oozed blood.

"Did you see them, Brianna? Did you? Did you?" Conal sniffed and scrubbed a dirty sleeve across his eyes to rid them of tears. "They took everyone."

"Yes, I saw them," she replied, scanning the cave. The dry, sandy floor was scuffed with footprints, the small ring of stones they had used on the warm balmy evenings of the last moon cycle was still intact, and wekaza webs hung from the roof in gossamer strands, appearing undisturbed for many months.

He watched her, his eyes full of hope, questions and fear. "Is it a Tyban? Why did they take everyone away? What are those horrible creatures with slimy skins and pug noses? What would a Tyban want with us?"

A flash of guilt seared through Brianna. It was she the Tyban wanted, but she wasn't about to reveal her secret right now, and she had no desire to refresh Conal's earlier taunts.

"I don't know what the Tyban wants, or if we can rescue them," she replied, struggling to keep her voice steady.

Conal nodded. "How do we fight a Tyban, Brianna? We're not Abrasaxon."

Brianna felt her heart miss a beat or two then it thudded erratically, and her stomach twisted in knots at Conal's words. *I am, but it's not going to help, only make it worse. If only I had control of my magic.* A sudden storm of anger extinguished the guilt clutching at her. *This isn't my fault. It's theirs.* Tennille's, the priestesses',

Mam's, even Da's and of course her life-force father Hakon's—those who had concealed the truth and failed to protect her. Not that it helped apportioning the blame, for now there was only her. Maybe that was the answer. *I can ransom myself.* Sickness washed over her at the thought, and even as she contemplated the idea she knew it was not the solution. The farther away she stayed from the Tyban, the better. "We need to get help."

"But they got everyone. There is no one to help," Conal protested.

"Not mortal help, but Abrasaxon."

The boy fingered his slingshot, cocked his head to one side and curled up his lip. "Sure, Brianna, we'll simply go ask them, wherever they are, and they will say yes."

"The Abrasaxon promised to keep us safe from the Tyban, so they have to help when we ask," Brianna said.

"Oh sure. And *you* know where to find them of course—a village peasant."

His insult stung and she really wanted to shock him by revealing her identity, but she had enough to deal with right now. "Well, there is no one else," she retorted. "And it's more complicated than that. Things you know nothing about that would scare you to death."

"Well, if you know so much, what're we going to do?" Conal mocked.

"I don't know." She dragged out a blanket and tossed it in his direction. "Try to get some sleep and we'll decide in the morning."

"I can't sleep. I'm hungry."

Brianna sighed as she dug deeper in her pack and pulled out some food. She didn't need his derision to make her feel guilty. "Here, this'll have to do until morning. Then we'll go back home and find some more."

Conal screwed his nose up at the bread and cheese she handed over. "It's not much."

"It's better than nothing, so shut up and eat up," she snapped.

With a sudden unexpected rush, fatigue washed over her, bringing with it a raw angst and dark dread about what tomorrow might bring. In her state of despair, she decided it was best to ignore the grumpy boy, and acknowledged that his fear was probably even greater than her own.

She turned her back on him, stuffed a candle in her pocket for easy use and snuggled down into her makeshift bed. It was cold, hard and uncomfortable. Suddenly she was unable to keep the tears from falling. All she wanted was to be home safe in her own bed, a mere mortal with an uneventful life.

But that life was now behind her, exploded beyond recognition by her mixed blood and the terrifying and unexpected arrival of a Tyban. She felt so alone, lying in the dark cavern side by side with the mayor's petulant son and tormented by her own chaotic thoughts. Resentment simmered along with her sense of betrayal — lied to by one set of adults and abandoned by another. She felt cheated by her father's failure to turn up and bewildered and frightened by the mysterious power that lurked inside her. Where were the Abrasaxon now that they needed them? Why hadn't they come?

Despite being Abrasaxon, she was in no way equipped to defeat the formidable foe that had attacked the village, but her father was. She rolled over and sat up. Hakon was a powerful Archon and he owed her. Moonlight and madness, she would just go and demand his help. Surely he would not refuse her request. Her mother had assured her that he loved her.

Apprehension settled into an icy lump in her gut. The Tyban had called her by name, it had recognized her magic and wasn't afraid of her. Surely her father's name would have been enough to strike fear into any Tyban. Were tonight's terrifying events linked to her father's failure to arrive? Had something happened to the Archons of the Abrogative Direktorate?

A cold shiver trembled through her. No. Surely not. What a terrible thought. The Abrogative Direktorate was indestructible, impenetrable and all-powerful. All mortals relied on their promise of eternal protection from evil magic and the Tyban who perpetrated it. If the Abrogative Direktorate was in trouble, then who was going to save them from the evil that had come to the valley tonight?

Yes, she needed to find her father.

Brianna tossed and turned through the cold, drawn-out night, tortured by the uncertainties, the possibilities and the dangers tomorrow held. By the time the first green fingers of dawn filtered through the shrubbery she was grateful to get up. Her body ached with tiredness, her muscles protested any movement, and her heart felt squeezed out of shape, but she was calmer now than she had been since she blasted Conal with her magic. She had a plan.

After she had packed up her bed, she gently poked the snoring Conal. "Get up, Conal. It's morning."

He groaned and mumbled something unintelligible as he sat up. He rubbed his eyes. "Do we get breakfast?" he asked.

Brianna almost laughed out loud at how normal Conal's question was, but sobered quickly with the thought that things were far from normal — and might never be again.

Without meaning to, she barked in response, "That's all you think about! Here, have this." She thrust more bread and some dried fruit at him. "It's all I've got." Despite her own gnawing hunger pangs, she didn't think she could eat anything. She struggled to get even a few sips of water past the constriction in her throat.

Conal ate in silence, devouring the scorned food with gusto.

Armed with her crossbow and sword, Brianna wrapped her scarf securely around her face to keep out the cold that had developed with the waning of the cycle and waited outside for Conal. The wet moon cycle was about to start and would be quickly followed by the ice cycle. The wind had died with the dawn, leaving a fine mist lying in the hollows and frost on the moss by the stream edge. Brianna scanned the valley. Nothing moved.

Still sleepy, Conal finally joined her. "So what now, Brianna? Are we going to rescue them?"

"No, Conal. We aren't even going to try. That Tyban has powerful evil magic. Neither you nor I are equipped to fight it and win."

"But we can't simply leave them," he complained.

"We have no choice. We need help. I'm going to find my — " She snapped her mouth shut on the word father, gulped and said, "I am going to find the Keeper of the Wisdom. Hildegarde will know what to do."

"But what if they've captured her too? They might have, you know," Conal bleated.

Brianna sighed, resentful that Conal had voiced her own fears. She squashed them down and glared at the boy. "It's not likely because Hildegarde has strong magic."

"But what if she has—"

"Then, Conal, we will go to the Abrogative Direktorate in the Sacred Mountains and ask for help."

"Yeah, right. As if they're going to help us—and that's if you could even find your way there."

His scathing tone cut deep into Brianna's own fragile confidence in her plan.

She turned to him. "Well, do you have a better plan, Mr. High and Mighty Mayor's Son? Because if you do, you better spit it out right now—and it had better be good, or else," she yelled at him, her face right in his.

He backed away from her anger. "I want to rescue them, we can do it—"

"No."

Conal cringed under her explosive negative.

"Well, we can just stay here, in the cave, and wait for someone to help us. Surely the boys will be back from the war, and there's plenty of food in the store," he muttered, all the while wringing his slingshot rubber into a tight coil and releasing it.

"We'd get captured or freeze to death. Besides, the boys who went to the war are all dead—no one is coming back."

"But..."

"No—staying here is not an option, so no more arguments. Today we have to go get supplies from the village. We leave tomorrow."

She could feel his indignation cutting the air between them as they climbed the slope to the village. They hid for a while in the orchard but finally, convinced all was clear, they slipped in between the houses until they reached the store. From the abundance inside, they filled their packs with dehydrated fruit and vegetables, mixed nuts, seeds and strips of dried gort meat. Aware they were heavier items, Brianna chose a limited amount of cheese and cured breket. They would have to hunt on the way to supplement their supplies.

"See all this food, Brianna. We could live off it easily."

"Fine, and when it's all gone, then what?"

Conal shrugged. "I don't know," he mumbled, keeping his head down so he could hide behind his lengthy bangs.

Brianna suspected he was crying so she deliberately turned away, trying to leave the boy his dignity. "I'll check outside to make sure the way is clear. We need to go past the blacksmith's on the way back to the cave to get water bottles and a stone for sharpening my knife."

By the time she had checked that it was safe, Conal was standing beside her, and no sign of tears marred his grumpy expression. Brianna smiled to herself—better grumpy than inconsolable. Expecting him to follow her, she ducked into the road and ran toward the blacksmith's shop, suddenly filled with an urgent need to leave the village. Fear crawled along her skin and seconds later she heard a wet, gluggy snuffle and smelled a stench polluting the air. She paused.

"Help me. Somebody help."

She couldn't decide if it was a trap or a genuine plea for help. She couldn't risk having a death on her conscience so, struggling not to gag, she drew her sword and slunk around the corner.

A juvenile male lay flat on his back in the middle of the road. His feet were bound and he slashed wildly at the space around him with his sword. The blade swung uselessly through the air as two ugly, stinking creatures warily circled him, a fraction out of reach.

Before she could duck back out of sight, one evil, distorted face turned toward her. Its mouth split into a grotesque grin. The huge, fleshy lips pulled back to expose yellowing, pointed teeth that grew at various angles, the tops cracked and broken like a blunt saw blade. The creature chuckled, a harsh rasping rattle that ended with a sickening gurgle. Its yellow-brown skin oozed slime and was marked with huge, weeping boils. Hooded in floppy folds of greasy skin, the deep-set eyes were flashing green slits that glowed with malevolent glee. A wave of nausea swirled even as terror clenched her stomach onto itself. Sweat drenched her trembling hand as she clutched the sword hilt tightly and stepped forward.

"Keep back! It spits!" the stranger yelled.

Brianna brought her sword up as the creature moved toward her and screwed up its face, making the pug nose almost disappear into the wrinkled folds. Without warning, it spat a stream of foul-smelling substance directly at her. There was no time to move as it splattered onto her boots. She stared at the smelly, sticky mess, disgust quickly turning to horror as the slime set into an inescapable binding.

Brianna struggled to free her feet as her attacker squealed in delight. Enraged, she swung her sword and slashed a jagged gaping wound down the beast's side. It staggered back, and high on her first success, Brianna hopped forward and slashed again, cursing as she missed by inches. The stranger was now on his knees, driving his second captor toward the wall.

Hop by hop, Brianna forced the creature toward the corner of the forge, but she couldn't get close enough to deliver a fatal blow. Suddenly Conal was there, his face a mask of hatred as he silently maneuvered into place, a large rock held high above his head. Brianna lunged forward, and as her sword slashed within inches of the concave chest, the creature backed right into Conal's target zone. The boy's face contorted with effort as he brought the stone down onto the flat skull. The creature grunted and turned to face this new threat. Conal immediately backed off, fitting a large, pale-green stone into his slingshot. A glob of spit landed beside his toes. He stepped around it and wound up his weapon.

With a sickening whack, his flying stone connected with the oozing skin. The creature screamed in rage as a blinding flash of light engulfed it. With a sharp crack and a puff of orange smoke, the creature melted into a small, greasy puddle on the ground.

Brianna gaped.

Behind her the other creature screeched as it shuffled hastily away. Conal scrabbled in his pouch. By the time he had another green stone in his slingshot, the creature was halfway to the temple. Conal eyed it, aimed his weapon, and let the stone fly. With a small splat, it hit the creature in the back and its squat legs crumpled. An unearthly wail split the air and as the orange smoke cleared all that remained of the second creature was a puddle of muck on the dusty road.

Conal yelped in triumph and leaped into the air, his slingshot held high. "Yes! Yes. Yes," he whooped then stuffed his precious slingshot into his pocket and pulled out his old dagger. "We'd better get back to the cave. There are probably more around," he said as he sawed through the rubbery bindings around Brianna's ankles.

Released from her imprisonment, Brianna hugged Conal. "Thanks for rescuing me."

He pulled away from her embrace, his pale face flushed a deep red.

Brianna hid her smile by poking the closest puddle with the tip of her sword. "I've never seen anything die so quickly from being smacked in the head by a small green stone."

"It was a Gomahra— Well, at least I think it was," the stranger muttered as he struggled to release himself.

"And how would you know? You're not even from around here," Conal sneered. "And you're a bit old to believe in moonbeams, aren't you?"

The stranger glared at him for a moment then returned to sawing through his shackles of Gomahra spit without a response.

"Leave it, Conal," Brianna hissed behind her hand before she stepped over and helped hack through the last bindings on the young man's ankles. "Who are you?" she asked.

It was hard to assess their new companion's age as he climbed to his feet and dusted himself off. His face was swathed in a scarf of heavy, woven cloth similar to her own. His long-sleeved tunic was grubby and his pants had a hole directly above the knee. Dark gray eyes assessed her. "I'm Amon. I've been fighting the Yabix for the last two years, but now they are all eradicated I'm trying to find a place to call home," he said.

Conal ignored the introduction. "What do you want in our village?" he asked.

Amon glared at Conal. "I came to get food, so I could continue my journey. I couldn't find anyone so I left two small nuggets of zletic on the dresser of this cottage, but I was attacked by the Gomahras before I could leave." He pulled his scarf down to reveal his face. He was young, but carried battle scars — an ugly slash down his right cheek and another partially hidden by his shaggy bangs of dark blond hair. His wide, full-lipped mouth tightened into a grim line. "I only wanted some food. I'm not here for trouble."

"You're here to thieve — to take what you want without payment," Conal blurted out.

"Never," Amon snarled.

"Oh come on, warrior, you can see the village is deserted — easy pickings for the likes of you." Conal screwed his face up in a mask of contempt.

"Enough, Conal," Brianna snapped.

"I'm not a thief. I pay my way or work for what I need," Amon said indignantly.

Conal danced from one foot to the other, clearly desperate to say more to the stranger.

"Conal, go get three water bottles and a couple of stones from the forge then come straight back here. We have to leave the village before more Gomahras come."

"Huh," Conal huffed as he retreated to the forge.

Amon turned to Brianna. "So, what happened here? Obviously it wasn't Yabix or the village would've been razed."

Brianna frowned. "A Tyban, on a scaled, fire-breathing whituka, came with the Gomahras and took everyone away."

Amon's face paled and he glanced around. "Tyban? So where are the good and glorious Abrasaxon when you need them? Hiding in the hills like they were when the Yabix struck?"

His tone was bitter and his expression reflected his anger.

She lifted her eyebrows to express her scorn. "The Yabix are not magic — they are alien invaders. The Abrogative Direktorate will not interfere in mortal affairs. They only promised to protect Okana and Okiyarra from evil magic and the creatures that perpetrated it," Brianna declared sternly. "Specifically the Tyban. And they have, up until now."

Amon grimaced and waved his hands in a half circle. "Well, where are they then?"

Brianna cringed inside, feeling as if she had actually failed to fulfill the Abrasaxon promise. "I don't know, but we need help."

Amon frowned. "There have been no Tyban this side of the ravine for centuries. Why now?"

Brianna shrugged and guilt stabbed at her, but she wasn't ready to share her secret.

Amon frowned. "Well, it's something evil and powerful to bring the Gomahras over the ravine. My grandfather used to tell stories of the days when evil Gomahras were free to roam all the lands and how a strange green stone called the Tomatite destroyed their evil. Legend says a powerful Archon broke the stone into a million pieces over one hundred years ago, and scattered around all the lands so the Gomahras could never return from banishment in the Black Mountains. Only at the risk of death can they cross the ravine..."

"And seeing you know it all, who's the thing on the whituka then?"

Amon flushed at Conal's belligerent tone, but merely shrugged. "I don't know."

"Mmph," Conal muttered.

The single unintelligible sound said more than was fair, and Brianna decided it was time to halt the exchange before open hostilities broke out between the boys.

"Do you have more of those stones, Conal?" she asked.

He searched through his pouch. "I have about a dozen."

Brianna held out her hand and he reluctantly placed one of the stones in her palm. It glowed translucent green and was icy cold. It was strangely familiar, and Brianna tried to remember where she'd seen a stone like this before.

Conal didn't offer Amon a stone. "Now what?" he asked, and eyed Amon's bulging pack with distaste. "I see you've gotten what you wanted. You'll be leaving then?"

Brianna restrained her desire to boot Conal in the shins for his blatant rudeness. There was no need to deliberately drive Amon away. She rolled the stone around in her hand and suddenly she remembered. Hildegarde had them in her medicine bag. She had never explained what they were for.

Amon swung his pack over his shoulder with barely a sign of effort and gave Brianna a rueful peek from under thick, curly lashes. "Actually, I thought I might stay a while. I like to repay my debts."

Brianna nodded acceptance. Amon would be a valuable asset to her plan with very useful fighting and bushcraft skills learned battling in the Yabix War. Conal would have to get used to having the older boy around. If he bothered, he might even learn something from Amon.

Without waiting for Conal to voice another jibe, Brianna motioned them toward the temple. She needed one more thing to complete her preparations for the journey ahead.

The boys followed her without question as Brianna pushed the unlocked door open. The abandoned air in the temple felt oppressive as they walked reverently past the altar. The untouched remains of the Luna Goddess' offerings still sat where Brianna had placed them with such care. The candles were now misshapen lumps of creamy white wax, the charred wicks tiny black splinters in the whiteness. Brianna purposefully turned away, refusing to allow grief and sadness room in her heart. She hesitated only slightly before she pushed the next door open.

Conal balked at entering the preparation room. "We aren't supposed to be in here," he whispered.

"What are we looking for?" Amon asked quietly.

This wasn't his temple, but Brianna could see he respected its sanctity.

"These," Brianna replied as she twitched the velvet cloth aside. On the shelf leaning against a metal stand were two very old, leather-bound books with hundreds of pages each. "The Destiny Books," she said as she turned to Amon. "They explain the mysteries of life to the people of Okana."

He nodded. "We have them too."

Conal backed away. "We can't touch them."

Brianna frowned. "I know the law, but my mother always said these books have all the answers our people will ever need, answers we need now!" With trembling fingers she opened the book with reverent care and touched the pages with a sense of awe. She was drawn to the text in a way she couldn't explain.

Conal hopped rapidly from one foot to the other. "Don't, Brianna — close it, now. Only members of the

Forum and the priestesses can touch the Destiny Books." His voice rose to a high-pitched squeak. "We'll be banished or turned into skerry rats if we dare open the books and read the sacred words."

Brianna hesitated, her hand on the dry parchment. Conal was right. Did she have the right to violate that law? Neither boy would understand how drawn she was by the black letters on the page — the way they almost spoke to her.

With a sudden flash of defiance, she turned to Conal. "Well, nobody will know — unless you tell. We need the guidance that can be found in these books if we are going to survive this."

"But it's against the law," he cried.

She knew the law, but she had heard the tiniest sliver of doubt in Conal's protest. With an impatience that hid how she really felt — afraid, confused and lost — Brianna stared down at him, determined to use that tiny doubt to crush his opposition. "In these circumstances, do you think the law really matters anymore? Those who would enforce it are gone, dead for all we know. Do you know what else to do? Well, do you?"

Conal backed away from her vehemence, his face white and pinched. He grumbled under his breath but kept his gaze on the floor. His mop of white hair covered most of his face, hiding his expression.

"I thought not. And you?" She turned to Amon.

He held his hands up, palms open as if to ward off an attack.

"Well, I suppose it'll be all right...in these circumstances," Conal muttered.

His agreement didn't really make Brianna feel any better as she turned back to the open book, but it was easier if she didn't have to fight him alongside her own fears. The aging paper crackled loudly. Conal flinched.

Brianna frowned. "I can't read it." She peered closer. "I don't understand..." she wailed as she flicked through some more pages. Panic fluttered at the edge of her determination. These books held the answers — but not for her. "It's written in some strange language." Her voice rose, her panic and frustration broke through her show of bravery.

Amon pointed to the illustrations. "Maybe we don't need to read the script."

His tone was even and firm and his suggestion calmed her. Brianna flicked through more pages and felt a sudden flash of excitement as she found a symbol she recognized.

She pointed. "That's the symbol for scorpion."

Amon gave her a hard look, and she shrank back from the glint in his eyes.

"They say the scorpion is only of the magic realm. It's not a creature of this world," he said.

Brianna nodded. "I know," she replied.

She saw undefined emotion flitted across Amon's face, and she felt a bit exposed by his reaction. He remained silent as she continued to turn pages. Page after page had illustrations of grotesque Tyban and alien-like whitukas, each followed by a page of writing she couldn't read. The humanoid Tyban had names, but many of the others didn't.

"Good thing it has pictures," Conal grumbled. "I don't understand this stuff."

Brianna studied Conal for a moment, and wondered if he would have understood it any better if it had been in the common village dialect. She felt a surge of sympathy for the troubled boy who hated school, but struggled with it in an effort to win his father's approval.

She heard Conal's indrawn breath echo her own as she flicked the next page over and let it settle. There was the Tyban, complete with the smoke-snorting whituka.

"See, I told you it would have the answers." Brianna touched the picture with her fingertip. She felt a tingle — an unpleasant tingle. She pulled her hand away then peered closer at the writing, wishing with all her being that she could read the text. Timidly she reached out and touched the page again, drawn to the intricate lettering. She laid her hand on it. The page buzzed against her palm. The text swirled and swam before her eyes. When it stilled, she could read it.

"Zelig — the Sleeping Death. This evil entity spirits mortals away into slavery by casting a sleeping spell... The slaves eventually die of starvation and overwork. Terrorized Okana and neighboring lands more than two hundred years ago... Archon Donavon defeated Zelig at cost to himself and banished the Tyban to the Black Mountains. Zelig actively seeks out those with weaker magic than his to feed on their gift and their life force to increase his own power..." The words died in her throat as burning agony raced up her arm and wrapped itself around her heart. She gasped for breath as the pain squeezed tight. Her knees trembled and her head pounded with incredible pain. Terror tore at her as her vision darkened. She tried to cry out, but her tongue was swollen and dry in her mouth. Panic seared through her as the magic of the book dragged her into Zelig's clutches. She must have made some sign or sound because suddenly she felt Amon's vise-like grip on her shoulders pulling her away from the book. Their combined effort finally loosened the magnetic hold, and, as she dragged her hand from the page, she and Amon fell back and landed in a crumpled heap on the floor.

"It had you under a spell—I thought you were going to be dragged into the book." Amon's voice cracked as he spoke.

"Me too," she said quietly. "Thank you for rescuing me."

She scrambled to her feet and ruefully rubbed her stinging palm and felt the blisters already forming on the skin. "Ouch," she yelped. Now she was angry—she wasn't finished with that damn book.

"How come you can read it, Brianna?" Conal asked.

She shrugged. "I don't know."

Suddenly impatient for answers, Brianna hurriedly flicked through the bulk of the pages, only pausing when the ugly enitites Amon called Gomahras appeared.

She glanced over her shoulder at Amon. "Pull me away if it gets hold of me."

He nodded.

Even though they were only illustrations on the page, she felt a deep sense of revulsion as her palm connected with the crackly parchment. This time she felt a cold tremor creep over her hand. The words swirled and jumbled several times before they settled.

She could feel Amon's warm hand on her shoulder as she began to read. "Gomahras—revolting creatures with minimal intelligence. Often used by more powerful entities for their grunt work. Have been known to infect mortals with Leperatic disease, which is ultimately fatal. The mortal undergoes a slow transformation into a Gomahra, beginning with suppurating skin boils, a debilitating cough and vision impairments. There is no cure. Archon Donavon banished Gomahras to the Black Mountains one hundred and fifty years ago when he discovered the Tomatite stone could destroy them. The Tomatite stone was smashed into a million pieces and scattered throughout Okana, Okiyarra and neighboring lands, striking fear into all Gomahras."

She fell silent as an icy chill invaded her bones. Her knees felt weak. It was as if her bones had melted, and she struggled to stay upright. As she began to sag, Amon's hands encircled her waist and held her steady.

"Better leave it now before it kills you," he whispered as he helped her to a bench.

She pulled free of his helping hands. "No, Amon. I can't stop now. I have to find the Abrogative Direktorate. They are the only ones who can help us."

"The Abrogative Direktorate? What makes you think they are going to help mortals like us, Brianna?" Conal sniped.

She glared at Conal, suddenly tired of his sarcastic negativity. She wanted to shake him, but instead she said quietly, "They will help me, because I'm not an itty-bitty mortal—I'm half Abrasaxon and I have magic in my blood..."

Her words trailed off as Conal began to laugh. It wasn't quite the reaction she had expected.

"You have magic. That's the funniest thing I've ever heard." He chortled as he looked to Amon for support.

Amon merely stared back at him, his face somber and disapproving. Conal's laughter petered out as he glanced from Amon to Brianna and back again.

"How do you think she came to read the book, Conal? I couldn't. You want to have a go?" Amon snarled.

Conal's expression darkened. "No, I don't want to read the books — it's against the law. Just because she has grand ideas of who she is... She was probably making all that moon dust up anyway."

"Oh shut up, Conal. You can think what you like, but I'm going to get help to save our families in whatever way I can."

Conal sobered now. He spun around on the bench until his back faced them. Brianna was angry and hurt by Conal's attitude, but she couldn't let it interfere with her plan. She turned back to the book. The pages fluttered and heaved as she flipped through them.

Finally in the middle of the book she found a reference to the Abrogative Direktorate. She laid her hand on the page. A rush of spicy energy surged through her as the text aligned under her touch. She read the full list of members — seven in all, including her father Hakon, Yosei, Orysat, Rueben, Shakur, Seidet and... One name seemed unclear, and even as she sought to decipher it, the lettering faded into dust. The text outlined the role of the Direktorate, its history and what could be expected by mortals.

Brianna already knew this, so she turned the page. She gasped at the beauty before her. An intricate montage covered both pages. Mythical animals from the twin lands' rich collection of myths and legends pranced across a changing landscape — the landscape that was County Okana — the Sacred Mountains and, on the other side, Okiyarra. Reverently, Brianna smoothed the pages. She could see both Kenon Village and the neighboring village of Oroton. The Sacred Mountains cut the map almost in half, marking Okana's borders. The rivers, plains and mountains formed a patchwork of colors. In the top right hand corner, on the edge of a lake high in the Sacred Mountains was the image of a castle — shining with the clear blues and greens of the living crystal it was made of.

Brianna touched the image, her finger resting for a moment in a solemn salute of respect. "This is where I need to go." Her tentative thoughts solidified into a determined plan as she felt the page tingle and vibrate under her finger.

"Why?" Amon asked.

Brianna stared up at Amon. "The Grand Archon of Okana lives there."

Amon raised his eyebrows, making it clear what he thought of the Archons. "What makes you think he will help us?"

Brianna hesitated. It was hard to reveal her secret, a secret still so new to her. It made her feel exposed and uneasy, but she pushed it aside — he might as well know it all right now. The stakes were too high to worry about her personal feelings. She smiled, letting a feeling of pride replace her uneasiness as she slowly drew her dagger. "Because he is my father."

Conal jiggled back and forth, his slingshot bouncing up and down on his hip. "Your father! A week ago you didn't know who your father was, Brianna — now you suddenly claim to be — "

She turned to face Conal. "I don't claim to be, I am. They told me yesterday after I sent you flying in the orchard. Not Tyban, but Abrasaxon."

"Who told you?" There was defiance in his eyes as Conal glared up at her.

"Tennille."

"Is this why you think you have magic?" Conal whispered, regarding her with scorn still a dark depth in his gray eyes.

Brianna chose to ignore his put-down. Instead she shrugged. "I don't know. My father was supposed to come and guide me, but he didn't. Then the thing — Zelig — turned up. Something is wrong, and only the Abrogative Direktorate can fix it."

"So what do you need the books for, then, if you already know how to fix it?" Conal demanded to know.

Brianna was afraid to look him in the eye — afraid to admit what she was about to do. She took a deep breath, straightened her back and lifted her chin. "I'm going to cut these pages out. The map will guide me to my Abrasaxon father. He is the only one who can fight this evil." Her voice was sure and determined — she had successfully hidden the inner quake of terror that rushed through her.

As she reached for the pages, Conal clawed at her wrists.

"You can't take pages from the books. It's sacrilege," he bellowed.

She pulled away. "I can."

He launched himself at her, his small fists pummeling her ribs. She grunted as the air was forced out and she staggered under the fury of his onslaught.

"You can't. Grand Archon's daughter or not, you can't!" he yelled. "You can't. You can't," he wailed over and over. His childish voice bounced around the gloomy room like a trapped sonat.

Suddenly Conal was pulled from her. Amon held him kicking and screaming, his legs and fists flailing uselessly in the air.

Amon gaped at her. His face was drawn and pinched, the scars that marked his face standing out white and rigid. "We have Destiny Books too. To violate them..." he muttered before he fell silent. Then he shook his head and looked up at Brianna. "It is a terrible crime. Is there no other way?" he asked.

Brianna rubbed her chin. "I don't know who else can fix this mess but my father, and I don't know how to find him without this."

Conal stilled for a moment. Brianna stepped up to the book, shaking as much from the cold and fear of what she intended to do as Conal's attack.

Amon stared up at her. "Do it then," he said.

Conal resumed his struggles, his screeches a stabbing pain in her ears. She hardened her heart against his distress and with three swift strokes she sliced the pages from the binding and lifted them out. The crackling of the pages seemed extraordinarily loud as she folded the dry sheets and tucked them inside her shirt.

She carefully shut the heavy book. "We must hide these books so that when the village is restored they will be here to guide our people," she said then leaned closer to Conal. "Then I, and only I, will answer for this violation — if that is what the people of Kenon decide."

With the deed done, Conal seemed to lose his will to fight and obediently helped Amon pull down one of the smaller tapestries that lined the walls. With reverent care, Amon and Brianna wrapped the books in it. Conal stood back and watched them, his eyes dark with worry and a determined refusal to get involved.

As they carefully carried the books from the temple, Brianna's stomach fluttered with nerves, the stolen pages pressed warm against her breast.

She would have some explaining to do one day. It might be a protracted wait, but she refused to believe she would not be reunited with her mother when this was over, and she comforted herself that their urgent need and the dire circumstances would mitigate what she had done. One day they would all be together, then they would celebrate — even she.

Chapter Three

The first drops of rain splattered them as they walked in silence to the graveyard. In the east corner was the elaborate crypt of Sir Kenton, the famous explorer and revered founder of Kenon.

"What are we doing here?" Conal asked, still sulky about the books.

Brianna drew her sword. "Conal, your great-great-grandfather is about to become the guardian of our Destiny Books," she said, and levered the black stone slab away.

An insidious whistle drifted on the breeze. Brianna immediately spied Zelig, flanked by four Gomahras, almost at the cemetery gates. Before she could react, Conal and Amon both straightened and turned toward the sound, their eyes already beginning to glaze over.

"No. Cover your ears. Don't listen," Brianna shouted as she jumped off the grave and slapped her hands over Amon's ears. With the sound gone, Amon turned and acknowledged her. He nodded, pulled some bread out of his pocket and mashed it into lumps. With a bit of fiddling, he managed to stuff it into his ears as Brianna removed her hands. It wasn't perfect, but it was effective. Conal had already plugged his own ears with his fingers. Brianna gave him some fragments of candle wax from the bottom of the temple candle she had in her pocket.

Zelig and the Gomahras advanced. Brianna tried not to panic when she realized they were trapped inside the enclosed cemetery. Amon had his sword drawn. Conal scrabbled up the highest headstone he could get to and pulled out his slingshot. He loaded it with a green stone and let it fly. One of the Gomahras went down with a grunt and a wail. The other three paused. Zelig urged them on.

He beckoned Brianna. "Daughter of Hakon, come."

Brianna shook her head and backed away, lifting her loaded crossbow. With Zelig immune to her mortal weapons, she aimed at the Gomahra farthest away. The bolt *whizzed* through the air and hit it in the chest. It squealed and collapsed on the ground, its stubby legs waving in the air.

"Daughter of Hakon, come."

The compulsion to move forward seeped through her, muddling her concentration as she struggled to load her bow, and driving her feet restlessly on the spot. She glanced around. Amon was slashing and stabbing one of the Gomahras and Conal, still secure on his perch, had competently dispatched another Gomahra with a Tomatite stone.

Zelig halted. Red eyes blazed in the blank darkness of his cowl as his henchmen fell to their assault.

He pointed a bony finger at Brianna. "You are mine, Daughter of Hakon. Mine."

"Never, Zelig. I will fight you to the end," Brianna yelled.

The evil Tyban threw back his head and cackled. "Fight me, little one? A half mortal against the great Zelig when the Abrogative Direktorate failed to stop me?" The Tyban laughed and laughed as he turned and rode away, leaving the last Gomahra to die in a puff of orange smoke and a faint cry.

She vaguely felt Conal tugging on her arm.

"Brianna, we have to go now. Get your pack. I've put the books in the crypt."

She struggled to focus. Zelig's parting words had shattered her confidence that the Abrogative Direktorate would save them.

"Brianna, hey, wake up. We have to go." Conal begged her to move.

She felt Amon lightly slap her cheeks with cold hands.

"Brianna," he yelled in her face. "We have to go."

She managed to drag her mind back to the present and focus her eyes. With a sharp nod she acknowledged him then reached for her pack. It was raining heavily and Brianna was glad because they could melt away into the gray curtain. Not that it mattered, though, because she knew in her heart that Zelig could find her easily if he had a mind to.

Back in the cave, she huddled in her own embrace by the fire Amon was coaxing to life. Conal and Amon watched her as if they were waiting for her to speak. She couldn't, not right now—not yet. Her thoughts were a chaotic jumble and she hunted through them, desperate to find anything worthwhile to cling to. She felt betrayed by her confidence and bravado that her powerful father would help them.

"Brianna?"

She met Conal's intent gaze.

"You really are Hakon's daughter?"

She nodded.

"Zelig was coming to get you—he knows who you are," Conal whispered, awe and fear making his voice husky.

She nodded again. All too aware of her own vulnerability to any Tyban with stronger magic than her own, she mentally apologized to Tennille for brushing aside her concerns.

"Do you think he was lying?" Conal asked.

"Lying about what?" she responded.

"Beating the Abrogative Direktorate," Conal said, still whispering.

Brianna glanced from Conal to Amon. They were both waiting for her to give them the answer.

She brushed her bangs off her forehead and straightened her jerkin, needing time to produce an answer. "I don't know, but the Direktorate has fought and conquered evil for centuries, so why would they suddenly be defeated now by one entity? Something has happened to let Zelig free of the spell that bound him. Maybe the Abrasaxon don't even know he's free yet and that's why they haven't come."

"Should we still go, Brianna? To your father?"

"Yes. We can't stay here. Zelig nearly caught us today and the Abrasaxon are the only ones who can help to rescue our families."

"But if the Direktorate is destroyed, who is going to help us?" Conal's words were almost a wail.

Brianna leaned forward and patted his shoulder. "There are other Abrasaxon with strong magic who are not Archons, like Hildegarde. There is nothing we can do here other than get captured."

"So it's decided then — tomorrow we begin the journey to the Sacred Mountains to get help," Amon announced as he slapped a frying pan on the coals.

"Yes. Tomorrow we begin," Brianna and Conal chorused in unison.

* * * *

Slimy, rubbery tentacles of Gomahra spit wrapped themselves around her neck and body, trapping her arms at her sides. Her dagger hung useless in her numbed fingers. Round and round they danced, chuckling, eyes gleaming with malicious intent. She twisted and turned, tried to crawl away from her tormentors, all the while screaming for help. Slimy Gomahra arms reached for her…

Brianna gasped as the cold reality of the cave pushed the nightmare away. She curled in on herself trembling and sweaty, her golden plaits around her neck and the grotesque inhabitants of her nightmare still lurking on the edge of reality. Unsure what had woken her, she listened intently, the fear generated by her nightmare still real. By the soft glow of the embers, she could make out the black lumps of her sleeping companions.

It was still raining outside — heavily, with a steady persistent thrum. Slowly she raised herself into a sitting position and peered toward the opening, but except for the sporadic flashes of lightning, she couldn't see anything in the total blackness of the moonless night. Very quietly she got to her feet and, dragging the cumbersome blanket around her shoulders, she went to the entrance.

The roar of gushing water filled her ears for a split second before a crack of thunder blotted it out. She peered down, blinded by the sudden transition from bright light to heavy darkness. Moments later a brilliant, jagged fork of lightning dove for the ground. It illuminated the whole valley, turning the gray curtain of rain into a million silver drops.

A torrent of swirling brown water raced inches from her toes. Logs, frantically struggling animals and the carcasses of those that had given up torpedoed past. Brianna jumped back with a squeak of alarm. The shallow stream that normally trickled a good five feet from the ledge was almost in the cave. She twisted the blanket protectively around her and hovered in the dark, unable to turn away from the macabre scene that snapped into brilliant focus with each flash.

She flinched at a light touch on her shoulder.

"Looks bad. Does it usually get this high?" Amon asked.

She licked her lips her gaze riveted on the water at her feet. "Never." The next flash of lightning confirmed what she feared. "I think...it's still rising."

He squeezed her arm. "We'd better move the gear."

A spasm of cold dread rushed through her but quickly melted into fury. The last couple of days had been a rocky, tumbling ride—from gaining a father, losing an identity, a family and a home, to now facing the prospect of drowning without a chance to right any of the wrongs in the world. *Damn you, Luna Goddess, for wrecking my life. Enough.* She pulled away from Amon and stomped into the cave, determined that he would not see the tears filling her eyes.

By the flickering light of the stoked fire, Brianna and Amon added the few cooking utensils they had used and their blankets to the tops of the packs.

Conal, dragged from a deep sleep, mumbled and groaned as he moved everything else to the very back corner. "It's not going to come in. It never has," he mumbled.

Brianna desperately wanted to have the faith Conal did. In all her sixteen moon cycles, water had never entered the cave — not even at the height of the wet cycle or the thaw — but somehow she couldn't shake the feeling that this was different, and she suspected it was Zelig's influence.

Brianna still had the two temple candles in her jacket pocket, and she checked her flint. Amon added more wood to the fire, and they retreated to the back of the cave. Conal seared them both with a withering look before he promptly burrowed into his blanket and went back to sleep. Amon wrapped his blanket around his shoulders and tucked the ends under his legs like a tent, and soon his head nodded toward his chest.

Brianna sighed and glared at them both before she closed her eyes. Moments later she was compelled to open them again and peer into the comforting glow of the fire. With the boys asleep she felt dreadfully alone, so she stared into the flames, hoping to hypnotize herself into sleep. Instead she wriggled and squirmed, trying to find a comfortable spot, until her blanket curled around her like a very loving squeeze taraqu squashing its prey. Impatiently she untangled herself and tried again. With her eyes closed, breathing slowly, she counted miniature black tunnel diggers in her mind and willed the night away. All the while the persistent sound of the rain and rushing water throbbed at the back of her mind.

Brianna woke with a start. She blinked, but the darkness remained. Stiff and numb with cold, she lifted herself on one elbow and peered in the general direction of the fire. Nothing, not even a faint red glow of embers. She couldn't believe it had gone out. Amon had piled it high with enough heavy logs to last until dawn. Pulling her rug closer, she huddled down and shivered with a paralyzing mixture of cold and dread as she stared intently into the blackness.

Tiny pinpoints of light flickered in the darkness. She stared, rubbed her eyes and stared again. They were coming closer. She stiffened and clutched her blanket close to her body as she steadied her breathing and watched the parade in fascination. She shrieked as something with hairy legs scuttled across her hand. She flicked her hand and sent the unknown creature flying into the darkness. She didn't usually mind wekazas, gezz and elsuda, but in the total darkness, the thought of them crawling on her was unnerving, and it was an effort to fight down the desperate urge to jump up and shake herself.

She fumbled blindly in her pocket for a candle and flint. Her hand trembled so much it took three goes to light the new, tightly rolled wick. Amon and Conal blinked in the feeble light.

"What now, Brianna?" Conal rolled his eyes and scrunched his mouth up in a gesture of impatience.

Then Amon chuckled. "It seems we're not the only ones with wet feet."

In two lines that stretched right out of the candle's feeble glow, thousands of tiny creatures marched relentlessly toward the rear of the cave and disappeared over the rocks into the unknown darkness.

"They won't eat much—unless they're as hungry as me," Conal mumbled, already burrowing back into his blanket.

Brianna shuddered. "Don't say that. It's not funny," she snapped, her level of tolerance for Conal's wisecracks at zero. She hated dark, enclosed spaces, and with the traumatic events of the last couple of days, she had almost reached her limit of endurance. Reluctant to show weakness in front of the boys, she wrapped her arms around her knees and wished desperately for the night to be over.

"Blow the candle out—you won't see them in the dark." There was a tiny hint of a chuckle in Amon's voice.

She gave him a withering look. He shrugged, totally immune to her displeasure, then huddled down.

"The fire's out."

"It's all right, Brianna. We'll get more wood for the fire in the morning."

Not satisfied with Amon's easy dismissal of her concerns, she sat wide awake and on edge, watching with morbid captivation the constantly changing parade as it passed her by. She didn't know how long she'd been sitting in uneasy silence, but as she eased her numb backside and stiff legs, she became aware of something much more sinister at the edge of the candle's dim halo of soft light. She reached out and tapped Amon's shoulder.

He jumped, already drawing his dagger.

She snatched her hand back. "Amon—it's me."

He turned sleep-glazed eyes toward her. "What now, Brianna. Can't you just sleep?" he growled.

She pointed. With the swift motion of a wet cycle tide, the floodwaters were sweeping toward them.

"Oh, mother of moons," Amon cursed. "We'll need to get onto the rocks at the back of the cave."

Brianna laid the candle on the ledge above her head and grabbed one of the packs, and grunting with the effort, lifted it onto the rocky ledge. Amon snatched up his own pack and hoisted it onto the ledge.

"Right, up you get," he said, clasping his hands together to form a step for her to scrabble up.

Barely waiting for her to get settled, he handed her the last pack before he went to retrieve the sleeping Conal, the tide already lapping at his feet. Without even bothering to wake him, Amon heaved him over his shoulder and plonked him up beside Brianna. The water swished around Amon's ankles as Brianna reached down and tugged on his belt so he could haul himself up beside her.

"What's it with you, warrior? Don't like to see people sleep?" Conal grumbled as he rubbed his eyes. He wobbled like a baby beginning to sit up as he adjusted to being awake.

Without a word, Brianna lifted the guttering candle stub and was pleased to see Conal's jaw sag when he realized the shallow lake now covered the cave floor.

"Ummm—well, you're forgiven, you two, for disturbing me," he muttered.

Amon settled down beside her as the candle flickered, spluttered and finally died. A heavy, immense blackness blanketed them, extinguishing all feelings of time, place and equilibrium. As if in a vacuum of nothingness they perched precariously on the narrow ledge above the rising water, unsure of what the future held.

Brianna reached into her pocket, but Amon's hand covered hers.

"Save it for later. We only have that one. We will be all right in the dark," he said softly.

At first the silence was deafening. Then Brianna became aware of tiny scrabbling and squeaking sounds all around her in the darkness. She hunched herself into a tighter ball, her skin crawling at the thought of their invisible companions. The darkness closed in, suffocating and thick. Brianna tried hard to keep her breathing even as the all too familiar panic rose up to swamp all reason.

She'd told herself it was foolish thousands of times, but the fear was always waiting in a small corner of her brain to rise up and overwhelm her if she was confined. A silly childhood game from years ago had created this whituka in her mind.

She'd been determined to win the game of hide-and-seek. It had been her birthday party, after all. The old trunk in the stables had seemed ideal, but unfortunately, her entrance had unbalanced some badly stacked timber, and when it had fallen she'd been trapped inside. It had taken nearly two days for them to find her and by then she'd been hungry, thirsty and maddened with fear.

Her mother's gentle ministrations had helped her back to sanity, but she'd never forgotten the sound of her own shrieks, muffled by her crypt, or the thirst, the darkness and the fear of that stifling, enclosed space. She had always been careful never to go too far back in the cave, always keeping the entrance in sight—until now.

The enveloping blackness closed in and Brianna fought down the urge to jump from the ledge and wade through the deepening lake until she could breathe fresh air and see the stars again. Instead she took calming breaths and listened intently to the boys' constant stirring. It assured her she wasn't alone, and she managed to fight down the panic. Hugging her knees tightly, she rested her face against them and settled down to wait.

* * * *

Time had no meaning in the perpetual darkness, but the cramp in her legs and numb bottom were a fair indication that it had been ages. Other than the odd comment, nobody had spoken since retreating to the ledge, each of them occupied with their own thoughts. Both boys had slipped in and out of restless sleep, showing no concern that Brianna remained bolt upright and wide awake.

Brianna tentatively stretched her back and her body protested the movement, stiff and clumsy from the enforced stillness, and as she eased one leg from its cramped position, her foot slipped from the ledge and became immersed in icy water. A tight band of panic clenched at her chest as she stifled a squeal.

"Brianna?" Amon asked.

"I'm lighting the candle, Amon. I need to see," she blustered.

It took three attempts, but at last the spark flared into life and settled into a steady glow. The shadows receded to the corners of the cave, leaving them in a halo of pale light as they perched on the narrow ledge. Below was a wide lake of black water, the roof of the cave a pale dome barely three feet above the water's surface.

Conal's fingers latched viciously onto her arm. "We're trapped. We're going to drown," he wailed before choking into noisy sobs.

All around them tiny creatures fluttered and wriggled as the volume of his sobs increased and filled the enclosed space with echoes that chased themselves around and around the cavern.

Brianna shuddered as she tried to unlatch his fingers. The last thing she needed right now was arrogant, self-assured Conal's dire predictions and blubbering collapse into terror-filled panic, especially when his imaginings were probably far worse than the real thing.

Her heart seemed to have climbed into her throat. Her words were a mere stuttering whisper. "I suppose we sit it out. We have enough food and plenty of water."

Amon dipped his hand in the inky water and let diamante drops fall onto the mirror surface. "The water's still rising."

Amon's blunt assessment had Brianna struggling to breathe as her next breath jammed in her throat.

At her choking noise, Amon glared at her "Don't you start—"

"I'm not starting—"

"You're scared too, aren't you, Brianna? Like when you were in that trunk."

Brianna felt like she'd been hit in the stomach. "Shut up," she hissed.

Conal retreated, his face pinched and sulky. Amon contemplated Brianna, his eyebrows raised, but she merely shook her head. It wasn't something she wanted to discuss right now.

Something tickled her hand and she jerked away. She lifted the candle higher, her hand tightening on the smooth coldness of the white wax. The golden glow lit the ledge. To her left was a trailing line of oddly assorted traveling companions — black, hairy wekaza tottering on spindly legs, small golden scorpions with transparent shells, scaly flick-tongues with short stubby tails and gentle black tunnel diggers with myopic eyes that blinked in the unexpected light — while bushy-tailed skerry raks scuttled in and out of the rocks.

The light wavered as Brianna climbed clumsily into a half crouch. Slowly she shuffled after the exodus, careful not to massacre the small creatures. They ignored her, intent on their tasks.

"Where're you going, Brianna?" Amon queried.

"I'm investigating."

He'd already cast aside his blanket as he asked, "Investigating what?"

She didn't have an answer, but checking where the creatures were going was better than sitting waiting to drown. She shuffled forward on her knees while her spare hand reached out to explore the craggy surface of the rock where the creatures were disappearing.

She jumped as something closed over her leg.

"What have you found?" Amon asked, leaning forward to see.

"A crack in the rock face. All those creatures have disappeared in there and aren't coming back. I don't think any of them are prone to suicide, so I thought it might be a way out. You know, if the water rises right up..."

Heedless of her intrusion, the creatures continued to stream past. As Brianna felt deeper in the fissure, she fully expected to be bitten by something sheltering in there, but her fingers only found empty space.

"Is it big enough for us?" Amon demanded to know as he pushed up behind her.

Brianna shuffled some small rocks out of the way. "It might be, if we can move some of these bigger rocks."

"Let me past, Brianna," Amon suggested.

The water had risen even more and the ledge was now invisible under a shimmering layer. Her legs were icy-cold and stiff from being cramped and still. As she tried to rise, she staggered. Amon offered his hand. She held it tightly, her fingers interlocked with his, in the hope that his tight clasp would ease her fear of tumbling into the black water. Assisted by his strength to stagger into a half-standing position, she squeezed herself back against the rock face. Amon eased past. For a millisecond Brianna felt the warmth of his body pressed against hers. An awareness and warmth she'd never experienced before rushed through her, but before she could recognize or appreciate the sensations, they were gone. As they worked together to dislodge chunks of rock and heave them into the water, Brianna was strangely more aware of Amon than she'd been before.

Conal jiggled up and down on his knees, impatient to help. "Is it big enough?" he asked for the tenth time.

Neither Amon nor Brianna wasted breath answering him.

Brianna eased closer to the opening. "I'm going in."

Her baggy clothes snagged on the rocks and she scraped her knees as she squeezed through. For a moment, a wave of panic threatened to immobilize her and she struggled to breathe.

Amon steadied her with a hand on her back. "Be careful, Brianna."

Once on the other side of the cavern wall, the crevice widened out and Brianna was able to almost straighten to her full height. Behind her she could hear muffled thuds as the boys continued to enlarge the opening behind her.

"What've you found?" Amon inquired.

His voice passed through the opening and floated from rock wall to rock wall distorted and faint.

"A tunnel. I'm going on." She lifted the candle higher so it cast a wider, if shakier, light.

Wading now through ankle-deep water, she moved cautiously forward. The roof dipped in places and she narrowly missed cracking her head a couple of times, all the while fighting down the need to turn around and run back to the safety of the boys' company.

Her heartbeat thudded dully in her breast as her candle guttered and threatened to go out. Alone in the dark and petrified of being trapped, she turned around and hurried back as fast as the candle flame allowed. Her breath came in sharp, painful gasps as panic squeezed her chest.

Amon was already through the opening when she reached it.

"It's pretty narrow and the roof dips in places, but there's a cool breeze," she croaked.

Conal stuck his head through the opening. "Is it a way out? Where does it go? What if it's a dead end...? What if it doesn't lead anywhere?" Conal's voice was rising to a shrill shriek.

Brianna's barely controlled panic began to increase as Conal quibbled about the tunnel. She wanted to move, be doing something — anything.

"Enough, Conal! We don't have time for childish hysterics. Pass the packs through," Amon snarled.

Brianna, grateful Amon's gruffness had silenced Conal into obedience, dragged her pack on and carefully held her remaining temple candle in front of her. It burned with a ragged flicker but didn't go out. Brianna felt vaguely comforted by the thought of her mother's capable hands shaping these candles for use in all the village ceremonies.

Just when she thought her knees would give out under the strain of walking partly crouched, the floor dropped away in a steep slope. The water ran faster, tumbling over scattered boulders, gurgling and splashing as it headed to an unknown destination.

Brianna rounded the next corner and felt her heart miss a beat. She stopped so suddenly Amon crashed into her.

"Sorry," she muttered.

He grunted and steadied himself. "What's the matter?" He peered over her shoulder.

She held the candle higher. A huge lake had formed across the tunnel. On the other side, the path rose steeply out of the water and disappeared into blackness.

Conal pushed past and went to stand at the edge of the water. "What now?"

"We cross. The water is rising fast—we don't have much time before this cavern will fill."

"Better go then," Conal said as he slipped off his pack, hoisted it onto his head, and waded in.

Amon followed but Brianna paused to remove her jerkin and wrap it around her head, painfully aware of the need to protect the crackling papers hidden in the inner pocket. Despite the Abrogative Direktorate and her Abrasaxon father failing her expectations, she was determined to search for him the minute they escaped from this. It was more than simply getting his help. She needed to know him so she could know herself. Accepting she could never have her old self back, she could, and would, forge a new one — if, of course, they survived the invasion of Zelig and the Gomahras, and this terrible tunnel.

Icy fingers of water curled around her body as she held her pack and the candle higher. She shuddered as a hooded moon taraqu wriggled in front of her, its body as thick as her arm. It could strike so fast you didn't even see it coming, and the only warning it ever gave was a flash of its icy blue hood. The venom from one bite would bring an agonizing end in seconds. She stepped sideways, but the deadly taraqu sailed past, intent only on reaching safety.

On the other side, Conal waded out and shook himself vigorously all over before dragging his shaggy hair off his face. As Brianna emerged from the underground lake she shivered in the sudden draft that whistled along the tunnel and quickly pulled on her leather jerkin to ward off the chill. As she felt in the outside pocket for the map the candle went out, leaving them in total darkness.

Brianna reached in front of her. "Amon?"

He took her hand. "I'm here. Where's Conal?"

Brianna felt him clutching her jerkin. "He's here."

An icy draft blew the candle out each time they tried to light it. Brianna flicked the flint again and again, desperate panic making her movements jerky and uncoordinated.

Finally Amon touched her hand. "Leave it. I have some rope, I'll tie it around my waist and then you tie it around yourselves."

He passed one end of a thin rope into Brianna's hands and she tied a loop around her waist before she handed the end into Conal's hands.

"Are you both secure?"

"Yes," Brianna replied.

"Give me a minute," Conal muttered.

Amon and Brianna stood patiently as Conal mumbled and cursed under his breath.

"Okay all done," he finally said.

They shuffled forward, holding hands.

Brianna heard a thud, similar to a ripe tolufa fruit when it dropped to the ground in a sudden ice cycle frost.

"Ouch!"

"Amon?"

"Keep your head down. The floor's rising," he grumbled.

Soon they were on their knees, pushing their packs in front of them. She couldn't breathe. Rocks scraped at her untidy plaits and loose clothes. A terrifying paralysis began to take hold of Brianna's limbs.

She pulled on Amon's leg as she hesitated.

"Come on, Brianna. Don't stop now," he urged.

Conal pushed from behind, but her legs wouldn't move. Hysterical screams built in her lungs, threatening to escape.

"I can't do this. I can't move," she wailed. Her eyes stung with threatening tears as she choked her cries down.

"Brianna, come on, one step at a time." Amon's voice was calm but firm.

"You can do it, Bri—" Conal barracked from behind.

"I can't!"

"Yes, you can," both boys said loudly in unison.

Brianna shook her head in a hopeless gesture that Amon couldn't see.

"Move, Brianna."

Amon's order was clipped and harsh, but Brianna heard the tremor of anxiety in his voice. She wanted to obey but she couldn't.

"I'm warning you, Brianna. I will do something very unpleasant to you if you don't move."

The tremor was gone. Now his voice was full of angry threat — enough for her to clutch what tiny remnants of sanity remained. With Conal pushing from behind and Amon tugging hard at the rope around her waist, she dragged her knees painfully across the sand. With her head down and her eyes squeezed shut, Brianna tried to ignore the rocks digging into her back as she shuffled forward. She would have frozen again but the boys wouldn't let her. Their combined effort kept her moving.

"I can see a light!" Amon yelled. His voice buzzed with hope and excitement.

Brianna opened her eyes and saw a pale glow. But the floor continued to rise, eventually forcing them to wriggle painfully forward on their stomachs, their packs almost jamming the space.

Brianna winced as her nails ripped away, and blood from her grazed palms was warm and sticky between her fingers, but with the end in sight her panic had faded to a dull thud of her heart.

Suddenly Amon's boots disappeared and sunlight poured into the tunnel. Brianna blinked as the glare blinded her, then Amon dragged her upward and she was free. Everything shimmered and swayed and her knees threatened to give way. Her heart danced with excited flips as she gulped in huge lungfuls of fresh air.

She observed the overcast sky and the one lone moon riding high above the horizon, and gave thanks for the fresh breeze that caressed her face.

Conal scrabbled up behind her, shielding his eyes from the brightness. "Where are we?" he muttered as he stumbled forward.

Brianna took one more deep, sighing breath and turned to inspect their destination.

A smile tugged at the corners of her mouth and she felt a rush of energy wash over her as she took in the austere furnishings, spell books and paraphernalia for creating spells and potions.

"Exactly where we need to be — Hildegarde's cave," she said very quietly.

Chapter Four

Brianna felt almost lighthearted for the first time since the Tyban had taken their families away. Hildegarde had Abrasaxon blood and, as appointed Keeper of the Wisdom, connections to the Archons. She would help them find Hakon.

Brianna wondered where the gentle old lady was. She had developed a deep affection for Hildegarde when she had been her mother's mentor in the healing arts and sponsor to become the Healing Priestess of the Temple of the Luna Goddess. Brianna felt none of the irrational fear others sometimes felt toward the wise old woman of the forests.

Amon and Conal crept cautiously up behind her.

"It doesn't appear as if the occupants have been here for a while," Amon commented. He brushed his hand through a thick layer of dust on the bench.

High in the cathedral roof of the cavern, sonats and eight-legged wekaza had taken up residence. Brianna surveyed the space and noticed for the first time that the cave had a deserted feel. Her sense of hope and relief faded, pushed aside by her darkest thoughts. The weight of responsibility rushed back to torment her. For one glorious moment, she had hoped the old woman would provide her with guidance.

"Perhaps she's gone down to the village." But even as she said it, she knew it was wishful thinking. Hildegarde rarely went to the village. Besides, Brianna felt from the coldness of the belongings that the old healer had been gone for several days at least.

Amon grabbed a set of snares from his pack. "Come on. Let's go and get our bearings. Tomorrow we'll go to the village for help. Maybe this Hildegarde will be there."

Conal cast Brianna a worried look but followed Amon outside in silence.

Brianna continued her exploration of the cave, heartily shaking the colorful wall hangings free of dust and straightening fallen objects. Finally satisfied that the cave was indeed empty, she borrowed Hildegarde's comb and soap and headed for the stream.

Farther up the slope, Amon was lying on his stomach, his arm immersed to the elbow in the slow-flowing water. Conal knelt beside him, staring eagerly into the gloomy depths. The moss was soft and cool on her scraped and bruised knees when she knelt down beside them.

With a quick jerk, Amon flicked a large, fat qymaten onto the bank. It flopped helplessly, glinting in the faded sunlight. Moments later another followed.

"That's enough. Let's go eat," he said.

Conal grabbed one of the gasping qymaten. "Good. I'm starving."

Amon and Brianna exchanged amused glances. Conal was always starving.

While Amon cleaned the fish, Brianna washed some of the grime from her skin and combed her tangled hair then replaited her braids. She felt almost normal again, except for the dull ache of loss that filled her chest and a vague, uneasy feeling that wouldn't let her rest. On the way back to the cave, she detoured through a small thicket and collected an armful of wood to supplement what Conal had found. A traveler expected to replace all goods used from another's home. Soon the delicious smell of roasting qymaten made her mouth water and awakened a ferocious hunger born of exertion and faded fear.

There was nothing left but two white skeletons attached to heads when they sat back, sated. Exhausted by the sleepless night and made drowsy by the food, they all dozed restlessly well into the afternoon.

The other two were still asleep when Brianna awoke. She tiptoed to the back of the cave and began to systematically search Hildegarde's home, searching for a clue to her whereabouts.

"What are you doing, Brianna?" Amon asked as he came up behind her.

She replaced yet another stopper in a jar. "I was seeking some clue to her whereabouts, but there's nothing. It's as if she's vanished without a trace — the same as the people from the village. These are her spare healing remedies, but she's taken her medicine bag."

Amon scrutinized Hildegarde's belongings. "Could she have been captured too?"

Brianna couldn't suppress a shudder. If Hildegarde was powerless against this evil, then what hope did they have? Maybe what Zelig had claimed about defeating the Direktorate was true after all. "Maybe… I think we should move on to Oroton Village first thing tomorrow," she said as she began placing Hildegarde's jars in her own bag.

Amon frowned. "You should leave her things alone."

"I don't think she'd mind if I borrowed some of her potions and remedies to take with us. We might need them. See, these are for hives and that one is for sore eyes and that—"

"Okay, so you know your stuff. Have you really thought about how hard and dangerous this journey to the Sacred Mountains is going to be?"

Brianna carefully placed a bag of herbs into her pack. "Yes, Amon. I have thought about that—a lot, actually."

Amon cleared his throat before he spoke. "Do you really believe the Abrasaxon will help you? I mean, who knows what they really think about us mortals? They have no need of us with their magic and all."

Brianna lifted her chin and stared hard at him. "Am I correct in assuming my potential magic bothers you?"

"Yes. It does," Amon admitted, a frown marring his face.

"Too much for you to stay and help me?" The silence stretched interminably as she waited for his answer. Her emotions swung from hope to despair. She wanted desperately for him to stay—they needed him. He was wood-wise and battle trained. He could live off the land. But she wasn't going to beg.

"I'll stay—if you want me to." The look he gave her was full of unreadable shadows.

She smiled. "I'd like you to, Amon."

Her quiet words didn't reveal the comfortable feeling of security that flooded over her at his affirmation.

"In that case, I'd better make myself useful and find something for supper," he said. "You and Conal should collect more wood. It's going to be a long, cold night, and we don't know what's out there." He turned to go.

"Amon..."

He hesitated, then half turned to face her.

"Thank you...for staying."

He grinned, turned and strode away.

The cave seemed very quiet with Amon gone, and unable to settle, Brianna woke Conal. He grumbled endlessly while they scrounged for dry wood. Finally, when they had a huge pile, Brianna stoked Hildegarde's small hearth at the rear of the cave. She left Conal to watch it while she returned to gathering small items that might be useful on their journey.

Amon returned empty-handed, his handsome face glum. "Nothing in the snares we set earlier. It's like the valley's been deserted. Even the teklick have stopped their clattering." He pointed to the horizon. "And there's a huge bank of black clouds coming from the direction of Kenon."

"Never mind, Amon. We have enough to make do — there's bread, cured meat, cheese and some nuts and dried fruit. Tomorrow we can get more at Oroton."

"Hildegarde will help us, won't she, Brianna?" Conal asked.

Brianna frowned. She didn't want to destroy Conal's hope, but the changes in the valley made her strongly suspect something very sinister had taken Hildegarde away.

"If she's there, she will help us."

"What if she's not?" Conal asked, sitting back on his heels, his face in slightly obscured by the lack of light.

"Then…" Brianna hesitated as she pulled out the map and spread it on her knees. She pointed to the castle. "Then we go on to the castle by ourselves and find my Abrasaxon father."

Conal jumped up and paced around the fire. "That's too far away. What about the people of Oroton Village, can't they help?"

Brianna sighed. "This is powerful magic. You saw what happened at home. Ordinary mortals can't defeat power like that, and they would probably end up being taken as well."

"Will he help you?"

Brianna regarded him for a moment. "Of course he will."

"He's the Grand Archon now," Amon warned.

"He's still my father. He will help, if I ask." Her voice was stronger now, driving out the tiny splinter of doubt that jabbed at the back of her mind. She buried it deep. "Hakon will help us," she repeated.

Amon gave her shoulder a squeeze. "It's decided then."

Brianna sighed with relief that Amon appeared to accept her family connections and committed himself again to the course of action she'd suggested.

Over a hastily prepared meal of toasted bread, fried cured breket and cheese, they studied the map and decided the best way to travel. They made a list of things they hoped the Oroton people would lend them, and at last there was nothing left to do but get through the night.

Despite her dragging tiredness, Brianna remained awake well into the night, moving restlessly to ease the aches and pains that stabbed at her body as she listened intently. Only the whisper of the breeze in the trees disturbed the silence. There were none of the usual night noises that Brianna was accustomed to and the eerie silence made her even more uneasy. Her thoughts whirled around and around. What if Hakon turned her away, rejected her now that he was Grand Archon of Okana? After all, they'd heard nothing from him in years.

On the other side of the fire, Amon shuffled restlessly, moaning softly in his sleep, and Conal began to snore as Brianna stared out of the cave at the single moon of the new season and wished everything back the way it had been.

* * * *

Brianna dragged one eye open and shivered. It was barely dawn. Her body ached and her hair was tangled and fluffed where she had tossed and turned. The fire was a pile of cold, gray ashes. With one hand she picked up a stick and poked them. A wisp of smoke curled lazily up. She stirred the ashes some more, groaning with the effort, but it refused to ignite. When the boys did not rouse at her noisy attempts to ignite the fire, she tucked the blanket tightly around herself, bent into an uncomfortable sitting position and sprinkled a handful of dry tinder on the ashes. The smoke increased. Futilely, Brianna tried to blow on it without exposing herself to the predawn chill. But the embers refused to catch and finally there was nothing for it but to get out of the blanket and coax a little flame into life. A fine misty rain blanketed the valley in a somber gloom that enhanced Brianna's sense of desolation.

The boys didn't awaken until the fire began to crackle, so, leaving them to wake up, she took the pot and stomped down the slope. By the time she got to the stream the circulation had begun to return to her limbs and she splashed the icy water on her face to banish the lingering mists of sleep. With lots of rough tugging, she tamed the tangles and replaited her hair before she filled the pot with water. All she needed now was a cup of hot tea and she would be almost back to normal. Well, as normal as one could be under the circumstances.

When she returned to the cave, she found the boys were nearly ready to leave. Amon strapped on his sword. "I'll just get my snares and then we'll be ready."

Conal jumped up. "I'm coming."

Amon frowned. "You coming, Brianna?"

She buckled on her sword. "It's better than staying here alone," she mumbled as she picked up her crossbow.

Below the cave, at first glance the valley had appeared serene and peaceful. The leaves on the gark trees had turned golden yellow overnight and now fell to the ground with soft pattering. But black clouds loomed above the horizon and everything was wet. Huge drops of water fell on their heads when they passed under the trees, drenching both them and the thick leaf litter beneath their feet. Brianna tried to shake off a sense of unease as she followed the boys. Something was wrong, but they were well into the grove of gark trees before it became obvious. Leaves were falling everywhere, not only the yellow and red that should be falling, but the green ones as well. Small shoots of grass had withered barely inches from the soil, and the syniah that sprinkled the meadow yesterday had dropped their petals. No living creature moved, no brightly colored teklick flitted across the sky or striped gezz buzzed beside delicate flemiko gathering pollen from the perfumed centers of the syniah.

Brianna touched Amon's arm. "Have you noticed?" she whispered.

He nodded.

"Noticed what?" Conal asked. His voice sounded loud and harsh in the quiet.

"Shhh." Brianna didn't know why she wanted him to be quiet, but she did. "The valley is dying."

Conal looked around, seeing the subtle changes for the first time. He stood very still. "Is it the Tyban?" he asked in a faltering whisper.

Brianna and Amon exchanged glances. It was almost too horrible to contemplate, but it would explain a lot and there was no point in pretending. Conal remained silent, but his expression was bleak when she nodded then turned to follow Amon along the path. The desire to peep back over her shoulder was almost overwhelming as they padded single file through the thicket to collect the other snares.

The overgrown path ended abruptly at the edge of a small cliff that bordered a circular clearing hemmed in on all sides by thick brush. Three narrow paths opened from different directions into the clearing. Not even the breeze stirred the wilting grasses. Brianna's breath caught in her throat at the unexpected majestic beauty of the male chirum. It stood so proudly, scenting the air. Tall antlers crowned its aristocratic head, wariness filled its moist eyes and its black velvety nose twitched. They froze, hidden by the bushes, and stared in awe at the regal beauty of the animal. A shadow drifted lazily across the clearing. The chirum flinched and bounded erratically off into the forest, leaving the clearing heavy with expectation.

In that moment Brianna shrank back into the deeper gloom, a tight grip on Amon's shoulder, but he needed no urging to hide. Her heart beat a faster, uneven tattoo behind her ribs. The leaves on the other side of the clearing rustled, the noise loud in the cloying silence. Brianna tensed. The shadows moved and filled the overgrown path. The soft thud of footsteps vibrated along her raw nerve endings. She peeked at Amon. He raised his eyebrows and pursed his lips in an expression of warning before he turned back to the clearing. Moments later, a Gomahra emerged from the path. Brianna stifled a gasp and lifted her crossbow, swiveling slowly to bring the yellow-brown, squashed-in snout into her sights. She wanted nothing more than to send one of her bolts thudding into the flat forehead, right between those evil, squinting eyes. Her finger twitched on the trigger, but suddenly the Gomahra wasn't alone.

Horror and grief swamped her murderous rage when she saw the captives being herded into the clearing. A dozen Gomahras, stomping on stubby legs, roughly pushed and shoved the stunned people into faster steps. The dazed mortals stumbled blindly, blank eyes staring at a distant point on the horizon. Brianna turned to Conal, holding out the green stone. He held up two green stones, and fury and frustration made his eyes flash brilliant silver. Amon tapped their shoulders and shook his head. They drew even farther back into the dappled gloom.

Conal stared wide-eyed, his mouth working, as the captives passed close. The sickening stench of the Gomahras almost made Brianna retch. Her heart thumped so hard in her breast she was terrified the Gomahras would hear it. None of the captured mortals resisted and Brianna cursed the power that held the villagers stunned into inaction, making them leave their homes without a fight. The Gomahras herded the people of Oroton Village across the clearing and down a path on the other side in a slow-moving, shuffling group. Tryton, the toymaker, and Keona, Hildegarde's daughter, trailed behind, helping old widow Sabra stagger along the path. As the last one disappeared, an oppressive silence descended, and all that remained of their passing was the lingering reek of Gomahra.

The three of them stayed crouched in silence, staring at the clearing well after the rustling leaves were still.

Unable to stand her thoughts a moment longer, Brianna tamped them down before they overwhelmed her. "Let's go," she said softly and turned away.

Conal grabbed her arm. "We have to find more stones. Then we can rescue them."

Brianna shook her head, knowing his sudden display of aggression was Conal's way of dealing with the uncontrollable. "No, Conal. We would never find enough stones to fight all the Gomahras."

Amon laid a hand on his shoulder. "And what about their leader, Zelig? How do we fight him?"

Conal pushed Amon's hand off, his eyes glinting with contempt. "Coward," he yelled. "That's what you are, Amon. A coward."

The older boy's hand shot out and grabbed Conal's arm in a vicious grip. He joggled him savagely. "Don't you ever call me a coward! Don't you ever!"

The color drained from Conal's face as he whimpered in shock at Amon's sudden aggression.

"Stop it, Amon! Stop it!" Brianna hissed as she clawed at Amon's arm. "We can't fight among ourselves."

A blank expression shuttered Amon's face as he let his hands fall to his sides. He appeared to be both sad and tired. "Sorry. Conal has to face the fact that there are only three of us and we don't have the resources to fight what's out there."

Conal sniffed and wiped his sleeve across his face to obliterate his tears. "So we simply walk away?"

A cold wind rattled the fallen leaves, and Amon surveyed the clearing. "Not walking away — marshaling reinforcements, developing a battle plan. We might only get one chance at rescue, so we've got to get it right. Let's get going."

Shouldering her bow, Brianna turned away and stepped into the clearing. A movement in the patchwork of light and shade caught her attention. She froze. Amon crashed heavily into her back. A sharp rattle of stones and a grunt pierced the silence.

"Shh, something's coming!" she muttered, shuffling backward into the bushes.

Brianna's knees felt weak as she crouched out of sight. Her breath came in tiny gasps as they waited. Amon's grip tightened on her shoulder, his fingers pressed into the hollow by her collarbone. He stood so still the tiny puffs of warm breath on her cheek were the only sign that he was alive. After a moment, the leaves at the opening of the path vibrated and parted to reveal a frail girl of about nine with red curls that cascaded to her waist. A sprinkling of freckles, a nasty gash and an ugly black bruise that discolored the left side of her face marred her alabaster skin. She limped badly on a crippled leg, supported only by a crude crutch.

"Tulia!" Brianna gasped.

"You know her?" Amon asked.

"She's Hildegarde's granddaughter." Brianna nearly choked on her words.

As the girl trudged past, Brianna bounded forward, Amon and Conal right behind her.

"We've got to stop her. She's going after the others," Brianna hollered.

They easily overtook Tulia. Brianna leaped directly into her path, but Tulia gave no sign of awareness and crashed right into her. Her legs continued to move of their own volition, driving her onward even as she only pressed harder against Brianna.

Gently, Brianna gripped her arms. "Stop, Tulia! Stop!"

The girl didn't respond, her legs didn't stop moving. Brianna knelt down in front of Tulia and stared hard into the green, almond-shaped eyes, willing a spark of recognition, but Tulia's expression remained blank.

Brianna gripped Tulia's shoulders. "Tulia — speak to me!"

The blank stare remained unchanged.

"Wake up, Tulia!"

No response. A sudden wave of panic and fear washed over Brianna. She trembled with its strength. She shook Tulia — harder this time — and shouted at her. Her words came out in jagged, halting blasts. She desperately needed to know that Tulia was still in that frail, battered shell.

"She's not going to wake up, Brianna. Leave it, before you shake her eyes out," Amon growled.

Brianna felt her desperation crumple into hopelessness.

Amon loosened his grip on the girl's shoulders. "Let's get her back to the cave before the Gomahras come back to find her."

When he scooped Tulia up like a sack of tubers and dumped her over his shoulder, she made no protest, but her feet kept moving up and down in front of his face as if taking her somewhere. Amon was staggering under his wriggling burden by the time they reached the cave.

Unceremoniously, Amon set her by the remains of the fire. "Guard her. Don't let her go! Tie her up if you have to. We need to eat. I'll see if I can catch a qymaten before they all vanish too."

Brianna nodded agreement before she turned to minister to Tulia, but the moment Amon released her she was on her feet and marching blindly away.

"You will actually have to hold her, for goodness' sake," Brianna yelled as Tulia escaped Conal's reluctant clutches and headed out of the cave for a third time.

Conal pouted, arms clenched tightly around his prisoner's frail waist. "It's all right for you. I can't stay like this all night. What am I supposed to do with her? Girls — they're always trouble."

Despite the horror of the situation, Brianna smiled at Conal's petulance before she collected a coil of rope from the back of the cave. "Here. Tie her up." She chucked the rope at his feet. "Gently."

"I can't do that. It wouldn't be right." For a brief second Conal's hold on Tulia loosened, and she began to walk away yet again.

Finally convinced that there was no other solution, Conal grabbed her, and, with Brianna's help, seated her in Hildegarde's large wooden chair. They bound her hands to the ornately carved arms and her ankles to the legs. Tulia sat there staring blankly ahead. The only movement a restricted wriggle of her bound feet as they still tried to carry her to whatever force called her.

Brianna struggled with the enormity of what they faced then she sighed. First things first, her mother had always said, and Tulia's physical wounds were something she could deal with.

Satisfied that Conal could now cope, Brianna turned to Hildegarde's multitude of healing remedies. Her heart ached because she had no idea how to break the spell holding the girl prisoner, but thanks to her mother she had a rudimentary knowledge of the healing arts. She quickly pushed aside the wave of grief and frustration that came with the thoughts of her mother and what she had lost. Now was not the time to wallow in self-pity — Tulia was her first consideration.

Brianna cleaned Tulia's wounds and bandaged them carefully, noting the younger girl didn't even flinch when she applied the stinging antiseptic salve. She wondered if Tulia had been beaten for being too slow with her crippled leg or if she had stumbled trying to keep up with the others. Either way, she was lucky it was only a few cuts and a nasty bruise, not a smashed cheekbone and jaw.

The early sunset brought a cold wind and rain fell steadily in a thick gray curtain. Conal stoked the glowing embers in the hearth and added several large logs.

Brianna grabbed his arm. "No. Don't do that."

"But I'm cold," he moaned.

"So am I, but we have to keep the fire small otherwise it will be a beacon to every Gomahra for miles around."

Conal flushed at her rebuke but only nodded and fiddled with his slingshot.

"We'd be like nesting shandina — easy targets."

"Well, if I had enough stones I'd kill the lot of them."

His expression twisted in rage and hatred, his voice full of bravado. But Brianna saw the fear lurking in his eyes and hoped it was enough to prevent him from trying anything foolish.

A rock rattled. Conal flinched. Brianna swung around, her sword clutched in icy fingers, her breath coming in sharp jerks. The seconds of tension stretched into eternity.

"It's me," Amon whispered moments before his face appeared above the ledge, ghostly white in the darkness.

"You shouldn't sneak up on people like that, warrior. You're lucky I didn't have time to let one fly. Could've killed you."

Amon glanced pointedly at the empty slingshot then up at Conal but remained silent as he joined them at the back of the cave. Brianna propped her sword by the hearth and silently begged her knees to stop trembling.

"Sorry if I frightened you. I didn't want to encourage any followers," he said as he laid one smallish qymaten on the coals and bent down to blow gently. "This is all there was."

Brianna shrugged. "It's better than nothing. We can supplement it with some cured breket and cheese, and there's still some bread. I also found a pot of dried anjoa fruit. We can have that for afters." She tried to sound casual, but couldn't keep the sharp edge from her words as she watched the small qymaten sizzle in the glowing embers and wrestled with the reasons behind the lack of animals and the dying valley. Was it Zelig — or something else?

They ate quickly by the soft glow of the fire. It wasn't fancy, but it took the edge off their hunger. She tried to get Tulia to eat, but it was futile, and she soon gave up in frustration, swamped by a flood of grief, for she knew the child would die very quickly unless they found a cure for her zombie-like state. She tried extremely hard not to think of the Kenon villagers.

"Try to get some rest. We've a hard walk tomorrow," Amon said as he picked up his sword. "I'll take the first watch."

Brianna didn't quibble about his decision, merely tucked a blanket around Tulia and crawled into her own blanket beside the chair. In the concealment of darkness her tears fell — tears of grief, fear and pain.

Chapter Five

"Wake up, Brianna!"

She cringed away from the rough shaking on her shoulder and the intrusion into her dream.

"Come on, Brianna! Wake up! The girl has gone! She must have gotten loose last night," Conal bawled in her ear.

The meaning of Conal's words finally penetrated the clouds of exhausted sleep, and she rubbed her eys to dispel her vagueness. "Where?"

"She's headed up the valley after the others. Hurry or we'll never catch her!"

"Let's go, she mustn't reach the castle. Where's Amon?"

Conal shrugged. "Dunno."

Rubbing sleep from her eyes and trembling from her abrupt transition to wakefulness, Brianna gathered up her weapons and scrambled down the slope with Conal and they bounded across the meadow into a narrow gorge cut in the rock by the fast-flowing stream. Conal plunged in and waded upstream without even a glance back at Brianna. She hesitated a moment and wondered if there was an easier way up the valley, but there was no time to search for one. She jumped into the icy water and followed Conal.

The narrow streambed had steep sides and was littered with sharp, broken rocks. Brianna used her sword for balance as she struggled to keep her footing against the gushing force of the water. Mist swirled through the gnarled trees, and Brianna shivered as cold tendrils seeped through her leather jerkin and touched her skin. An air of decay hung over everything. Not a shandina whistled a dawn greeting song or a mud firozt croaked. Unease squeezed around her and dread sat heavy in her gut.

The ground rose steeply where the stream gushed noisily out of the spring. Conal pointed to the rocky slope on the right of the small waterfall and without a word they began to climb. The ground was damp and covered in slime that seeped into her clothes. Brianna's body was aching by the time they were halfway up the ridge. Her pants were torn and sweat beaded under her bangs.

"There she is. Almost at the top!" Conal cried.

Brianna threw down her weapons and sprinted up the hill. Her breath came in tortured gasps. Fortunately Tulia's lameness slowed her, and as she topped the rise Brianna lunged, closing her hand around Tulia's good ankle in a desperate grip. The younger girl toppled onto the wet grass as Brianna thudded to the ground, sludgy mud caking her face and filling her mouth and nostrils.

"Yuk!" she spluttered, blinking her eyes and wiping the putrid mud away with her spare hand. As her vision shimmered and cleared, she stifled a squawk.

An enormous castle fashioned out of black rock, shining with weeping dampness, filled half the plateau, carved out of the hillside. Four turrets jutted into a black cloud of mist that swirled around the slimy walls. Flesh scavengers hovered on black leathery wings in rising drafts that brought an awful stench wafting across the gully.

Conal landed beside her with a grunt. "Curse the Luna Goddess, look at that!"

Brianna frowned at his expletive but focused her gaze on the valley floor. The villagers of Kenon and Oroton shuffled in and out of a small opening leading to the underground shafts of Okana's biggest zeltic mine, bringing baskets of rocks from underground — heads down, shoulders hunched. Brianna stared in morbid fascination as her gaze shifted from one familiar face to another. She couldn't see her mother. Where was she? Was she still alive? Brianna cringed against the painful contraction of her heart and almost lost her grip on Tulia's ankle.

Sharp cracks and thuds filled the air. Brianna shifted her gaze and found a group of men in one corner breaking rocks.

"Da," she murmured.

Her stepfather was in the center of the group, flanked by two of the grotesque Gomahras. He was chipping laboriously away at a huge block of stone.

With a light scrabbling and a couple of garbled curses, Amon suddenly crouched by her side. He dumped a large hare between them and grabbed Tulia's free leg as it snapped up and down in front of him. "I wondered where you two were going when I saw you dashing down to the stream. I thought maybe the Gomahras had come."

"Sorry, Amon," she said. "There was no time to find you or leave a message. Tulia escaped. I don't know how."

Amon's face colored slightly. "I loosened her bonds this morning before I left. They seemed so tight and I was sorry for her, but I didn't mean for her to escape."

Brianna choked back tears and the censure that was on the tip of her tongue. "We would never have found them if she hadn't escaped, but I don't think we can do anything to rescue them. Look at it, it's awful, all of it!"

Amon nodded, his expression shamefaced. "At least we know they're still alive."

In front of them, the mute girl wriggled against Brianna's imprisoning hands. Brianna tightened her grip on her ankle, determined that Tulia would not join the others. "We have to go. There's nothing we can do here."

"See those moldy moon dust Gomahras guarding them." Conal's face scrunched in disgust.

Amon screwed up his nose. "Where's the Tyban?"

"I have no idea. Gone to get more slaves, I guess," Conal spluttered, his hatred and frustration almost tangible.

"What does he want them for?" Amon asked.

"As miners. This is one of Okana's richest zletic mines," Conal grated.

Brianna felt a flutter in her mind — soft and gentle, but intrusive. She shook her head to clear it. She wondered if it was Zelig calling, but the others didn't appear to be affected. It came again, this time more insistent. She slapped her hands over her ears. It made no difference.

"Don't fight me, Anna – it's Da."

She heard her stepfather's voice as clearly as if he were standing right beside her. Cautiously she lifted her head and peered across the gully. Her da was staring straight ahead, his hands stilled on the rock.

"Go from here, Anna – now. Zelig is too powerful to fight. Get your father. Your mother is safe for the moment, as am I. Go, Anna, before he smells you, smells your magic. Go. Go. Go. Get help. Do not fear your gift – use them on the journey. Now go. Zelig comes this way."

"The sleeping sickness... A cure?" Brianna whispered in her mind.

She saw her stepfather shake his head now. *"Hakon will know."*

Zelig appeared in a swirl of black smoke and her head was immediately empty of words. Below, she saw her stepfather bend to his work. All that remained were the emotions left by her da's intrusion into her mind.

"Come on. We've got to leave. Now!" The depth of Brianna's urgency was fired by the feelings that had flooded her mind. They were strong and unrelenting – fear, anger, impotency and frustration, but even stronger the urge to get away from the castle.

"Let's go." Fear made her words clipped as she jumped up.

"But aren't we going to do something?" Conal asked, still staring at the castle.

"No!" she snapped. "We need to go!"

Ignoring both boys, she struggled to scramble down the slope with Tulia perched on her hip. She didn't wait to see if they followed her, the feelings from her stepfather so urgent they were almost a painful throb in her mind – *'Go, go, go!'*

"Silly young fool! We can't tackle that lot. There were a hundred Gomahras at least." Amon's words were a low growl as he caught up with her headlong flight and matched her frantic strides down the slope.

Conal careened behind them in a landslide of rocks. "We can't just leave them there!" His whining voice was a high-pitched statement of reproach.

Brianna didn't even spare him a glance.

Amon shrugged. "What do you suggest? We go charging in there? All three of us — sorry, four — with our swords and crutch swinging and a battle cry to scare the enemy out of his magic?"

It was not fear that held Amon back, but common sense. Unfortunately, unable to admit the hopelessness of such action, Conal could only see his reluctance. He wanted someone to blame, to take responsibility for his pain, and he went on the attack.

"Don't tell us you're afraid, Amon," Conal sneered. "You're the warrior. Fighting is your specialty."

Amon's mouth tightened and his face paled as he swept Tulia out of Brianna's arms and onto his shoulder before he turned away.

"So you won't help. You're going to walk away without a backward glance."

Brianna touched Conal's shoulder in warning. "We're all going to walk away. It's the only way to save them. We must go!"

Conal jerked his shoulder out of reach of her hand. "I can understand him, but you, Brianna? You're going to leave your own mother in that hell? How can you?"

Brianna gave Conal the evil eye. She wanted to shake him, to make him understand what she and Amon already understood but restrained her impulse because she appreciated how he felt. Every step down the slope was a struggle with her own desire to charge in there and fight. Uncertainty tortured her mind. Instinct and love would have sent her hurtling over the hill, sword slashing. But deep down she knew the foolishness — the futility — of that, and with that knowledge her tentative plan to find her Abrasaxon father hardened into certainty.

"It's what she would want, Conal."

"How would you know?" he sneered.

Brianna smiled vaguely. It was no use trying to explain because she didn't understand it herself. "I just know, that's all."

Conal lapsed into sulky silence but fell into step beside her as they hurried after Amon.

Back at the cave, Brianna ignored Conal's flouncing and sulking and calmly went about her preparations. She knew exactly what she wanted to take, and began to add some extra potions and liniments to a large leather bag that could hang over her shoulder. Her hand hovered over the last small pot, the one that contained a glistening red powder and was marked with the symbol of the scorpion.

As she lifted it out of the drawer, a stabbing pain seared her hand. "Ouch!" Holding her bleeding hand, she peered into the drawer, for a moment thinking she had been bitten. "Oh, it's beautiful!" The zletic dagger glowed with a sharp black gloss from where it nestled in a bed of velvet.

Apprehension sizzled along her skin as she reached for its deadly beauty, but as her hand hovered over it Amon reached past her, his strong muscular fingers almost caressing the glowing metal.

She grabbed his wrist. "Oh no you don't! That dagger is mine!" She couldn't explain her sudden need to possess the weapon, but she knew she must have it, and that knowledge shocked her.

Amon glared at her. "What gives you the right?" he snarled.

Annoyance flushed over her as she lifted her chin and glared at him. "I found it first. It's mine."

Her fingernails clawed into the softness of her palms as their eyes locked in a deadly battle of wills. Her mother had always accused her of being strong-willed and stubborn, and this was one fight Amon was not going to win.

"It's mine!" she stated again.

Amon ignored her statement of ownership, snatched the dagger from the drawer and backed away from her. Deep inside, Brianna felt an intense pulse grow — the same unidentified power that had felled Conal. She stared hard at Amon, willing him to give her the dagger. The tension built around them, an uncontrolled vortex of power. With a sudden, unexpected twitch, the dagger wrenched itself from Amon's grasp and flew across the room to slam, point down, into the bench right in front of Brianna. They both stared at it in stunned silence. It quivered gently as Brianna grappled with the emotions swirling through her. There was a sudden rush of black wings and a loud, angry caw. A raven's talons dug into her shoulder. She stood motionless, unsure what the bird intended. Hildegarde's raven cried again and fixed beady yellow eyes on Amon. His face paled and he retreated, hunched over in a protective stance. The raven cawed again and in a flutter of wings swooped at him before disappearing out of the cave. With the threat gone, Amon straightened.

"Have it then, if it means so much to you. It's only an old woman's toy," he said scornfully as he turned and stomped away.

Sweat poured from her brow and she felt drained of energy and scared at the sudden awareness, for the first time, of the unknown, untested power that throbbed within. The Abrasaxon magic she hadn't wanted and genuinely feared had somehow become part of her, and it might prove useful before the end of this nightmare.

She examined Tulia, tied in the chair. The younger girl desired and expected to have the gift of magic, felt entitled to it as Hildegarde's granddaughter. Brianna was sure Tulia would handle her gift more competently when it came than Brianna was handling hers A shiver of trepidation vibrated down her spine about her unknown destiny, but her future was here, now, whether she wanted it or not. While she fretted for the old Brianna, lost to her so unexpectedly, and was apprehensive about the new one taking shape out of the ashes, she also worried how she would be shaped by the journey ahead, and if she would indeed survive it at all.

The dagger fit her palm so well it could have been made for her. Still feeling guilty about snatching it from Amon, she studied its beauty for a moment before slipping it into her boot with her hunting knife. She had no idea why she wanted to possess it, or what use it might be, because it was too small for fighting or cleaning game. All she knew was it felt right to possess it. And at this time of uncertainty, that was all she had to guide her — what felt right.

It was raining again, a fine, silvery mist drifting down and leaving everything shimmering with glistening drops. Brianna was worried about Tulia. She hadn't eaten or drunk since they found her, and she didn't know for how long before that. It was beginning to show. Tulia's aristocratic face had thinned, her nose was pinched and her beautiful eyes sunken and lifeless. The paleness of her skin seemed almost translucent as it stretched over a fine bone structure, accentuated by the hated freckles. Brianna didn't know how much longer Tulia could go on. Already she had become so frail—her dark red curls fluffed like a fiery cloud around the small face with its fading, yellowish bruise. The green eyes remained open, the unblinking stare unnerving.

Brianna regretted the argument over the dagger, so leaving Conal to guard Tulia, she carried her pack down the slope to where Amon was constructing a crude stretcher.

"Can I help?"

As Amon gave her the once-over, a mixture of emotions flitted across his face like shandina through trees. He didn't reply, merely handed her some twine as a gesture of acceptance. But Brianna had seen the wariness in his eyes and knew Amon was now apprehensive of her. She didn't blame him, for she was a somewhat nervous of herself at the moment.

Half an hour later, they had a sturdy structure. Amon kicked it halfheartedly. "It will have to do. Let's get Tulia onto it and get out of this awful valley before we die with it or worse, are pressed into slavery."

Tulia didn't struggle as they strapped her onto the litter, although her legs still moved. Brianna hadn't seen Tulia's baby brother with the others and she wondered where he was. Tulia had been fiercely protective of Dodi since the mysterious accident that had left her with a lame leg and Dodi unable, or unwilling, to talk. Tulia would never have left him on his own unless forced to.

* * * *

Tulia whimpered again. They'd been walking for hours under gray clouds. Conal had been complaining for ages he was hungry, but Brianna and Amon both ignored his pleas—not because they were unsympathetic, but because they wanted to reach the village before the freezing cold and soaking rain that came with the dusk drove them to shelter. Neither of them wanted to spend a night in the open. The floor of the valley had turned into a steady slope upward. Side by side Amon and Brianna continued to trudge relentlessly, backs bent under the weight of their burden. As the path steepened on the last rise before the village, he grunted with renewed effort.

"Give us a push, Conal," Brianna ordered.

Conal frowned at her, readjusted his pack, and began to push. Brianna tightened the rope over her shoulder and tugged harder, digging her feet into the loose shale that littered the path. All three gasped in labored breaths as they struggled.

"Come on, you two. Tulia's village is not far over this rise." Brianna panted as they dragged the stretcher loaded with Tulia and their two packs up the hill.

At Tulia's cottage, they didn't bother to knock. The remains of the family's last meal moldered on the table.

Amon inspected the room, his thick blond eyebrows drawing low over his eyes in a deep, furrowed frown. "I'll get some wood," he muttered as he beat a hasty retreat from the smelly room.

Brianna screwed her nose up at the odor. "Come on, help me get this clean then we can eat."

He gave Brianna a pained flick of the eye, but obediently set down his pack and began to clear the table. They didn't bother washing the plates, just dumped everything in the bin, which Conal took out the back.

Moments later, he walked back into the room. "Phew, that stank so bad even the terrates scratching in the dirt wouldn't eat those scraps. But see what I found in the terrates' house."

He opened up his jacket and nestled in a grubby bundle were ten eggs.

Brianna grinned. "It appears we feast tonight. I've found more breket, bread and some greens in Phoebe's garden."

The door flung open as Amon lurched in, a bucket in one hand and a neat bundle of wood tucked under the other arm. "I've milked the gort that was bellowing in the stable yard."

With three sets of hands, the meal was soon on the table. They ate in silence. Brianna tried to get Tulia to swallow a sip of gort milk but it was hopeless. The child was fading away before her eyes and a terrible ache knotted in her stomach. *What if Tulia dies?*

"Please, Tulia, just a drop of milk," Brianna pleaded.

She even tried forcing the milk between Tulia's lips, but it merely dribbled out and ran down her chin. Brianna mopped her dry and turned away, a mixture of desperation, fear and anguish choking her throat closed. Conal had retreated to his blanket, claiming exhaustion, so Brianna squatted down beside Amon and stared into the flames. She could feel the precious map rustle next to her breast, but one glance over her shoulder told her Hakon's help would be too late for Tulia.

Intent on their individual thoughts, they didn't hear Conal's return from his failed attempt at slumber until he hunkered down beside them. He poked a blackened stick through the coals, stirring up a shower of orange sparks.

He shuffled his feet uncertainly as he cleared his throat. "Are you sure we can't rescue them? There are plenty of villages to the south. Surely they would help us attack the castle." His voice was soft, imploring almost, with no trace of his customary whine.

Amon sighed. "I don't know, Conal. I've had plenty of experience fighting Yabix, but this is different. I don't think more swords or warriors are going to help."

"It seems like we're running away, not fighting. I could fight, use a sword."

Brianna shook her head.

"What if the Tyban has...everybody" — he flicked a glance in Brianna's direction — "including Hakon, under" — he pointed at Tulia — "that spell? What if we're the only ones he hasn't got?"

"Hakon's much too powerful for that. Besides, he has the Abrogative Direktorate to help. Don't worry. My Abrasaxon father will know how to fix it... We simply have to ask him."

Conal leaped up. "What if your father won't help us? What if we can't find him?"

Brianna stared into the flames for a minute or two before she met Conal's expression with a worried one of her own and said very softly, "I don't know. I really don't know."

Conal's face crumpled at her words. He said nothing, though, as he turned and went back to bed.

Amon poked the fire and added another log. "There are no guarantees in this, are there?"

Brianna stared into the embers. "No, Amon, but we have hope for the moment." She stood. "Will you take first watch?"

Amon nodded. "Get some sleep, Brianna—if you can."

* * * *

She moaned in protest, rolled over, and burrowed back into her blanket the moment Amon touched her shoulder, desperate to recapture her precious dream. The bright meadow, her mother laughing as she unpacked the picnic, Da pushing her on the swing, high into the warm summer air, thick with flemikos. His cheerful, funny, fatherly jokes to her each time she whizzed by that made her giggle so much she had nearly fallen off.

"Brianna."

"No, go away," she grumbled.

Amon jiggled her shoulder gently. "It's your turn to keep watch."

She sat up, surprised to find her cheeks wet with tears. Hurriedly she wiped them away, acutely aware of the searching look Amon gave her. She stood. "Sorry. I was dreaming."

He touched her shoulder lightly, a grimace twisting his face. "It'll be all right, Brianna."

She nodded then shuffled to the fire, her blanket wrapped around her. After adding a couple of logs to the already crackling blaze, she huddled down in the chair and stared into the flames. It was a lonely vigil and every minor noise in the unfamiliar house sounded threatening, and in between, when the silence closed in, her fearful thoughts grew large. In the distance Brianna heard a mournful wail and trepidation crawled along her spine at the unknown creature calling into the night. Seeking solace, she added another log to the fire and huddled closer to the comforting glow.

At last the green dawn seeped into the room. Brianna sat up, discarded the blanket, and eased the map from her jerkin. In the soft firelight, she carefully examined every detail of the journey to the Crystal Castle. The rivers, swamps and mountains appeared daunting obstacles on the flat page and Brianna could only guess the dangers of the real things, but deep in her heart she knew this was the only way. She sensed Amon behind her.

"Here is Kenon," she said softly, taking a quick peep at Amon's grave face. "We are now here in Oroton." She laid a grubby finger on a group of cottages marked on the map. Then she traced a path directly toward the mountains. "All we have to do is follow the setting sun to find the Crystal Castle and Hakon."

Conal joined them, still rubbing the sleep from his eyes, and peered down at the map. Brianna waited for objections to her plan.

Amon seemed very thoughtful. "It's a dangerous journey through unknown wilderness — swamps, mountains and Nixets," he muttered. His finger slid across the cute diminutive people drawn on the map. "I don't fancy taking on a Nixet, but at least we won't have to worry about Yabix."

"What's a Nixet?" Conal asked.

"Hmm…" Amon hesitated. "Nixets are little people, about as big as my foot…"

Conal gave Amon a skeptical look. "Have you ever seen one?"

Amon grimaced. "No, but I don't doubt they exist. Legend has it that they used to help the big people — us — but sometimes they liked to play tricks as well. One day they played a trick on an old man who was actually an Archon, and he was so mad he took away their ability to become invisible. According to legend, he comes every year to check if they've collected enough jewels to buy their ability back. This is why the Nixets won't help us, they're obsessed with finding jewels to pay the ransom. If they think you might have a jewel, they can be pretty nasty, and they have powerful magic."

Conal shuddered. "Perhaps we should stay here."

"And wait for the Gomahras to come?" Amon asked.

Brianna frowned at Amon. "Don't worry about the Nixets, Conal. We don't have any jewels they might want. Besides, it's only a legend from old times. Even if they did exist once upon a time, I doubt they still do."

"All right, I'll go. I have my compass." Reverently, he pulled it out of his pocket. "Kenton gave it to me, before he left for the war." Conal touched the map with his forefinger, the bitten nail ragged and dirty. He traced a line across the map. "I reckon we need to head due west with perhaps a couple of detours for rivers and swamps."

Amon chuckled. "Yes, Conal, straight into — Ouch."

Brianna glared at Amon to reinforce her kick to his ankle. "Great, Conal. You're chief navigator then," she announced.

Conal grinned, and his face glowed with importance. "But I'm eating first."

Amon chuckled again. "Got to get those priorities right."

When Conal turned away, Amon raised his eyebrows and mouthed 'sorry' to Brianna.

She smiled back. It was a nice feeling, knowing Amon would do his bit to head off Conal's tantrums and sulks. Hastily they scraped together a meal then, while the boys went in search of more supplies, Brianna tended Tulia's wounds. Feeling safe in the cottage with the door closed, she left Tulia unbound and the girl marched around and around the cottage like one of the wind-up toys Tryton had always made for each child's birthday.

Conal returned with his pack bulging and an untidy bundle for Brianna in his hand. She unpacked her herbs again and stowed the new contents at the bottom of her pack. Tulia wandered aimlessly about, getting in the way.

"For a red moon's eclipse! If you're not doing anything, Conal, please try to keep her under control," Brianna huffed as she was bumped a third time.

Conal scowled. "Why me? She's not mine, you know!"

"Somebody has to do it," Brianna snapped as Tulia brushed past her again, eyes staring vacantly. "I don't want to tie her up if I don't have to."

Conal sighed. "You'll expect me to do it instead."

Brianna continued to repack her herbs. Suddenly she was shoved sideways. The small gray bottle flew from her fingers and spun in the air. Brianna lunged to catch it, but it slipped past her fingers and crashed onto Tulia's head. The stopper burst open, releasing a fine red powder.

"Oh no!" Brianna moaned. "Now it's wasted."

Tulia sneezed violently and doubled over in a fit of coughing. Brianna felt a shiver of fear — she didn't even know exactly what the powder was. What if it was dangerous?

"Seven moons, Brianna, what the moon dust are you doing?" Conal complained. "You've spread that stuff everywhere."

Tulia sneezed again, rubbed her eyes, and brushed the powder from her head. She fixed her gaze directly on Brianna. "What're you doing here in *my* house?"

Brianna froze, then lunged forward and swept Tulia into her arms. "Tulia! Oh moonbeams, you're awake. You've come back to us."

Tulia wriggled against her confinement. "Don't hug me, Brianna." She pointed at Amon. "Who's he?"

Amon stood stock-still in the doorway with a large bundle held to his chest. "Moonbeams, she's awake. What happened, Brianna? How did you wake her?"

"So, who is he?" Tulia demanded in an imperious voice as she pushed free of Brianna's hold.

"He's Amon, a warrior. He's going to help us."

Amon continued to stare at Tulia as he placed his bundle on the table. "Is there any damage, you know, from the spell?"

Brianna glanced from Tulia to Amon. "I don't think so…"

"I'll have you both know I'm not damaged, merely a bit confused as to why you three are in my house." Tulia scowled around then. "Where are Mama and Dodi?" Even as she asked, her eyes filled with fear. Her memory had returned. "Dodi, Mama," she wailed.

Brianna put an arm around the frail shoulders, but Tulia pushed her away. "Are they still here?" she asked.

"No, the Gomahras are gone."

"And what are Gomahras?"

"Whitukas," Conal announced. "They've come to get all us mortals."

Tulia's expression crumpled and she plonked into the chair. Tears welled up in her eyes, but she hiccupped instead of humiliating herself by sobbing. The child looked up at Brianna. "Well, that's all very well, but what are *you* doing here?" she asked again this time perching her hands on her hips.

"The Gomahras took everybody in Kenon Village but Conal and me. We're going to get help. We found you in the valley. Everybody else is captive in a big, black castle at the top of the valley."

Tulia frowned, her eyes wide. Her bottom lip trembled slightly. "Not Grandmamma too?"

Brianna shrugged. "I don't know, Tulia, but she wasn't at her cave."

Tulia pouted, vigorously wiped the tears from her eyes and studied her new companions. Brianna knelt before her and pulled her into her arms.

Tulia extracted herself from Brianna's embrace. "So it seems I will have to find a spell..." Her gaze flicked from one to the other, her lips pursed into a thin line. "Seeing as there is no one else to save them."

"Well, actually, Brianna has a plan," Amon said.

Tulia grimaced at Brianna. "And this plan is?"

Brianna hugged her tight. "We're going to find my life-force father."

Tulia pulled away from her. "Your life-force father? You don't know who your real father is."

"My father, according to Tennille, is Hakon—the Grand Archon. He'll help us." Brianna deliberately didn't meet Amon's glance. She didn't want him seeing her doubts.

Tulia stared at her, eyes wide open and unblinking. For a moment Brianna thought she had gone back under the spell.

But then she spoke in a tiny, high-pitched squeak. "Hakon is your father?"

"Yes, Tulia."

Tulia folded her hands in her lap and continued to stare at Brianna. "Well, that changes things, doesn't it?" she said. A sharp edge of disdain made her words clipped.

"So why did she wake up, Brianna?" Amon asked, still watching Tulia closely. "Do you know what suddenly broke the spell?"

Brianna bent to retrieve the jar. "I spilled this red powder over her. You know what this means?"

Amon nodded, grinning. "If we can find enough of that powder, we can release everybody." His smile faded. "Unfortunately, we don't even know what it is, let alone where to get it."

Brianna dropped the almost empty jar into her bag. "It has the scorpion's symbol on the lid so maybe my father —"

"It's pollen from the blooms of the Scorpion's Heart Syniah," Tulia said quietly, rubbing the powder between her fingers.

"Where do we find it, Tulia?"

She shrugged. "It's very rare. Only Grandmamma or the Archons would know."

"Well, she's disappeared and the Archons are far away."

Tulia nodded, fresh tears welling up in her eyes even as she stood up straighter. "Then it will be up to me, as

Hildegarde's granddaughter and future Keeper of the Wisdom, and you, Brianna, to find her."

"I think we should follow Brianna's plan," Amon said.

Brianna pulled out her map. "We will use this, Tulia, to find my father."

Tulia's eyes opened wide as she stared at the pages in Brianna's hand. "You took pages from the Destiny Books! You'll be punished for that, Hakon's daughter or not."

"Yes, Tulia, I know, but for now it's time to go." A sense of foreboding weighed Brianna down as she turned toward the door.

"But I can't go, *I* have to find Dodi." Tulia crossed her arms and stamped her foot.

"The Gomahras have him," Conal informed her bluntly.

Brianna shook her head. "No, I didn't see her brother with them."

"Is there anybody else left?" Tulia asked.

"No," Brianna said.

Tulia followed them outside, but her brow puckered in disbelief when she saw the stretcher. "You can't take me on that, I'm too heavy."

Amon frowned. "We brought you all the way from Hildegarde's cave on it, and yes, you are heavy, but you won't be able to keep up with us. Do you have any other suggestions?"

Tulia nodded. "My domnak might still be in the stable down there." She pointed along the street.

They walked at her slow pace to a rickety stable behind the bakery. By the time they were halfway down the road the domnak was braying a hungry welcome. As Tulia opened the stall a shadow darted past, sending her tumbling into an inelegant heap.

"Got you!" Amon yelled. A thin, dark-haired child hung from Amon's strong hand like a limp tunnel digger. He whimpered plaintively.

Tulia scrambled up. "Thank goodness! It's Dodi."

The child stopped wriggling. Amon lowered him to the ground and he scuttled into his sister's arms. After a quick hug, she held him away from her and studied his condition before she asked, "Oh, Dodi, they didn't enchant you?"

He shook his head, his tight, dark curls bouncing around his chubby, tear-streaked face. He pulled away from her and mimed the grotesque face of a Gomahra. He tugged at Tulia's arm and signaled with his hands. She shook her head. "I couldn't stop. It was a magic spell."

Dodi slapped his own chest hard then held his hands under the side of his face, his eyes shut.

Tulia grinned. "You couldn't hear because you were asleep in the cellar. You've been into Father's fermented anjoa juice again. Well, I suppose at least Mama's not here to punish you this time."

When Amon appeared from the stable with the saddled domnak, Dodi darted behind his sister.

Tulia placed her arm protectively around him. "Dodi, this is Amon. He didn't mean to frighten you. He's going to help get Mama, Father and Grandmamma back."

As Dodi sidled around Tulia, Amon smiled at the child then he pulled two roasted gark nuts from his pocket, squatted down, and held them out to Dodi. "I'm sorry I grabbed you. I was protecting your sister and Brianna."

117

Dodi reached out with a grubby hand and took the nuts. He immediately popped the biggest one into his mouth and grinned around it, showing juice-stained lips and indicating to Amon that he didn't hold a grudge.

Chapter Six

By mid-afternoon they were slopping through black ooze. Florescent-blue water had collected in puddles and the straight, smooth trunks of the celinda trees rose into the pale sky, huge feathery branches stirring gently in the breeze. The huge spiny fronds of the sawa plants slapped at Brianna's face, leaving it damp and tacky With Amon leading the way they made slow progress though the mire. All around, loud plopping noises and ripples in the water were evidence that this wet, smelly place was home to something other than the tiny black kachine that bit so hard they made Brianna jump and yelp.

Through the trees, Brianna could hear the grumbling croaks of the slimy, green firozt, but as they drew close, an eerie silence fell. Amon held up his hand and everyone shuffled to a halt behind him. Brianna's feet slowly settled into the sticky mush.

"Where's the map, Brianna?" Amon asked.

She sloshed up behind him and pulled out the map, careful to keep a tight hold on it. "What are you thinking, Amon?"

He pointed to where the swamp was marked on the map by a rainbow puddle of colors. "I think we need to go around. It's too dangerous to cross this place—it's full of bogs and quicksand."

Brianna agreed with him, but she despaired of the day or two it would take to walk around the swamp. Did they have that long? How many days could people live without eating or sleeping? She felt the heavy weight of tears in her throat and had to swallow hard to stop them from escaping. She sighed.

Conal lurched up behind them, compass in hand. "Come on, you two. Decide which direction we're going—we need to get moving before these bloodsuckers eat me alive." He swatted at the undulating black clouds of kachine. "The sooner we get across, the better."

Amon frowned at him. "That's exactly the problem, Conal—it's too dangerous to cross without a guide."

Conal flicked his bangs out of his eyes and laid the compass on the map. "See, this is where we go. Can't go round. It would take too much time." He pointed out over the swamp. "See—there and there and over there. You can see the dry patches. All we have to do is stick to them and we'll be all right."

Brianna sighed again. There was nothing to be done but go around. She wanted to kick and yell in protest, but they would be no use to their families at the bottom of a bog.

A high-pitched screech shattered the still air. The hair on Brianna's neck stood on end, and sweat that tingled with fear rose thick on her skin. She spun around.

Tulia and Dodi had been herded by dozens of miniature mortals onto a mound of firm ground.

Their bright rustic-style tunics stood out vividly against the muddy background. All the tiny men wore perky little hats decorated with feathers, which they had pulled down over bushy eyebrows and pointed ears. The rest of their leather-brown faces were covered in beards, some short and neat, others bushy or straggly. They barely came halfway to Brianna's knees. She glared down at them. They stared back at her with beady black eyes that gleamed with cunning. So these were Nixets! Brianna examined the miniature mortal look-alikes because, despite her anger at being hijacked, she was curious about these legendary beings often talked about in the myths of Okana.

Tulia howled as one poked at her toes with an ornate staff. Amon had warned them that Nixets had powerful magic, otherwise they would have been easy to deal with — stomped on like firozts.

With six large strides, Brianna and Amon came to stand in front of Tulia, arms held out protectively.

"Don't be so rude, Nixet king," Amon ordered. He slammed his hands on his hips and leaned over to scowl at the undersized man standing by the scuffed toe of his boot.

Brianna could see he was slightly taller than the rest. His luxuriant beard almost reached the ground and was flecked with silver. Around his neck he wore a gold chain and in his hat was a gold pin topped with a sparkling red jewel.

The Nixet peered up at Amon, wrinkling his nose. "You smell, Bigfoot," he complained.

Amon's scowl deepened. "You're still being rude, Your Majesty."

"Hah!" scoffed the Nixet king. "I'll do what I want, Bigfoot! This is our marsh. Why have you come?"

He stabbed Brianna's foot with the staff. A searing pain shot up her leg but she refused to flinch and kept her foot planted firmly in the slush.

"We go in search of the great and powerful Hakon, her father," Amon stated loudly. He pointed to Brianna.

Immediately an excited babble broke out. The Nixets huddled together, gesturing wildly as they yabbered at one another. Brianna fought down a stab of fear. Obviously mention of her father had brought this tizzy on, and thoughts of kidnap flitted through her mind.

Finally the Nixet king turned back to them. He sketched a small bow to Brianna. "We have heard of the Daughter of Hakon, and we respect her search. We will allow you to pass unharmed." The man's face glowed with a greedy flush as he rubbed his gnarled hands gleefully together then declared haughtily, "But a toll must be paid for the privilege to cross in safety."

Brianna bit hard on her tongue to stop the harsh words of protest clamoring in her mind from escaping. Anger and dismay were obvious in Amon's expression as he bowed to the Nixet king.

He didn't protest, only nodded sagely and said, "This is fair. If we pay what you ask, will you promise us safe passage with a guide?"

Brianna wondered what Amon was up to, but she figured he knew more than she did, so she clamped her mouth shut, not wanting to interrupt these delicate negotiations.

The Nixet's smirk widened. "Of course, Bigfoot. But first, you must retrieve the Morning Dawn Pearl for us from Moonshine Lake."

"Moonshine Lake?" Amon repeated as he frowned down at the midget-sized entity.

The Nixet chuckled. "A day's travel in that direction, Bigfoot, but remember this—the only time to dive is when the third moon rises high in the sky." The Nixet surveyed his gathered subjects as if seeking their approval. "Yes, we'll lead you through the marsh, but"—he suddenly turned and pointed his staff at Tulia—"she shall be our hostage until the pearl is safely in our hands."

Amon stepped forward. "No."

But even as he spoke, a blinding flash of light zoomed past him and enveloped Tulia in a halo of glowing embers. She screamed once and was gone.

The Nixet king held out his hand and a large bubble floated down to settle on his palm. Enclosed in the translucent casing was Tulia. Tears poured down her face as she pushed helplessly against the sides of her prison.

"Help me, Brianna, help me."

The words fluttered in her mind just like Da's had. She faced Tulia and pushed the words out of her mind. *"We'll save you, Tulia, don't cry. We will find the pearl."*

"I'm not crying... Take care of Dodi..." The words faded and Tulia plunked herself down in the middle of the sphere and covered her face with her hands. *"I'm scared."*

Anger washed over Brianna. *How dare these wretched creatures threaten Tulia?* She slipped her sword from its scabbard. "You horrid creature! Let her go!"

Amon placed a restraining hand on her shoulder. "No, Brianna," he muttered.

"That's right, warrior. Keep her under control. Little girl, being Hakon's child may protect you from my wrath, but if you wish to ensure your friend's safety, do as you're told." He peered down into the bubble. "Your beautiful maiden will be released in good time. No harm will be done, but..." Evil flitted across his face while his fingers closed threateningly over the fragile bubble. He snickered. "One mistake and I'll crush her like a flemiko."

Amon raised his hand to ward off the warning. "We mean no harm, Nixet king."

The Nixet opened his hand again, holding the bubble delicately between finger and thumb. With exaggerated care he slipped it into the pouch at his waist. "Now go, Bigfoot, before I change my mind," he ordered with a dismissive wave of his hand.

Dodi made a strangled noise and gestured toward the Nixet's pouch, his face scrunched up, tears threatening to spill down his cheeks. When Conal tried to talk to him he pulled away, his rosebud mouth turned down in a stubborn pout. He tucked his chin to his chest, folded his arms and stomped one small foot.

"Dodi, we have to go." Brianna moved closer. *We'll be back soon, Tulia.* She formed the words in her mind, still struggling with the concept of mind messages and how easily she could communicate with others.

The child shrugged and stood stiffly.

"Dodi." She tried to make her voice firm and low, copying her mother. It was meant to be a threat of dire consequences if he didn't obey.

Dodi dropped his head and stared at the ground. The Nixets scowled.

"Pick him up, Brianna," Amon ordered. "Let's go."

With one eye on the Nixets, Brianna stepped forward and scooped Dodi up. His wail shattered the tense silence. The whole swamp came alive with squawking and the fluttering of wings, while all around them millions of kachine and elsuda puffed and billowed in myriad iridescent clouds. The firozt clattered away in frantic rhythms.

Brianna clamped her mouth shut against the floating hordes and the nasty words she really wanted to spit at the Nixet king. Instead she heaved her kicking, yodeling bundle onto the domnak. The frightened animal danced slightly sideways at the unexpected burden, but Brianna snatched up the bridle, determined not to give the animal a chance to indulge its stubborn nature before it began to walk forward.

They traveled quite a distance before Brianna's heartbeat slowed and Dodi's tantrum had calmed to a series of inelegant sniffles and a blotchy face.

Brianna tried to send a mind message to Amon. She got no response so she tried Conal. Again silence. She glanced over at Dodi.

"We'll get the pearl, Dodi, and rescue Tulia as soon as we can."

"Go away, Brianna. I want Tulia." Dodi's petulant words prickled in her mind. Brianna flinched at their touch.

"Oh, moons' curse, you can communicate."

A cold silence was all she got in response.

Anger at the Nixets still sizzled inside her, but beside it was a bright warmth of discovery and acceptance. She could mind message. Wow.

They plodded on late into the night, only the croaks of the firozt disturbing the morose silence that surrounded them. Finally, exhausted, they rested on top of a huge fallen tree trunk until sun show. Nobody slept.

* * * *

Their pace was slower as they moved on in the cold light of the pre-sun show. Brianna was so tired — her legs ached and her eyes were scratchy. Her body itched with the dampness of her clothes and a growing lump of resentment toward the Nixets weighed her down. How dare they divert them from their task? This delay might mean the difference between life and death for some of the villagers.

As soon as the sun appeared, the kachine and the elsuda took flight to hum and bite. No amount of slapping or Hildegarde's ointments deterred them from attacking any exposed skin for a quick meal. Tested almost beyond endurance, Brianna was grateful to realize they were walking up a slight slope and absolutely ecstatic when they finally left the swamp and the torment of the kachine behind.

The sun was almost at its full height before they heard the sound of firozt and the tinkle of water. Brianna dropped her pack and pulled out her map. "See here," she said, holding it out. "It shows the lake."

Amon studied it. "Unfortunately, it does not show where the pearl is, and we have to dive in the dark."

He sounded grumpy. Brianna winced, immediately sorry that she'd spoken.

Tall spiky reeds surrounded the pool, but they could hardly see the dark, glistening water in places for the huge saucer-shaped leaves that floated serenely, spinning lazily in some unseen eddy deep in the water. They halted with grateful sighs on the small, pebbly bank. While they waited, Brianna wondered who would dive for the pearl. Certainly not she.

She was ashamed to admit she could hardly swim, but then she'd never had the time to play in the millpond like many of the other children. She glanced at Amon and wondered whether he could swim. Beside her, Dodi had finally lapsed into exhausted sleep, but Brianna could see it was far from restful. He twitched and groaned, trapped in a dream of his mind's making.

Conal explored in a desultory way, turning stones and scuffing the pebbles.

Amon watched Dodi for a minute. "Dodi and Tulia are very close for a brother and sister with several years' age gap."

Brianna stared out over the water. She smiled and wondered exactly how much Tulia would want Amon to know about her unfortunate escapade into magic that had crippled her leg and left Dodi without speech. She decided to give him a simple answer to begin with and only elaborate if he asked for more. Without turning to Amon, she said quietly, "They've been inseparable since the accident."

"Accident?"

"Two moon cycles ago, when Dodi was barely two, he and Tulia went missing overnight. Strange things were said to have been seen or to have happened in the woods that night. Nobody really knows what. Dodi has not spoken since, and Tulia has developed an obsession with magic."

Amon reclined on his back staring upward as he absorbed her story. "And nobody knows what happened?"

Brianna shrugged. "I believe Hildegarde knows. I saw the burns to Dodi's hands and suspect Dodi saved Tulia from whatever it was that night by using his gift before it matured."

"Does this mean Tulia does not have the gift?"

Brianna shrugged again. "Maybe. All I know is that she wants it so badly, she will be shattered if she isn't chosen."

They fell silent as Conal returned through the gloomy twilight that had settled on the pool.

He quickly scrutinized the pond then averted his eyes. "Who swims for it then?"

Brianna flicked her thick plaits over her shoulders. "You, Conal. You're the best swimmer in the village."

Conal glared at her. "Just because I can doesn't mean I want to, and you can't make me either."

Undaunted by Conal's hostility, she leaned toward him and said quietly, "Well, you should, you're the best diver."

"So?"

"And you can stay under the water longer than anyone else I know." Brianna scowled at him. "You were always showing off at home."

"So?" Conal spat.

"So, what are you afraid of?" Brianna asked, hoping to taunt him into taking up the challenge.

Conal stiffened and jutted his pointy chin in the air. The dimple in the middle deepened with his indignation. "I'm not afraid of anything," he spluttered.

"In that case, you won't have a problem with retrieving the pearl from the pond," Amon said softly.

Brianna saw the hope in Amon's expression. He wanted to delegate this particular job.

Conal shrugged and his top lip curled up into a sneer. "Do I have a choice?"

"No," Amon replied. "Because I swim like a firozt with four broken legs."

Despite his angry bravado, Brianna had seen the fear in Conal's eyes. Her heart went out to the mayor's younger son, victim of a privileged existence and his father's obsession with his elder son. Bullied or ignored at home, Conal had taken delight in showing off his superior swimming skills to the sons and daughters of the peasants. But this was different.

This was a strange pool, and the huge responsibility of Tulia's life rested on his shoulders. Up until now Conal had never taken responsibility well, seeing it as something to be cast aside or avoided at all costs. But Brianna knew he would dive for the pearl, if only to save his reputation.

Normally pale, Conal was now a sickly green color. His mouth was drawn into a tight grimace and he clenched his fists at his sides to hide their tremble. He stood stiffly on the bank, his gaze on the unknown body of water.

"All right, I'll go." Brianna clambered to her feet, already lifting her jerkin over her head.

"No, Brianna. He'll go as soon as the moons have risen and I'll go with him, as a lookout," Amon declared with a glare at Conal.

Conal nodded reluctant agreement, his face a kaleidoscope of expressions. Brianna suspected he was weighing up the knowledge that he would have company and whether that made a difference.

The hour grew late. Dodi woke and sat silently beside Brianna, tears still sliding down his cheeks, but his whimpering had become nothing more than erratic hiccups. The first silvery moon rose and sailed across the moss green darkness of the sky, which was broken only by the twinkling stars. In quick succession, each moon rose and traced a silvery arc overhead. It was time. The Nixet king's warning echoed in Brianna's mind. She wondered why it had to be at the height of the third moon rise. For even with all six moons floating in the sky, there would hardly be enough light to see around the hollow, let alone under the water.

The pool was dark, the glassy surface marred only by the muted reflections of the three silver moons. Even the elsuda leaves had stopped spinning, as if the eddies underneath were gone. Not a living creature had stirred since they arrived. Warily, Brianna studied the hollow, certain she could feel evil eyes boring into her undefended back.

She saw nothing, so turned back to watch the boys wade into the brackish water. The surface suddenly rippled as thousands of tiny qymaten scattered away from the two-legged intruders. Amon drew his dagger and waved Conal into the water.

At waist depth they began to swim, completing a slow circle in the center of the pond before Conal dove. Brianna held Dodi's hand, and he clutched her fingers so tightly they began to go numb. It seemed like an eternity before Conal surfaced.

"Can't see a thing," Conal gasped. "It's black as pitch down there." He paddled aimlessly then started to swim toward the shore.

"Where're you going, Conal?" Amon demanded.

"Out. No point in diving in the dark."

Amon immediately waved him back. "Oh no you don't. Use your hands if you have to—we need that pearl."

Conal frowned as he wiped water off his face. "But..."

"Are you prepared to let Tulia die?" Amon growled.

Conal hesitated at Amon's harsh question.

"Go," Amon ordered as he struggled to keep himself afloat. His expression showed no mercy.

Conal dove again. Seconds later the three moons reached their full rise, the fourth barely peeping over the mountains. Brianna gasped. The murky darkness of the water turned crystal clear and she could see Conal swimming aimlessly. Huge gray clams littered the sandy bottom. With the water now clear, Conal swam from shell to shell inspecting the insides. He started with the largest, but after he had inspected half a dozen he shot to the surface, gasping for air.

Amon squinted up at the moons. "Better hurry, the moons will begin to wane soon."

Conal swiped the water from his face, frowning. "Maybe you should try it, warrior, instead of issuing orders. But then, you don't swim so well, do you?"

Amon's face flushed an angry red. "You get going, boy. I'm right behind you."

Brianna waded in up to her knees. "Try the smallest one — out there on the ledge." She pointed to the sharp protrusion halfway up a ridge running along the far edge of the pool.

Conal's frown deepened, but he spun around in the water and peered down at the ledge, at the pink shell, delicate and frail, that rested on a bed of weeds.

"What makes you think the pearl is going to be in that baby thing?"

"Please try it, Conal."

He shrugged. "Fine — if you like wasting time." Conal dove neatly.

Amon trod water as he scanned the surrounds for danger.

Brianna quickly realized Conal was having trouble opening the small clam. "Amon, you need to help him. He can't get it open."

Amon waved in acknowledgment, took a deep breath, and forced himself below the surface in a clumsy dive. Brianna held her breath as she watched both boys struggle to open the shell.

It seemed to take ages before the lips of the shell parted and there, lying in the bed of soft, pink flesh, was a huge pearl, creamy white and absolutely perfect. Before Conal could retrieve it, both boys needed air and together they glided to the surface. Brianna waved her approval and the boys grinned back as they filled their lungs with air in preparation for the next dive.

Once below the water, Conal drew his dagger and carefully cut away the pearl. Reverently he lifted it out of the shell and slid it into his pouch.

Brianna sighed. Mission achieved. But as she turned to leave the water, a slight movement against the cliff face caught her attention. She stared intently, but saw nothing. Yet she felt the danger, the evil. A feeling so strong it felt like a physical beating in her breast. She waved at the boys and called out a warning, but they couldn't hear her. They were so busy congratulating themselves as they rose to the surface that they didn't even glance in her direction.

Dodi hopped nervously from foot to foot, and pointed. There was a stream of black bubbles spurting from the cliff face. Brianna checked the progress of the moons. They were almost past full rise and at any moment the light would be lost. She looked back at the pool. A dark blotch appeared in the agitated water.

Amon stopped rising. One huge tentacle held him firmly. Seven others waved wildly in front of a huge, gray-domed head that swayed from side to side. The creature's one bulging, myopic eye swiveled erratically as it struggled to see the prey it had captured. Pinned against the ledge, the snapping beak gnashing only inches from his face, Amon struggled frantically to free himself, his eyes fixed on his captor. Unaware of Amon's plight, Conal bobbed up and started to swim to shore.

"Conal! Go back! Something's got Amon," Brianna hollered and pointed.

At her frantic shrieks Conal hesitated, turned, and churned his way through the water. Huge bubbles now whipped the surface of the pond into a dirty gray froth. The reeds waved wildly and the sand and pebbles on the bottom swirled up in a thousand tiny, abrasive tornadoes.

Brianna ripped her tunic over her head and dragged off her boots, sword and trousers before she splashed clumsily into the water. With her hunting knife clenched between her teeth, she could hardly breathe as she crossed the pool in her awkward dog paddle. At the spot where she had last seen the boys, she splashed and kicked in a clumsy dive down into the now-murky water.

Conal grabbed her arm. He was holding Amon by the waist to stop the creature from dragging him away. Conal pointed to the surface. She nodded. Amon's face was a white blob in the dirtied water, and she wondered how he'd managed without air for that length of time. Her lungs were already straining to their limits, but she clawed her way down Amon's bare chest until she could hook her hand in his belt. The tentacle twitched and pulsed as she began to hack at it. It didn't retreat under her onslaught. The slimy, rubbery flesh was so cold it numbed her fingers. She tightened her grip on the dagger. Thick orange liquid oozed out of the wound and obscured her vision completely. She slashed harder, but she didn't seem to be doing much damage to the tentacle.

As red spots spun before her eyes, another pair of hands was beside hers, hacking with vicious strokes. Conal had returned. Her grip loosened as she battled blindly with the tough gray flesh, all the time worried that they might take some of Amon with it. She shot up for air then hauled herself back down. Rage at this creature and the Nixet's deception stirred until it thumped through her veins. Energized by her anger, she slashed deeper and faster.

Something brushed her foot. She jerked it away and continued to hack. Conal tugged and pulled the strands of leathery skin with his bare hands. Her arms ached. Her legs felt heavy as she pedaled slowly to keep herself suspended. Something tickled the back of her neck. The water stirred around her. Blackness rushed in with ringing pain as a vicious blow smacked into the side of her head. Her grip on Amon loosened and she began to sink. With a shake of her head, she fought unconsciousness. Something tugged at her shirt and hair and she kicked feebly and grasped Amon's legs to claw herself upward. Only a few strands of flesh remained. Amon strained against them. She sawed and Conal pulled. The last clinging strands sprang apart. Amon shot upward.

Struggling to stay conscious, Brianna felt her hunting knife slip from her grip. Conal pushed her upward until she burst through the surface of the water with a rush, right beside Amon, coughing and choking in a desperate effort to drag sweet air into her starved lungs. They burned as she gasped again and again—then she coughed violently again and spat the foul-tasting water from her mouth.

"Yuck, yuck, yuck," she spluttered.

Amon was barely keeping his chin above water. His mouth was set in a tight grimace, his face smeared with gluggy orange muck.

Conal spat out fluid and pushed his dripping hair off his face before he jerked his head toward the shore. "Let's get out of here," he gasped.

Nothing disturbed the surface of the pond. Even the firozt were silent. Using one another for support they paddled to shore, staggered out of the water, and collapsed on the beach. Brianna's head rang and thudded with the effects of the blow, and Amon groaned as he rolled over, holding ribs that were already turning black.

"Are you all right, Brianna? You and Conal saved my life."

Brianna nodded weakly and winced at the pain that flashed through her head. "I don't plan on fighting a war right now, but I'll live. What about you?"

Amon felt his ribs cautiously. "Nothing broken, this time," he muttered ruefully.

"Conal?"

Conal peered at his finger. "Nothing but a small nick from your knife, Brianna." Blood still oozed slowly, so he wrapped the tail of his shirt around it and held it tight.

Dodi took Brianna's hand and tried to pull her up. When she protested, he moved to Amon, then Conal. To satisfy the child's need to have them on their feet, Conal allowed himself to be pulled up.

"Come on, Dodi. Help me resaddle the domnak."

The child remained downcast.

But Conal took his hand and whispered in his ear, "And then we'll go get Tulia."

Dodi tried to smile as he pulled away from Conal and picked up the bridle.

Slowly Brianna eased herself to her knees. The world spun in and out of focus and for a moment all she could do was wait until it stilled. When it did, she climbed unsteadily to her feet.

Amon was watching her closely. "You aren't going to collapse on me, are you?" he asked.

Brianna focused her eyes on Amon. He was half sitting, his head cocked to one side, pain twisting his mouth into a lopsided scowl.

Brianna frowned and waved her hand in dismissive gesture. "I'm all right... I think..." Her words faded as she locked looks with Amon.

She shivered, suddenly aware of the way her wet shirt clung to her breasts and was riding up her bare thighs. Unexpectedly, she felt acutely aware of the rise and fall of Amon's bare muscular chest and his long legs encased in wet trousers. She saw warmth in his eyes that hadn't been there before, and she self-consciously pulled her shirt away from her body.

Amon eased himself up and went to stand by the lake. He stared out over the water. "What do you think it was, out there?"

Behind his back, Brianna quickly pulled on her pants. "I don't know." She went to stand beside him. "But I'm sure the Nixet king knew it was there," she snarled.

He took her hand and squeezed it gently. "I'm really glad we're all safe, and we have the pearl to exchange for Tulia."

Brianna felt the strange tension between them ease, and sighed. This was no time to complicate things.

She returned his clasp. "And we'll find Hakon too."

Conal scrunched up behind them. "Ready to travel?" he asked.

They nodded.

Brianna held out her hand for the pearl. "Give me the pearl, Conal. I'll put it my medicine bag for safekeeping."

He gave her a venomous look. "I got it."

"*We* got it, Conal," Brianna said firmly. "It was a team effort."

Conal frowned, retrieved the pearl and opened his hand. Brianna gasped at the pearl's perfect beauty — creamy white with a delicate blush of pink. She took it and stowed it deep inside the medicine bag.

As Amon leaned down to pick up his pack, Conal dragged it out of his reach. Amon frowned.

"I'll carry it for a while," Conal said quietly as he swung it on his back.

Amon appeared ready to argue, changed his mind, and with a brief nod of thanks to Conal, he turned and walked steadily up the beach.

"Let's go and deal with these wretched Nixets," Conal announced as he took up the domnak's bridle and led the way back to the swamp.

Nobody was inclined to make conversation as they trudged down the slope, and Brianna was grateful for the silence. Her thoughts rampaged through her head — her Abrasaxon father, the horrible reason for this journey, the brief elusive feelings between her and Amon, and the sure knowledge that she had the Abrasaxon gift of magic and absolutely no expertise in using it. They were all jumbled, and her head ached as she tried to analyze them. Finally she gave up and trudged behind the others in blank silence.

* * * *

They were well into the swamp when sun show came, and the Nixets were waiting in the soft light.

The Nixet king stood atop a decaying tree stump. His eyes narrowed as he took in their disheveled state. "You have the pearl?"

Amon nodded.

The Nixet's frown immediately transformed into a leering grin. "Let me see! Let me see." He chortled as he rubbed his chubby hands together.

Despite her uncertainty, Brianna couldn't help smiling at the diminutive creature's display of glee. She closed her fingers protectively over the beautiful jewel. They had almost lost their lives retrieving it, and she was reluctant to hand it over to this horrid manipulative creature.

"You agreed to lead us safely through the marsh if we delivered the pearl," Amon said quietly.

All signs of happiness left the Nixet king's face. "How dare you make demands of the Nixets?" he snarled and stabbed his staff into the decaying wood of the stump.

Amon gave a terse smile and quietly replied to the tiny man, "I'm not making demands, Nixet, simply opening up negotiations."

The king stared up at Amon with his beady eyes narrowed. A flicker of evil red lit up the dark centers. "Nixets don't need negotiations," the king declared loftily.

Again Amon nodded. "I know that too, Nixet king, but I'm hoping you will be fair and reasonable."

The small creature scowled for a moment then his face cleared. "Of course Nixets can be fair and reasonable."

Brianna could see Amon was trying not to smile. He managed, after a struggle, to adopt a serious expression and appear duly impressed.

"This is what I've been told," Amon concurred calmly.

"It is true. Nixets have their own code of honor, not always understood by the Bigfoot."

"So, Nixet king, will you lead us through the treacherous marsh for the price of a pearl?"

"Of course, this is what we agreed," said the Nixet king.

Brianna fingered the pearl before she reluctantly passed it to Amon. They both knew the Nixet wasn't to be trusted, and she wondered why he'd said nothing about Tulia.

The obnoxious creature scowled with impatience. "Hurry up, warrior, or the deal's off."

They had no choice, so Amon held out his hand.

The Nixet king smiled gleefully, his tiny feet stomping an excited lively dance on the log. "You have it! You do have it!" he shrieked.

Amon nodded. "The pearl is yours when we reach dry ground," he reiterated firmly.

The Nixet smiled slyly. "Then we have a deal, warrior. Let's go." He signaled with his staff and the Nixets gathered in single file to lead the way.

At last the Nixet king brought them to a halt. They stood huddled in a wet, muddy group, the stench of the marshes rising in a fetid cloud around them.

The Nixet king scrutinized them, disdain contorting his face. "Not very good travelers, are we?" he sneered.

Brianna had a terrible urge to stomp on his precious gray-haired head, but she restrained it with a struggle. Amon's set face signaled his own thoughts about the obnoxious creatures.

The Nixet king pointed with his staff. "The end of my kingdom is over yonder, warrior. You will reach it by sunset. Hand over the pearl."

Amon's expression was grim. He cast a glance around him. "But we are still in the swamp."

The Nixet king shrugged. "So?"

Amon frowned. "Our deal was to be guided across the swamp."

The Nixet king shrugged again. "This is near enough."

Amon turned to the Nixet king, pearl in hand. "Here's your pearl. Now give me Tulia."

The Nixet king began to laugh. "Since when has a warrior made demands of a Nixet king?" he snorted.

A surge of rage rushed over Brianna—they were being played with. She began to wonder if the edge of the swamp was as close as promised, but one wrong word and the Nixet king would unleash his formidable powers. They would all be doomed to live forever in the marshes as green firozts, or shrunk to Nixet size, their only purpose in life to do Nixet chores. Brianna watched Amon, terribly afraid that he was running out of options.

Amon smiled. "I'm not making demands, Your Majesty. I desire to complete our bargain with all haste, so we can continue our journey."

The Nixet king frowned at Amon's conciliatory words. Obviously he didn't like being reminded that he was expected to keep his bargain with these unwelcome Bigfeet.

Slowly he took out the bubble. He studied Tulia carefully. "I've seen prettier," he grumbled, turning the transparent ball around in his fingers. "Besides, she's lame, and no good to the Nixets like that." He leered at Amon. "Give me the pearl," he demanded.

Amon turned the pearl gently in his hand. He looked from it to the Nixet then held out his other hand for the bubble. The Nixet king appeared loath to keep his side of the bargain.

Brianna saw movement across the corner of her vision. "No..." she cried.

But even as she shouted the warning, in a flash of green and brown a Nixet leaped up and snatched the pearl from Amon's palm before he could close his fingers. Seconds later the thieving Nixet delivered the pearl to his king with a jaunty bow.

Brianna would have dived after it, but Amon's hand on her arm held her back her. She didn't fight his restraint, but the rage building inside pulsated through her limbs and cramped her fingers.

Amon's expression was frozen, his complexion white, his eyes dark with rage. With an outstanding display of calmness, he held his hand out. "It's time to complete your side of the bargain, Nixet king."

A cunning gleam appeared in the Nixet's eyes. "Why should I?" he asked as he clutched the huge pearl to his bony chest.

Brianna could sense Amon's desperation. It showed on his face even as he tried to conceal it.

He chose his next words carefully. "I have always believed Nixets never reneged on their bargains. I trusted you on the reputation of all the generations of Nixets that have gone before."

The Nixet continued to stare in fascination at the pearl.

"Do you hear me, Nixet king? I trusted you."

The Nixet king smiled benignly. "Of course, warrior, but only because you had no choice."

Amon sighed.

The Nixet's smile widened. "But today, warrior, I am feeling contrary." He flicked his staff in the direction of Tulia's bubble. "So, she will stay with us. Now go, and never return to my land." The Nixet king captured the bubble between thumb and finger and squeezed gently.

Chapter Seven

Dodi's unearthly screech sliced through the air. Brianna grabbed his shoulders and held him against her. He struggled, making high-pitched grunting noises as he fought her embrace.

The Nixet king smirked — the pearl in one hand, Tulia in the other.

Rage slashed at Brianna. She ignored its unleashed heat, concentrating on her internal heat — white-hot and controlled. Letting it build, she focused her stare on the Nixet king, her stance rigid. Her hand began to tremble. Slowly she lifted her arm, extended out straight in front of her, tight and inflexible all the way to her fingertips. With mechanical precision she bent her wrist up until her palm was at a right angle to her arm. The power throbbed along her arm, forming a pulsing mass in her hand. Breathing deeply, she tried to distill the magic from her mortal anger, consciously trying to direct it, harness it.

She jutted her chin out in a defiant gesture. "Release Tulia, and let us go." Her voice was a steady monotone.

The Nixet king grinned at her. "Or what, little girl?"

Brianna could feel the power gathering, and was petrified that she would not be able to hold back much longer. "I'm warning you, Nixet king, let her go or you'll be sorry."

Amon frowned at her, a sharp fracture of real anxiety in his eyes, but he made no attempt to stop her — whether out of fear or acceptance of what must be done, Brianna didn't know. In a vague corner of her mind she sensed that this would be a turning point in her relationship with Amon.

The Nixets were now spread out in a menacing circle, almost surrounding them. Still Brianna stood, arm outstretched, stiff and throbbing.

The king frowned now. He looked from the pearl to Tulia then back at Brianna. The frown melted into a sneer. "You don't scare me, little girl. You're bluffing."

The mortal rage twisted around the magic power, tightening her control. Her palm burned. She glared at the Nixet king. She eased her control on the power inside her the minutest fraction. A flash of white light shot from her hand. It hit the Nixet king in the chest. He reeled backward, made a grotesque expression of agony and slumped to the ground.

As he landed with a splat, the light changed to pink, swirled around the pearl and Tulia, then retreated to Brianna with the two precious objects encased in its cloud-like mist. Without conscious thought, Brianna held the pearl and Tulia in her hand — a hand that still smarted from the heat, but was now relaxed.

The Nixets screeched and crowded around their fallen monarch. He lay in the mud, his bearded face gray, eyes closed. Brianna let the held breath *whoosh* out of her lungs when a quick check by a wizened old Nixet revealed that the king still lived. She was relieved that she hadn't killed him.

Two of the older Nixets turned to the children and waved their staffs. Brianna frowned, shoved the pearl and Tulia into her pouch and raised her hand, which immediately pulsed with power. She had no idea exactly how powerful these Nixets were or if her newly emerged skills could match theirs.

The Nixets stood frozen. Brianna saw the uncertainty in their expressions. They were as unsure of her potency as she was of theirs.

Amon backed slowly away, dragging a sobbing Dodi with him and gesturing for Conal to follow. He put Dodi on the domnak and took up the bridle, ready for a hasty departure. Amon touched Brianna on the shoulder.

She ignored him, her stare fixed on the Nixets. "I propose a new deal, Nixets. We will leave unmolested — "

The oldest Nixet frowned and waved his staff. "You're not going anywhere. Those who attack the person of the king die!"

Brianna raised her hand and sent a blast of fiery white light toward the Nixet. It exploded at his feet — rocks, plants and mud splattered everyone. For a brief moment a small crater oozed in the mud. The Nixet appeared worried as he stared at the fast-filling hole. Brianna signaled with her other hand for Amon to move off. She heard him go and felt bereft at his departure, but she stayed put, determined to ward off the Nixets. The Nixets waited in silence and made no protest when Brianna sent out a translucent pink cloud that scooped up the unconscious Nixet king and brought him to her. She dumped him over her shoulder still wrapped in remnants of the pink cloud. The babble that arose from the Nixets hurt her ears. The older Nixet advanced, his staff pointed at her. Brianna lifted her hand again and placed it on the Nixet king.

"One more step and the king dies," Brianna grated in warning.

The Nixet froze. Brianna backed away. The Nixets didn't move. With just one quick glance over her shoulder, she kept backing away until she judged she was out of reach of any magic they might cast. Then she turned and sloshed at a clumsy run after the others. The mud squelched into her boots and sucked at every footstep. Every few paces she checked over her shoulder, but there was no sign of the Nixets. The ground was getting soggier, and at times Brianna sank to her knees. The Nixet king was heavy, despite his small size, and Brianna was worried about Tulia still trapped in the bubble, but now was not the time to investigate.

At last she caught up with Amon. He glanced past her.

"They aren't following?" he asked.

Brianna pointed to the Nixet king slung limply over her shoulder. "They'll wait."

Amon frowned, obviously not happy with the way things had turned out. She suspected she would now be the object of his fear and contempt because in most of Okana and Okiyarra a mortal of mixed blood with magic was someone to be feared or at the very least wary of. She felt defensive. It wasn't her fault, the magic had just happened.

"What happens to him?" Amon asked with a glance at the unconscious king.

"I suggest we leave him and the pearl at the first rocky outcrop we find near the edge of the swamp."

Conal glowered. "They don't deserve the pearl."

"Two wrongs don't make a right," Brianna said as she heaved the Nixet onto the domnak.

Conal pouted. "You didn't tell me you could do that."

Brianna shrugged. "I wasn't sure I could."

The sulky boy gave her a disbelieving look as he turned away.

Before they moved on, Brianna carefully lifted Tulia's bubble out of her pouch. The child sat hunched on the floor of the bubble. She peered up through the translucent covering, her face white and tear-streaked. Brianna tapped the surface of the bubble ever so gently. When Tulia saw it was Brianna, she smiled weakly.

"It won't be long now, Tulia. Hang in there until we're out of the swamp."

Tulia nodded and Brianna carefully placed the bubble and its precious cargo back in the pouch.

Brianna fell into step behind Amon.

"Walk in my footsteps, everybody," he instructed.

Caked in mud and surrounded by the swamp's evil stench, they trudged on until at last the ground became solid, with the mud and slime giving way to rocks and dry grasses. The sun was low in the sky, and ahead of them loomed a substantial rocky outcrop — silhouetted by the last rays of sun.

"This will do." Brianna halted in the shade of the rocks and dumped her pack before she lifted the Nixet king from the domnak.

As she propped him in a sitting position on the ground, he muttered something unintelligible and pulled at his beard.

Amon and Conal stood back, watching the miniature man with wary fascination. Dodi stayed on the domnak, his cherubic face screwed up into a mask of hatred. Brianna felt a shiver of fear run over her skin as the king came to. She didn't know if she could repeat the white blast, and she didn't know quite how the Nixet king was going to react when he realized what she had done. In an effort to make his response as civil as possible, she picked up her water bottle, filled the lid and handed it to the still-dazed king. He sipped several times before he spoke, and his eyes darted from one to the other as he assessed his situation. Now he fixed a beady glare on Brianna. There was grudging respect in his eyes.

"So, Hakon's daughter — you have inherited the gift, and it seems almost as powerful as the Grand Archon's."

She nodded, still worried about what this cunning creature might do.

"So I should have been a great deal more careful about being contrary."

Brianna stood straighter, braver after seeing the effect her magic had on the Nixet king. "Yes, you should have."

The king climbed to his feet. "And what do you intend to do with me, Hakon's daughter?"

"I will release you to return to your people unharmed, but only on the condition that you break your spell on Tulia and promise to leave us to continue our journey in peace."

The king seemed relieved. "Consider it done!" he said as he snapped his fingers. He muttered two short unintelligible words and suddenly Tulia stood beside them.

Brianna gave her a quick hug and Dodi clung to her hand, his eyes wet with unshed tears.

The king straightened his clothes and looked up at Brianna. "And the pearl?"

"You ask a lot, Nixet king, after the deplorable way you have acted, but when we go, we will leave the pearl with you."

"But..." Conal protested as he stepped toward the Nixet.

Instantly he was stopped by Amon's iron grip on his arm. Brianna knew how Conal felt, but she didn't want to push her luck with her untapped power — or that of the Nixet.

The Nixet king smiled. "So, Bigfoot, our business is concluded."

"It is," Amon muttered.

The Nixet's smile faded as the inner evil seeped out through his skin. "Just this once, warrior, you have been fortunate. If you're wise, you won't come this way again. Next time I will not be so unprepared for one as powerful as Hakon's daughter. Now be gone from my sight."

Brianna felt her heart sink into the seething mass that contorted her stomach. That horrid little man had used them, and now he was closing the only way home she knew. The desire to step on him was unbearably strong, but she gritted her teeth, heaved her pack onto her shoulders and trudged off in the direction of the mountains.

The answer to their dilemma would be found ahead in those mountains, lying like sleeping whitukas, dark and mysterious. If all went well, they would be in the foothills in a day or two. Brianna sensed the others falling into step behind her, but she didn't dare to even glance over her shoulder in case the Nixet king was about to cast a spell at their retreating backs. She didn't want to see it coming.

The light was almost gone, but Amon didn't want to stop. Brianna heard somebody stumble.

Tulia's anguished cry rent the air. "Dodi!"

The child was sprawled among the boulders, his chin bleeding profusely as plump tears trickled down his cheeks. He didn't make a sound as he climbed clumsily to his feet.

Tulia shot Amon a venomous look. "See what you've done? We should have stopped ages ago."

There was a mumble of agreement from Conal.

Brianna came back to stand beside Amon. "Amon isn't to blame for this. I am. I didn't want to pitch camp right under the Nixets' noses."

"Well, we are not all big tall warriors like you," Tulia said softly.

"Never mind, Tulia. I think we're far enough away now to stop." Brianna dropped her pack and glanced at Amon for confirmation.

He peered around the darkness. "This appears safe enough, I suppose."

They lit a small fire that provided comfort more than warmth, and quickly ate chunky sandwiches made from bread and cheese, washed down with hot tea Brianna had brewed from some of Hildegarde's herbs. With the gnawing hunger satisfied, Tulia and Dodi huddled together in one blanket, reluctant to be separated again after their ordeal. Conal rolled into his blanket beside a small overhanging boulder left of the fire. Brianna sensed that he still felt some resentment toward Amon and envied the superior skills and strength the older boy had. But Conal had no understanding of the horror Amon had gone through to be like that. It was not something that came easily or without a price. Amon gave them each a brief look, stoked the fire and prepared to leave the camp.

"Where're you going, Amon?" Brianna asked. Although he didn't have his pack she was unexpectedly worried he was leaving them.

He gave her a grim smile. "I'm only going to set some snares. We can't rely completely on our supplies."

"Do you need help?"

"No thanks, Brianna. Somebody should stay here and watch over them. I won't be far away."

"Are you angry at me for what I did to the Nixet king? Using magic?"

Amon frowned before he gave a vague smile. "No, Brianna, I'm not angry, merely uneasy with powerful displays of magic."

"I can't help it. I didn't ask to be born half Abrasaxon."

"I know, Brianna. It will take some getting used to, that's all. Be back soon."

Brianna hugged her knees tightly as she watched him trudge off into the darkness. She'd only known Amon a few days and was surprised at the feeling of loneliness that washed over her as he disappeared. While she waited for his return she stared into the dancing flames, trying not to flinch at every minute noise, and wondered how much danger there was lurking out there in the darkness. There were no large predators this side of the mountains, and from reports of the war, the alien Yabix had been eradicated completely. Of course there was Zelig and the Gomahras.

Even though Amon had not spoken about his past, Brianna suspected he was still troubled by his experiences. He hadn't really wanted to help them at first, but very quickly he'd become an important part of the team. She liked him – he was handsome, funny and caring. He was also brave and smart. A warm wave of sensation edged with a tingle of excitement seeped through her as she remembered the strange tension between them at the lake, and she wished things were normal so she could explore these new feelings.

The other thing that played on her mind was the manifestation of her gift. Amon had only made a vague comment about her magic display with the Nixets and she wondered if his uneasiness with her ability would come between them. While Brianna's initial denunciation of her gift had faded, she worried about the future, after everybody was rescued. Would she find a place in the world or would ostracism be her lot?

At a sharp rattle of stones, she jumped to her feet and peered into the darkness. Moments later Amon emerged from the blackness. He touched her shoulder, squeezing it quickly in reassurance.

"Amon... Can we talk?"

He smiled and brushed his fingers over her shoulder. "Later. Try to rest, Brianna. We have a strenuous walk tomorrow."

She felt rejected, but didn't protest, just wrapped herself in the blanket and curled up to sleep. He hadn't wanted to talk about what had happened, and she interpreted that as a bad sign. The night stretched interminably. The hard rocks stabbed her body, leaving oddly shaped indentations in her back, arms and side while her doubts and fears stabbed at her mind. In the moments she stared at the stars, she heard the others toss and sigh as they struggled with the night. Again she wished desperately to be home, safe.

* * * *

When the sky began to lighten, Amon went to retrieve the snares. The others had slept at last, and before they woke, Brianna went to fetch some water from the small stream they'd passed prior to setting up camp yesterday.

She met Amon on the way back, two white floppy-eared tahua dangling from his hand.

"Good hunting."

He nodded. "They'll do for tonight. There seems to be plenty of game this side of the marsh."

Brianna nodded. "Everything's still alive here. It must be Zelig's influence in the valley that's killing everything..." A sudden buzz in her head tore the next words out of her mind.

"Help me. Oh, moons' curse, I don't want to die. Help."

Brianna smacked her forehead to dispel the words from a voice she did not recognize, but the fear and desperation they carried remained in her mind like a stain. A loud roar filled her ears and echoed around the clearing. It was followed by a sharp clatter.

Brianna jumped, her nerves jangling with fear. "What's that?"

Amon flung down the carcasses and drew his sword. He broke into a run as he left the camp.

She checked the children. They were standing stock-still by their blankets, expressions of terror on their faces. Brianna's heart clenched in sympathy — they'd all faced so much in the last few days. They didn't need another whituka to battle.

Brianna struggled to catch up to Amon as he bounded up the slope, stunned at his instant battle-ready response. Moments later she halted beside him. He stood frozen, his face an ashen gray. He made strangled choking noises as he tried to find his voice.

Finally he did, and bellowed, "Yabix! Run, Brianna."

Brianna stared at the huge creature in the meadow below. She gulped. It was awful. The ballads sung by passing musicians had definitely not done justice to the horror of the real thing. The Yabix was like a six-legged wekaza, except that it stood ten feet high, upright on the back four legs as it swept its two front legs, armed with pincers, over the head of a young woman. Loose blue-gray skin flexed and bubbled around heaving muscles and flesh, jagged patches sloughing as the creature moved. The unknown juvenile female was backing away from the creature's advance, her spear and shield held defensively in front of her. Two serpent-like heads lunged down at her with huge, gaping mouths filled with sharp yellow pointed fangs that dripped slime. Long forked tongues flicked from side to side, tasting the air — seeking the taste of its prey. The woman thrust with her spear but the Yabix agilely stepped aside and the spear passed uselessly by its ribs. The misplaced thrust unbalanced the woman and she stumbled forward, landing on the ground. The Yabix reared over her and roared.

Small hands clutched at Brianna's clothes as Dodi and Tulia pressed close, whimpering with terror.

"Fiery moons, a Yabix," Conal muttered.

Her stomach turned at the acidic fumes emanating from the creature. A tight band of fear gripped her chest. Her legs trembled and refused to move forward. She stood frozen, staring, her sword half drawn.

As if suddenly sensing others, the creature stopped mid swipe and lifted its two heads high, the tongues thrust fully out into the air. It roared again as it towered over the helpless stranger and stared in their direction.

"Stay back, all of you. I'm going in to rescue the girl," Amon yelled as he charged down the slope, his sword held high over his head and a curved silver dagger held stiffly out in front of him.

Sensing imminent attack from a more worthy foe, the Yabix threw up its heads and lumbered forward to close the gap. Four glowing red eyes now squinted with evil intent. Amon steadied himself before he lunged forward, his sword aimed directly at the Yabix's exposed belly. It reared up with a rumbling hiss. Amon's sword glanced off the scales, but immediately he brought his sword back for another thrust.

"I'm going to help," Conal yelled as he drew his sword.

Brianna had no chance to stop him before he hurtled toward the battle.

"Tulia, Dodi, go hide somewhere — do not come out until it's safe."

"Brianna," Tulia wailed.

"Do as I say, Tulia."

Brianna drew her sword and launched herself down the slope, hoping that Tulia did as she was told. The unknown woman was back on her feet now, tormenting the Yabix with well-placed stabs from the rear. Her flimsy shield was held high to ward off the thumping swipes that rained down on her from the spiny tails.

Amon danced back and forth, trying to find an opening between the two front legs and the two swishing heads.

Conal surged forward. "Ahhh!" His battle cry rang out as he rushed in, sword flashing in the sunlight.

"Conal! No!" Brianna and Amon yelled in unison.

"Take that, Yabix!" Conal howled and stabbed furiously at the scaly back.

The Yabix squealed in pain as the boy ripped his blade through the tough membrane and embedded it deeply into the spongy flesh. Blue-gray liquid gushed from the wound. Conal stared at his blade in horror. The Yabix roared and spun around, slimy arms with razor-sharp claws slashing the air.

Conal backed away, his face ashen. "Warrior, help!" he squeaked as the realization hit him that this creature was not playing. It intended to kill him.

The maddened creature began to stalk Conal, its ugly mouths slavering blood-flecked foam. Conal, now armed only with a small hunting knife, backed away.

"Keep going but watch those tails, they have a reach of fourteen feet," Amon yelled before he joined the young woman behind the creature, his sword poised, ready to strike.

Obediently Conal backed away, barely fast enough to stay out of reach of the lumbering Yabix's tails.

He waved his arms provocatively and yelled, "Come on, you ugly brute. Come and get me." His sword still hung in the creature's flesh, heaving up and down as it moved.

The huge gray tails twitched then lashed out with sightless accuracy. Conal backed hurriedly out of reach, his gaze darting back and forth between the two writhing lengths. Close enough to strike, Amon brought his sword back then drove it forward, shoving the blade up to the hilt in the pulsating gray mass. A terrible screech rent the air. Amon tugged at his weapon, but it was stuck fast. Desperately he twisted and pulled, but already the tails were swinging around to slap at him. Frantically, he tried once more to free the weapon. Brianna fretted. That was three strikes and still the creature did not die. Amon had told her it often took five or six solid strikes against a Yabix to kill it. Warriors in the war had always tried to fight them in pairs to kill them more easily.

Brianna watched as the dark-haired young woman jumped forward and thrust her spear deep into the flesh beside Amon's quivering sword.

"Watch out!" Brianna cried.

It was too late for Amon to duck. The viciously armed tails struck him a savage blow to the head. His head jerked back, he swayed on the spot then collapsed to the ground.

"Run, Amon! Amon! Get up, Amon!" Brianna urged.

Amon staggered up, reached blindly for his weapon, but found only air. The writhing mass of heads, arms and tails reached for him again. One of the Yabix's heads snapped forward and sharp, venom-filled fangs sank into Amon's shoulder.

Brianna charged in, her sword swinging wildly. "Let him go, you beast!" she yelled.

The Yabix flung Amon like a rag doll thirty feet up the slope and turned to face Brianna. The razor-sharp claws flashed through the air. Evil-smelling fluid gushed from the three puncture wounds already inflicted.

Brianna saw cunning intelligence flicker in its four bloodshot eyes as the Yabix assessed her strength and anticipated her next move. She raised her hand and willed her magic to materialize. It began to build, but too slowly, so she abandoned her efforts. Brianna sensed the woman move in beside her, but she didn't have time to acknowledge her presence. Together they made strike after strike, but only managed to inflict superficial wounds.

In desperation, Brianna lifted her hand again. This time she felt the power surge down her arm and centralize in her palm. Mentally she willed it forward, and the blast came. White-hot light ripped through a thick muscular neck, immediately behind one of the Yabix's heads. The creature didn't even have time to move before the severed head hit the ground in a shower of bloodied flesh, writhing tongue and red, glinting eyes. The stump of its decapitated neck waved around blindly as the remaining head swiveled to face its new foe. It roared. Brianna raised her hand again and conjured up another deadly blast.

This time she caught the Yabix in the rump. It staggered but still did not fall. "Moon lights – die, you bastard."

She blasted again, but this time the blast was so weak it did nothing more than sear the scaly skin. Knowing she was weakening and unable to summon up more magic power, she gripped her sword tightly and slowly moved closer, only vaguely aware of the stranger beside her. When a tail lashed out, she ignored it, waiting until her circle was three-quarters complete. Then she lifted her sword and rushed madly forward. The Yabix tried to swing around, to cover its blind side, but Brianna moved too quickly. She raised her sword and drove it deeply into the undulating flesh, feeling it jerk as it slid through the tough skin. She twisted it sharply and dragged it out again before sprinting out of reach. The Yabix roared and swiped savagely at empty space. Gasping for air, Brianna waited. That was six strikes. It seemed like an eternity before the creature shuddered. Its tails went limp, its huge clawed hands hung at its sides. It screeched again, raised its remaining head to the sky, then — tongue hanging out and eyes glazing over — it toppled slowly to the ground.

Brianna's knees buckled and she sat heavily on the ground, her sword slipping from nerveless fingers. With trembling hands she wiped the stinging sweat out of her eyes and inspected the young woman standing in front of her. Her greeting died in her throat as her mind groped to make sense of her vision. Except that the stranger had the most intense gray eyes and the darkest of hair, Brianna might have been looking in a mirror.

"Hello, sister. I am Issah, second daughter of Hakon. I've been trying to find you."

Brianna's mouth sagged open. She tried to speak, but although her mouth moved and her throat convulsed, no sound came out. Issah waited in silence for her response.

"You all right, Brianna?" Tulia asked as she limped up.

Brianna nodded and with shaky hands handed over the medicine bag. Tulia gave one appraising glance at Brianna's dark-haired look-alike, then gathered up her skirts and lurched up the slope as fast as her crippled leg would allow.

Brianna fought to hide the tremors and confusion rattling through her. "I didn't know... Nobody told me

I had a sister. I didn't even know who my father was until a few days ago... I don't know..."

"You probably don't know what to think or how to feel, Brianna. Maybe you're even angry about the secrets. You probably even resent me," Issah informed her calmly.

Brianna had not been able to keep the pique out of her voice and yes, she was angry. She was jealous, and hurt that she'd been lied to, and she couldn't discuss it right now with this girl in front of her because unshed tears and constricted sobs strangled her throat. There was nothing she could say right now that would not be cruel and dismissive.

"I need to see Amon," she muttered as she turned away from the girl called Issah and watched the Yabix twitch.

It at last lay still. Only then, certain it was dead, did Brianna feel the tension ease out of her body. Slowly she pushed herself upright onto weak and shaky knees. Cold tremors rushed over her body in debilitating waves. She held onto the rocks to steady herself. Sweat dampened her skin and as she licked dry lips, she tasted salt. She swallowed, making her dry throat rasp. After a long moment, she felt strong enough to move, and on legs still unsteady, she staggered up the slope. Without invitation, Issah followed her.

Tulia was kneeling by Amon when Brianna got there. He writhed, his face covered in gray slime, the triangular puncture wounds on his shoulder weeping venom and blood, the flesh already swollen and discolored.

"Lie still, warrior. You're hurt."

Tulia's gentle voice must have penetrated his pain. For a moment he relaxed then, with stubbornness born of war, he forced his eyes open. "Conal? Where's Conal?"

"Conal's fine. Lie still, so I can get this muck off." Tulia held him down with all her tiny weight.

But Amon continued to fight her. "The Yabix..."

"It's dead." Brianna forced her tone into a matter-of-fact flatness as she fought the nausea that threatened to overwhelm her stomach.

With unsteady arms, he pushed himself into a sitting position and peered down the slope. "I can't see, Tulia! I can't see!" He clutched wildly at her arm.

The Yabix had tumbled into a gory heap at the bottom of the slope, but there was no sign of Conal. Together Tulia and Brianna pushed Amon down.

"Lie still, Amon. Rest now," Tulia urged the struggling man.

"No! Where's Brianna?"

"I'm here, Amon." She touched his arm. Tears trickled down her cheeks. She sniffed inelegantly and wiped them away with her sleeve.

"And the girl?"

"She's fine, Amon." Brianna touched his shoulder in a gesture of reassurance.

He clutched at her hand. "Go on without me, Brianna. I'm doomed. A single scratch can kill, never mind about a full-toothed bite." He struggled to speak, his throat swelling closed from the poison. "First the blindness, then the slow, rotting death, the poison eating away at your insides. They all went that way..." The words choked in his throat.

"No!" Brianna cried, startled by the depth of her feelings for him.

Tulia shook her head, her wide, thinnish lips drawn into a wry smile. "Don't worry, warrior, you're not getting out of your responsibilities that easily. You took us on for better or worse and now you have to stick with it until the end. Now lie still so I can apply this salve, then you will drink my potion."

"All your salves and potions are useless," Amon mumbled.

"Be quiet, warrior!" Tulia snapped. "My potions are strong."

He turned his face in her direction and reached up to stop her. "Don't waste it on me…"

Tulia slapped his hand away. "Don't argue with me."

"Where's Conal?" Brianna asked.

Tulia smiled and pointed to the bushes halfway down the slope. "He's being sick."

Brianna gave Tulia a grim smile. She was all too familiar with how Conal's stomach was feeling. Behind the bushes, she found him hunched over a rock, his face a sickly green.

"You shouldn't have tried to tackle a Yabix."

"It was horrible," he muttered.

"The Yabix?"

A choking noise came from his throat. "Yes, and the killing."

"Amon warned you that killing is not all it's cracked up to be. It's awful, dangerous and more often than not leads to your own death, not heroism and glory," Brianna said.

"So why? Why do they go to war? Why did Kenton want to go so badly he defied Father and snuck away in the middle of the night?" Conal wailed.

Brianna shrugged. "Sometimes the generals paint a picture of glory — sometimes the recruits believe so strongly in the need to protect loved ones, or they have no choice. Somebody had to rid the land of our enemy."

"Why can't we all live in peace?"

"I don't know the answer to that. Maybe when we can all be more tolerant of our differences, accept one another's failings, try harder, maybe then..." She squeezed his shoulder. "It's no different to us fighting Zelig or the Gomahras. Sometimes you simply have to. Here..." She handed him the water bottle.

Conal rinsed his mouth out and washed away the remains of the tears he had pretended weren't there, then he drank several large gulps.

Brianna stood up. "Will you help me get Amon's sword, please?"

* * * *

With both swords cleaned, they returned to the others gathered at the top of the slope. The girl, Issah, stood a small distance from the injured Amon. With her arms folded across her chest, she stared down at him, stiff and silent, apparently oblivious to the tears that trickled down her cheeks. While Dodi stared unashamedly up at the stranger and Tulia peeped at her from under her lashes as she tended Amon, Conal abruptly marched right up to her and demanded identification.

"So who're you?"

When Issah flinched at Conal's bluntness, Brianna felt guilty about ignoring her, and obliged to introduce her.

"Everyone, this is Issah."

She immediately felt bad about not introducing Issah as her sister, but she needed time to come to terms with this unexpected development herself before sharing the information with her friends. Issah frowned at her and Brianna felt a tickle brush over her mind. She glared at

Issah, touched her forehead and then flung her hand outsharply. *"Get out of my head,"* she messaged.

Issah's glared but, when Brianna did not elaborate on her first statement, Issah remained silent.

Tulia barely spared Issah another glance as she tended Amon. Conal scowled but acknowledged her with a nod of his head, and Dodi continued to stare up at her with wide eyes.

Other than the blunt introduction, Brianna ignored Issah, which was rude and unkind, but she definitely couldn't cope right now with her revelation and the connotations that came with it. Would her Archon father even want to know her? After all, she was only half Abrasaxon. He had a full-blood daughter to follow in his footsteps. He would have no need for her. Did he even remember her? Her thoughts hammered relentlessly in her brain as she helped make Amon comfortable.

After they had forced Amon to swallow a small amount of Tulia's nasty-smelling potion, they carried him back to camp on a makeshift stretcher of belts and branches. He struggled to breathe and could not see but agreed with Brianna that they should move on as quickly as possible, as Yabix rarely lived a solitary life, preferring to live in groups to breed, hunt and raise several pairs of twins each moon cycle.

Issah followed them in wraith-like silence after she had retrieved her sword and small pack from near the dead Yabix. At the first rest stop, she reached out to Brianna — in comfort or question Brianna didn't know and refused to face. She abruptly shrugged Issah's hand off her arm and turned to pick up the stretcher poles. Without a word, Conal picked up the other ends, and together they carried the heavy burden of the now unconscious Amon back to camp. As they approached, the domnak brayed loudly in welcome and Brianna flinched, knowing everything for miles would hear that raucous noise.

With barely a movement of air and shadow, Issah ran lightly past them. Moments later, the domnak fell silent. As they drew closer, Brianna could see Issah leaning close to the domnak's face, and it was nodding up and down, exactly as if it was listening to the stranger.

As they began to pack, Issah came to stand beside Brianna. "Sister, I know you are angry and confused, and your friend is hurt, but I have come to find you. We need to talk. Father always said if I needed help and he wasn't available, I was to find you."

Brianna hefted her pack on her back before she faced Issah. "Why?"

"It's a complicated story. We need to talk, Brianna, but not here. When we camp for the night will be soon enough. I see you are already heading in the direction of the Crystal Castle."

"Yes. I was going to find my Abrasaxon father — to get his help."

"And that is why I have come to find you, because he needs your help. The whole Abrogative Direktorate needs your help — our help."

"What help would I be to the Abrogative Direktorate? I'm only his abandoned half-breed daughter..."

Issah grabbed her arm in a vise-like grip. "No, Brianna. Do not talk of yourself in this way. It's not true," her sister scolded, her eyes filling with tears. "Father would be horrified if he found out this is what you think of yourself."

Brianna pulled away, but bit down on the scathing retort that had come to mind. Instead, she said bluntly, "We have to go, Issah. Are you coming with us?"

Issah nodded and fell into step behind them.

Chapter Eight

Several times in the night Brianna helped Tulia force more of the potion down Amon's throat and bathe his face and neck. His skin was blistered and felt fiery to the touch. He stirred restlessly on the stretcher and cried out as if tortured by nightmares.

When they had finished, Brianna guided Tulia out of Amon's hearing. "Is he going to make it, Tulia? Can we do more for him?"

Tulia's expression was filled with worry. "I don't know, Brianna. I've done all I can." She sighed. "If only Grandmamma was here. She would know what to do."

Brianna squeezed Tulia's hand. "You've done the best you can, Tulia. Without your healing skills, he would have died on the hill."

All through the night, in between applying Amon's treatments, Brianna hunched under her blanket listening to his ragged breathing, tensing at the pauses, relaxing when she heard another breath being drawn in.

* * * *

She groaned in protest at being roughly shaken. When she dragged one eye open a fraction, she could see Issah's feet. It was barely light enough to see her hand in front of her face.

"Brianna, we must talk. Wake up."

Brianna groaned again and tried to huddle down, but Issah was relentless and, eventually, Brianna pushed herself into a sitting position, yawned, and rubbed her itchy, stinging eyes.

"I'll wait for you just behind those boulders. I have fruit and nuts for you to eat. Don't delay."

As Issah disappeared toward the boulders, Brianna tried to rein in her irritation. She didn't want to deal with tangled family ties and obligations right now. There was enough to deal with, saving Amon and finding her father... Her thoughts stopped for a moment as she remembered Issah saying he needed help. She sighed, remembering all too well when not so long ago she'd craved adventure. Well, now all she wanted was a quiet, simple life.

By the time she joined Issah behind the boulders she was wide awake and resigned to hearing what this young woman had to say. She settled herself comfortably on the smaller boulder, fully expecting this to be a lengthy discussion.

"Brianna, you have every right to feel angry and resentful toward your parents and those who kept the secret, but it was done with the best of intentions—"

Brianna snorted her disdain.

Issah held up her hand. "Please, Brianna?"

"Sorry," Brianna whispered as she struggled to keep her mind open to Issah's story.

"Our father was the second son of the most powerful Archon family in the universe as we know it. He fell deeply in love with your mother, Katrina, and, not expecting any obligation to the Abrogative Direktorate, he made a covenant with her. Shortly after you were born, his older brother, Latidon, already Grand Archon of Okana, was overcome by an evil entity called Saquin as he fought to save twenty mortal children from being turned into Gomahras. The children were saved, but Latidon did not recover."

"Couldn't someone else have taken his place?"

"No, Brianna—each Archon holds the guardianship of all the evil entities his or her family have conquered since time began. Guardianship is inherited. In time, I or my brothers will inherit our father's place on the Direktorate and guardianship of all the evil entities conquered by our family. Without a family member to inherit, the entities can rise again."

"He has another *whole* family. What about me?"

Issah gave a sympathetic smile. "He has never stopped loving your mother and you, even though he unbound his covenant with her before he returned to the Crystal Castle. His covenant with my mother, Alameda, was arranged purely to produce full-blood heirs, although I think they have grown fond of each other over the years."

"So why have you come for my help, Issah?"

Issah leaned forward, her voice a mere whisper. "Archon Donavon never had offspring, so when he passed, his nephew was expected to step up to the obligation. When, at the last minute, his nephew failed to step forward, something went terribly wrong. In the few seconds it took for our father to realize the nephew was not going to take Donavon's place, a rift formed between good and evil. Before our father could take on the burden himself, many of the spells were weakened, and entities crossed back into our world. Moments later, every member of the Abrogative Direktorate vanished."

"What about the other Abrasaxon?" Brianna asked.

"Many fled the castle immediately."

"Why?"

"They knew the extent of evil under Donavon's guardianship and feared for their lives."

"And your mother?"

Issah glanced at her feet for a moment then back at Brianna. The shine of tears made her eyes bright. "Saquin came to the castle a few days ago, rounded up the remainder of the Abrasaxon, including my mother, and herded them into the dungeons. I managed to escape by hiding in the kitchen rubbish pile. Then I attempted to weave a traveling spell so I could find you, but it wasn't very strong. Shortly after it faded, I came across the Yabix."

"But, Issah, what can we do when the Abrogative Direktorate has been overcome by this evil and a castle full of Abrasaxon flee in fear? I'm only beginning to have the gift, and you obviously aren't that skilled either…"

Issah leaned forward, took hold of Brianna's hands and whispered confidentially, "But, sister, don't you realize that you and I together are at least one and a half times more powerful than our father alone? I have all his power—albeit unrealized yet—and you have at least half his power, maybe more if the Abrasaxon blood dominates your mortal half."

Brianna gaped at her sister as her mind struggled to comprehend the meaning of the information she offered.

"Don't you see, Brianna? This is why you had to be kept a secret until you were old enough to manifest the gift. Those without magic cannot enter the magic realm of the Abrasaxon. Father was coming to get you right before he disappeared, to bring you to the Crystal Castle to be trained…"

"Trained?"

"Yes, sister, trained, right along with me."

While they had been talking, the sun had risen. Brianna felt its warmth on her back, but it failed to dispel the chill that ran in her blood and melded with her bones. Her thoughts raced around her head as she tried to make sense of what her sister had told her. It was a hard task to rationalize the secrecy she'd been subjected to, and also to accept the depth of the power she held.

"So, Brianna, will you work with me to save both Abrasaxon and mortal? Saquin is a formidable enemy. Only together do we have the power to defeat him."

Brianna glowered at her sister for a moment. "And together, do we have the power to also defeat Zelig and the hordes of Gomahras currently overrunning Okana and at this very moment enslaving the mortal population?"

"Zelig?"

"Yes, Issah. He came to the village with Gomahras in tow and took the people away. That is why I was coming to get help from my father."

Issah's face was pale in the early morning light. "There is more than one Tyban and henchmen in our world right now?"

"Yes. And Zelig knew who I was—he called me Hakon's daughter."

Issah frowned. "So you and your power are no longer a secret. It is worse than I thought. If they trap us both, they will be able to milk our powers and they will be unstoppable. There is no time to waste. We need to get to the Crystal Castle, release the captured Abrasaxon and find the Abrogative Direktorate."

* * * *

They made good time, despite the stretcher, by following a rough track carved through the valleys and hillocks. The gark trees that lined the path provided shade, and on the lower side a small stream ran swiftly between jagged outcroppings of white rock. They followed the track across the stream and into a grove of trees. Here the bushes had begun to encroach on the track and the gark branches met overhead. It was cool, gloomy and very quiet.

Brianna felt twitchy at the lack of forest sounds—no shandinas or kachine buzzed around them or firozt croaked in the stream.

Amon moaned from his stretcher and pulled at his bandages. "I smell Yabix. Moonbeams, the stench. Let me see. I must see. I can smell them," he screeched.

Tulia dosed him with more sleeping medicine, so he quickly fell silent and drifted into unconsciousness.

Amon's claims made Brianna uneasy.

"Do you think he can?" Issah whispered.

"Maybe, Issah. I wouldn't be surprised." Brianna glanced around then back down at Amon. "But I think right now he is definitely delirious."

At last Brianna could see a break in the tree tunnel. She increased her pace, keen to be out of the enclosing vegetation, and was pleased that the others hurried behind her.

With a flap of black wings, a raven flew at her. Brianna threw her hands up and startled back as the bird's talons clawed at her chest. It cawed and scrambled its way up to her shoulder despite her frantic attempts to knock it away. It clattered its beak and whistled softly in her ear and dug its talons into the flesh of her shoulder, right through her jerkin and shirt. It croaked softly again and Brianna understood the warning at the same moment as a cacophony of sounds reached her. Roars, rattling armor, sniffling and snorting—the sounds of many creatures. With the raven still perched precariously on her shoulder, she crept forward and slid behind the last tree.

Issah inched up behind her and peered over her shoulder. Her grip tightened on Brianna's forearms. "Oh, fiery moons! Dearest sister, what do we do now?"

Brianna placed her right hand over Issah's and squeezed, unable to verbalize the abject terror that held her motionless. She had no answer.

"What's the holdup, you two?" Conal mumbled as he pushed in beside Brianna and peered out over the meadow. "Moonlight's curse," he muttered. His voice was barely audible above the increasing noise from those gathered in the meadow. "Brianna..." He hiccupped before he vomited at Brianna's feet.

She peered down at him. His ghostly white face was wet with tears, his hands trembling as they clutched her jerkin.

"Are we going to die?" he asked.

"Not if I can help it. Now go back to the others. Issah and I need to think this through."

Brianna was shocked that he obeyed her without a verbal challenge, and as she glanced over her shoulder at the cowed lad creeping back to the others, she realized how much she missed Amon's companionship and worldly advice – particularly now.

She turned back to the horror before her. The battle line was drawn – hundreds of Gomahras armed with stakes on one side, all drooling and spitting, and on the other at least one thousand Yabix with multiple heads weaving back and forth, tongues scenting the air and razor-sharp tails slashing from side to side. The combined stench was sickening, but as Brianna's stomach roiled and clenched, she knew it was not from the stench, but from stupefying terror.

The only thing that stood between the two armies was a gruesome creature clad in shiny suka armor – a hugely muscular Tyban with dark skin, short spiky silver hair, large yellow glowing eyes and elongated pointed fangs that showed below the full top lip.

"Kybotek, Raiser of the Dead," Issah said, her words barely audible. "He must have brought the Yabix back to life – hundreds of them."

"We need to go far away, Issah."

She nodded, but before they could drag their gazes from the horror in front of them there was a swirl of black smoke, a flash of light and a deafening crack. Brianna gasped. Zelig had arrived.

He raised his staff and silence fell. "You intrude, Kybotek. You have exceeded your mandate."

The dark-skinned humanoid laughed – a rough, grating rattle. "I seek my bride. My spies tell me she is in Okana, so I have come to retrieve her."

"If your bride is indeed in Okana then I will sniff her out—white magic has such a stench about it—then you can claim her." With that, Zelig lifted his face to the sky and inhaled the air. "I believe your wait will be short, Dark One," he announced. Then he began to whistle, softly at first, then louder, more insistently.

As the insidious sound touched her mind, Brianna knew it was too late to retreat.

Issah began to move away from her, her eyes glazed over. Brianna lunged forward, grabbed her sister by the waist and dragged her to the ground. With no thought to dignity she straddled her while she retrieved the red powder from her bag. As she fumbled to find it, Conal walked past, and right behind him was Dodi, with Tulia clinging to his belt. Even with her heels dug in, she was being dragged slowly forward through the loose shale by her smaller brother.

Brianna scattered some powder on Issah, and as soon as she saw recognition in her eyes she jumped off. "Issah, get the others together. Can you do a traveling spell for all of us?"

Wiping the powder from her eyes, Issah shook her head. "I don't know. I have only done it for one before, and that didn't work so well, but I can try..."

"I'm going after Conal. Help Tulia hold Dodi. When we get everyone together, we will try the spell. We need to get away from here." Brianna ran past Tulia and Dodi and quickly caught up with Conal.

Conal pulled away from her, his face already glazed over into vacant blindness. To make matters worse, Amon, left unattended, had staggered up from his stretcher and soon passed them, his feet moving in unison with Conal's in answer to that terrible rhythm Brianna could hear just at the edge of her mind.

"No! No! Block your ears!" she shrieked, but they didn't hear her. She ripped a strip off the bottom of her shirt and stuffed her ears full of scrunched-up material.

Conal and Amon moved down the slope toward the waiting throng of evil, Amon's blindness no barrier to his movement forward. Tulia remained at Issah's side, the two of them hanging desperately onto Dodi. His chubby feet worked overtime as he hauled against Tulia's ferocious grip.

"Dodi!" she screeched as her brother began to drag them forward toward the gathered army.

A malevolent chuckle rumbled across the meadow and up the small hillock. "You will come." The voice was abrasive and harsh.

"Go faster, Brianna. You've got to stop them!" Issah cried, hopping from one foot to the other.

Brianna ran after the boys marching blindly toward the restless army of horrors milling in the field below. Even her feet were shuffling to the insidious call of Zelig's whistle, faint though it was through the cloth stuffed in her ears.

The whistling got louder. Deep inside, Brianna felt the call of Zelig.

Conal and Amon were almost halfway down the slope. Amon's bandages flapped in the wind that now ripped at their hair and clothes, but both boys ignored it and marched steadily forward. Brianna was gasping and coughing by the time she reached Conal. She grabbed his arm but he ignored her. Desperation gave her strength she didn't know she had, and with one savage tug she wrenched him roughly off his feet. He hit the ground with a thump. She immediately bounced onto his chest. Conal's legs continued to kick and his eyes stared vacantly up at her. Afraid the wind would blow the precious powder away, she tipped it into her palm then rubbed it through Conal's hair and over his face. The powder stuck like paint as it blended with Conal's perspiration, and his white-blond hair took on a faint pink hue. In an instant he sneezed, and his eyes snapped into focus.

"What the...? Get off, Brianna...you're mighty heavy."

He pushed at her, but she was already rising to search for Amon.

"We have to stop Amon. Zelig is calling!" she yelled above the wind.

She had sprinted on by the time Conal comprehended the situation, then he charged past her, straight at Amon. With the accuracy of a bolt and the weight of a small gort, Conal tackled Amon, bringing him down with a crash. His bandages flapped grotesquely as they slipped down to reveal a swollen, mottled face and vacant, gummed-up eyes.

It took only a split second for Amon to fight off Conal and stagger to his feet, but it was enough for Brianna to reach them. She pulled on Amon's collar and upended the last precious grains in the bottle down the back of his shirt and in his hair.

He flinched, stood still for a moment then spun around, reaching out with flailing hands to identify who was attacking him.

Brianna had felt the cloth in one ear loosen as she jumped at Amon, and Zelig's whistle was now inside her head. She felt the world begin to fade—blackness around the edges of her vision—and her legs began to move of their own volition.

"Use the powder," Tulia yelled.

Brianna heard her vaguely through the evil haze of Zelig's spell, but could not help herself. There was no powder left.

She tried to summon her untested magic, but nothing happened, and she could feel herself sinking into the web of Zelig's power. In a desperate attempt to save herself she shoved her fingers into her ears, but the whistle came from inside her head and she succumbed to the call.

Some invisible force held her arms pinned to her sides while her legs kept marching to oblivion. An awareness of the other world remained — she could see herself crossing the meadow, hear her voice hollering the temple chants but she couldn't reach that other world. Zelig's call was too strong. She gathered her rage to feed her power, but Zelig must have sensed her potential and his insidious whistle rose to a higher pitch — a pitch that hurt her ears and beat her brain to mush. Her tenacious grip on the power within slipped and diminished and she could no longer feel Amon's and Conal's hands, but she guessed they were still holding her because, despite the steady stomp of her feet, she was not getting any closer to the evil that called her.

"No! No! No!" she bellowed down at the evil entities waiting for her in the meadow. Her eyes were barely able to open and focus in the onslaught of pain that gripped her mind.

"Do you hear me, Zelig? You will not win!" Her words were slurred. She was having trouble forming coherent thoughts. A stab of fear cramped her breathing and twisted her stomach — she was losing the battle.

In a last-ditch effort to beat this evil and save herself, she closed her eyes and concentrated, past the pain that zigzagged across her brain, deep down inside, to conjure the power. A searing heat spread through her. Now she could feel the boys' hands as they clutched her shoulders and legs. Her feet still shuffled until a pair of tiny hands clutched her ankles in a grip that burned her skin and vibrated with energy — energy feeding her own, and somehow she knew it was Dodi.

The whistle still cut through her mind, but it was weaker now. She felt rather than heard the loud cackle of laughter.

"Hakon's daughter, you will not win — you are mine."

Brianna cringed inside her mind against the voice that mocked her. Her head felt as if it were going to explode as the voice pounded around and around.

"Okana is mine! Okana is mine!" Zelig bellowed.

Brianna cringed against Zelig's verbal invasion in her head. Blackness closed in, everything shrank and zipped far into the distance. She heard Conal and Tulia cry in unison.

"They're coming. They're coming."

She waved her hand and muttered the spell before her friends' voices faded. Brianna let the blackness come. If she hadn't beaten Zelig by now, she had nothing left to fight him with.

Chapter Nine

Gentle hands wiped her face and body with a damp cloth. She heard snatches of soft conversation that was hurriedly hushed. A few droplets of tepid water trickled against her mouth, and Brianna licked them lightly from cracked lips.

Then she forced her eyes open. Above her was a canopy of soft green sky sprinkled with the last of the night stars. As her mind struggled with the concept, Tulia's white, pinched face blocked her view.

"How do you feel?"

Brianna tried to move and groaned. She closed her eyes to still the dizziness. "Awful. What happened?"

Issah knelt beside her. "We're safe for now, Brianna. You fought Zelig and used a concealing glamour charm on us long enough for me and young Dodi to conjure up a traveling spell. It was a very rough ride, and didn't last, but it got us away."

Brianna tried to sit up, but Issah pushed her down.

"You and Dodi?"

Issah smiled, leaned closer to Brianna and whispered, "Tulia is extremely disgruntled because she understands now she has not been chosen. I saw she'd been crying when we landed, but she wouldn't discuss it with me."

"Poor Tulia."

"Tulia has other talents. She truly has to accept. Anyway, we will stay here tonight and begin the climb in the morning."

"Where are we?" Brianna asked.

"On the mountain pass to the Crystal Castle. On the other side of this mountain is the lake—and home," Issah said.

"And Amon?"

"Your companion is strong. He is improving, but he is still unable to see."

Tears filled her eyes and threatened to spill over. "Oh no," Brianna moaned.

Issah touched her shoulder. "Don't worry, sister dear. There are things that can be done, but first we have to reach the castle and free the others. Now rest. We have a hard climb tomorrow."

It was nearly dawn when a mournful wail floated down to them from the summit. There was a scuffle and a whimper then Tulia was at her side, her face pale in the gloom. Seconds later Dodi threw himself to the ground and buried his face in her lap.

"What's that, Brianna?" Tulia cried. "Are we going to be attacked by another evil whituka?"

Brianna squeezed Tulia's trembling hands. "I don't know."

"It's a Sokomara—they're incredibly ugly, but gentle. I saw one once—a great lumbering animal with velvet skin that lies in rolls because it is too big for it and a wide, slobbering mouth with a huge overbite on the bottom jaw. It has wings and flies, using its muscular tail for a rudder," Amon said quietly.

"Amon is right, Tulia, there is no need to be scared. They're ugly but generally harmless, although they will fight and kill if attacked. What I love about them is they're quite affectionate if you have a tame one. Their fur is so soft and their ears are huge." Issah indicated with her hands the size of the ears. "They use them for echolocation to find food and navigate because they have poor eyesight and hunt at night."

"Really?" Brianna wasn't sure if her sister was telling the truth or not.

Issah nodded as she leaned closer to them. "They say the single tear a Sokomara releases at any moment of sadness is precious and can cure many ills, but it has to be given willingly by the Sokomara or it dries to salt. Now back to sleep. We have a big day tomorrow," she admonished the frightened siblings.

Despite Issah's and Amon's assurances, Tulia and Dodi stayed cuddled to Brianna for the remainder of the night.

* * * *

It was slow going up the narrow track carved into the side of the mountain. Tulia struggled to keep up without the domnak, which had been left behind by the traveling spell, and Amon crept along with a slow shuffle, one hand on the cliff face, the other swinging a tree branch to check the path in front of him. Conal scouted ahead with his sword drawn and a serious expression on his face.

They had been climbing for some time when the track turned back onto the mountain and followed a natural canyon carved into the rock. As the floor of the canyon began to drop, they had to squeeze past huge boulders of red and yellow with sharp, angular edges. They struggled on until finally their path was completely blocked. Brianna called a halt, and they all flopped down in the shade of the boulders.

Amon's face was white with exhaustion, sweat beading on his forehead, and Tulia was barely dragging her lame leg forward with each step. Brianna sank to her knees in the cool sand, almost ready to lie down and stay there — forever. Her confrontation with Zelig had taken far more out of her than she could have ever imagined. Conal sprawled beside her. Issah put Dodi down, then poked and prodded the blockage, throwing or rolling away the boulders. After a moment Conal joined her, but instead of moving the boulders, he climbed to the top and peered over.

"It's not too big, and the canyon opens into a valley on the other side. I can see the sun glinting on something in the distance. Maybe it's the lake."

"Well, get down and help us clear it then," Issah ordered. "I can't do a traveling spell because I don't know where we might end up."

Both Brianna and Tulia scrambled to their feet and began moving boulders. Dodi helped Amon find boulders and together they rolled them out of the way.

Suddenly a rumble grew around them, getting louder and louder.

Brianna felt the boulders shudder under her hands as she reached for a new one. "Something's happening!"

Issah snatched up Dodi, ready to flee.

The rumble stopped abruptly and silence surrounded them.

"Come on, you lot. We'll never get it clear if you stand there gawking." With a grunt, Conal rolled away a boulder almost as big as himself.

A small shower of rocks crashed down on him. As he ducked and covered his head, the whole tumble of boulders heaved, shuddered and moaned. The roar rose to a terrifying thunder that vibrated in their bones. The largest boulder began to sink into the earth.

"Conal!" Brianna screamed in warning, but it was too late.

Conal was swept downward in an avalanche of jagged rocks. Tulia screamed again and again before she buried her face in Brianna's shirt. The sand beneath them heaved and shifted. Brianna clutched Tulia and scrambled backward from the gaping hole even as her feet were dragged from under her. The boys were pulled forward. Dodi barely had time to hook his hand through Amon's belt before they fell in a shower of rocks and sand. Brianna reached out, but only her fingertips touched Amon's — then he was gone.

Issah gave a guttural cry as the gaping hole widened. Everything in the depression was being consumed. The sand dissolved into sluggish, grainy yellow liquid that pulled Brianna and Tulia forward when the canyon floor collapsed inward. They clung to each other as they slid inexorably toward a thunderous roar. Brianna gasped as she hit cold water with a breath-squeezing smack. Instinctively she kicked upward. Her hands scooped the weight of the water down until her head broke through the surface. She gasped a lungful of air and wiped her eyes free of liquid.

"Issah, Tulia, Amon, Conal, Dodi!" she howled above the rush of water. Only the roar of the torrent answered her. She spun around and around as the flow of the river swept her past the walls of a huge cavern that had been honed smooth by centuries of the passing flow. There were no handholds or ledges to facilitate an escape. Then she saw Tulia paddling frantically to keep her head above the surface.

"Tulia!"

Her red curls, the color of blood, were plastered flat to her head. Her eyes were dark with fear. The girl turned and tried to swim against the flow to reach Brianna, the only safe object in a terrifying mass of angry turbulence.

"Float, Tulia, I'll come to you."

For a moment she kept swimming, but as the meaning of Brianna's words sank in she ceased the struggle and paddled only enough to keep from drowning. As Brianna began to swim toward her, she felt Tulia's eyes on her, drawing her in, willing her to come closer.

At last they touched fingers, but Brianna didn't dare get too close in case Tulia tried to grab her and dragged them both to the bottom.

"Are you...are you all right?"

Tulia stared wide-eyed back at her and whimpered. The waves splashed her face, diluting her tears.

"Tulia, dump my bag, it's dragging you down."

Tulia's expression hardened with stubbornness. "No!"

"But..."

"I'll manage." Tulia kicked harder, her mouth barely above the water.

Brianna's breath came in gasps, the cold constricting her lungs. "Have you seen the others?"

Tulia nodded again and pointed downstream. "Amon had Dodi," she spluttered through the wavelets that threatened to swamp her. "And I saw Issah — she was swimming with the current, trying to catch up with Dodi and Amon."

"And Conal. Did you see Conal?"

Tulia only shook her head, unable to speak any more through her furiously chattering teeth. The dull ache of fear clamped around Brianna's heart, and her breath came in jerks and gasps. She fought off the grief and fear. After all, Conal was the best swimmer of the group.

Unable to solve the dilemma, she hooked her finger through Tulia's belt and gave herself up to the unstoppable flow of the river. As the tunnel narrowed and lowered they became enveloped in stagnant darkness.

Brianna kicked a bit harder to raise her mouth away from the waves and called. "Amon, Dodi, Issah, Conal."

Her voice sounded loud and distorted as it echoed again and again off the smooth walls, as if to mock her audacity in raising her voice in the river's sanctity. Struggling to stay afloat, she considered discarding her crossbow, still strapped to her back, but rejected the idea almost immediately, especially as she had lost her grandfather's sword in the tumble into the river.

"I'm afraid, Brianna."

All signs of the contempt, superior attitude or jealousy that often tinged Tulia's words were gone.

"Will we ever see daylight again or are we destined to die in this blackness?" Tulia spluttered.

Brianna struggled with the tremors that threatened to crack her voice. "All rivers eventually come back outside, even if we have to wait for it to reach the sea. All we have to do is stay afloat. And I'm sure the others are floating up ahead somewhere in the darkness. Conal is a better swimmer then either of us, and we're still here."

"But what about Dodi? He can't swim very well."

"Amon will make sure he is okay."

They rushed on, only the roar and gush of the river breaking the silence.

Brianna's panic rose and fell. She felt less isolated when they were talking, as even knowing Tulia was right next to her couldn't dispel her fear.

"Let's sing, Tulia."

Without waiting for her agreement, Brianna began to hum one of the moon festival songs they sang every year in the temple. At first Tulia's singing was nothing more than a gurgling whimper, but as they progressed through to the chorus her voice joined Brianna's in high, piping sweetness.

Their choral efforts bounced back at them, invisible waves of reassurance that they still existed in the black, tumbling void that rushed them onward.

After several songs, Tulia's voice faltered in a gurgle of water.

Suddenly frantic, Brianna reached out and clawed at Tulia's clothes. She boosted her up. "Don't stop kicking, Tulia."

"I'm tired, Brianna, and cold... So cold," Tulia muttered through clattering teeth.

Her voice faded.

"Keep talking, Tulia. You must concentrate, survive."

"I can't. I can't do it anymore," Tulia whimpered.

"You can." Brianna gripped her arm hard. "And you will. I'm not having you give up. Do you hear me?" Brianna didn't even realize she was making a terrible racket until her words vibrated back at her, crashing onto her eardrums like thunder.

Tulia sobbed now, and Brianna berated herself for her harshness. She hadn't meant to upset her, but she was so scared — scared of losing Tulia, scared of being in this awful river all alone.

She kicked herself higher and drew in a deep breath of stale air that scratched her water-tortured lungs. "Amon, Dodi, Issah, Conal!"

The names bounced back at her from the impenetrable darkness, deriding her desperation.

Brianna couldn't feel her legs, but knew she was still kicking because her head bobbed slightly above the swirling water. Desperate to get a grip on the passing of time, Brianna counted Tulia's spluttering hiccups and mentally tallied them into minutes as she struggled to keep her panic under control.

Despite her reassuring words to Tulia, uncertainty and fear nagged at her about the survival of the others. There had been no replies to her calls. The short journey and the struggles they had endured had bonded them in a way everyday living never would, and the thought of losing any of her friends sparked an unbearable pain in her heart. She didn't know how she would go on if she lost them. Without Issah, her new sister, there was no way she could beat the three evil Tyban who had been released by Donavon's death or even their evil helpers. There may be others who escaped at the same time. An unknown number of evil creatures roaming Okana and hunting down mortals and Abrasaxon alike. If the Tyban were not defeated then Okana and

Okiyarra would become nothing more than playgrounds for evil and slave yards for mortals.

After what seemed like an eternity, Brianna sensed that something had changed. She tensed, listened and stopped kicking for a moment. It was hard to tell, but the river seemed to be going faster. The roar that pounded in her head seemed louder and was punctuated by distinct splashing sounds. By scooping her hands deep in the water she managed to spin around, but all she found was darkness until after another slow circle in the ever-moving motion forward, she saw it—a tiny pinprick of light. Like a distant star on a cloudy night it wavered and blinked, then it was gone. She kicked harder to lift herself higher. Nothing. But she was sure she'd seen something. Her heart beat faster in anticipation—she'd seen something.

"Kick, Tulia. The river is moving faster."

Tulia let out a tiny squeak.

"Kick, Tulia," Brianna ordered, slicing through Tulia's protest. She'd seen it again. Now it was steady—hovering just above the water and surrounded by a soft glow. "See ahead, Tulia. A light."

Brianna coughed and spluttered as water gushed into her mouth. The turbulence was dragging them back and forth even as the flow rushed them toward the unsteady flicker of light. The patch had grown into a glowing arch in a pool of blackness. "It's an opening. Swim, Tulia." She felt hope warm her as safety came within reach. With renewed energy, she kicked harder.

Brianna could now see Tulia, her red hair dangling across her small face—a sickly shade of blue-gray and pinched thin, her mouth clenched into a determined line. "Swim," she urged.

Tulia kicked harder, yet struggled to keep above the swirling white water. The small white caps of snowy froth smacked in exploding puffs on their faces, filling their noses, mouths and eyes. Brianna scraped the water away, not willing to have her sight of safety obscured.

Pain stabbed through her legs and suddenly Brianna was aware of rocks dragging at her clothes, scraping beneath her feet. The contact was so forceful it stabbed painfully through the chilled numbness of her limbs. She scrabbled for a foothold, held, then slipped. The swirling water and Tulia's weight dragged her forward.

She pulled Tulia close as they catapulted into a shallow rock pool, where the water hesitated only a moment before it rushed out of sight over a cliff. Mist rose from below the cliff precipice, the roar of the falling water deafening as it pounded at them like a physical force. Brianna was dragged across the rocks. Each one battered her repeatedly as she tumbled like a rag doll in the seething turbulence of the water. Tulia was wrenched savagely from her clutches as the rocky outcroppings gave way to the endless expanse of sky, leaving them nowhere to go but into oblivion. Each foothold slipped away — each handhold on shiny wet rocks, worn round and smooth by the water's relentless abrasion, snatched out of her reach. Brianna's foot jammed against a rock. The force of her halt jarred her hips and spine with an agonizing snap. She was still, but the water continued to tear at her with maniacal fingers, desperate to take her on its endless journey.

With an awkward twist at the waist, Brianna reached for Tulia as the girl zoomed past. Only her hair was within reach of Brianna's grasping fingers and she grabbed the floating tresses with a merciless grip. Tulia cried out in pain and Brianna cringed in sympathy, but was not prepared to allow the alternative. Keeping herself steady with her foot wedged against the rock, she dragged Tulia into reach of the tumbled boulders then pushed her into shallower water. A voiceless waif coated in a dripping cloak of shapeless clothes, Tulia anchored herself with her good leg and provided a fragile link with the shore. Together, clawing bit by bit over each other, they inched their way to the shore, crawling onto the wide rocks that gave the pool its shape.

The rocks were smooth, flat and warm from the sun. Brianna moaned and sank into a boneless heap, pressing her face and hands onto the unforgiving surface, desperate to assimilate the warmth. Her legs were bruised and bleeding. Every muscle ached as the sun caressed their bodies, melting the numbness that had shielded them from the true pain of their battering. Every movement now brought agony but Brianna reveled in the pain — it meant she was alive.

She looked around and saw a patch of blue at the water's edge. "Issah," she screamed as she pushed herself to her feet and staggered to where her sister lay half submerged in the river. "Issah! Oh, fiery moons, please be alive," she sobbed as she dragged her sister's inert body from the icy water.

Tulia leaned over Issah's face. "She's breathing. She's alive."

Relief swamped Brianna as she gathered her sister in her arms and cuddled her. Issah had a large bruise on her forehead. She moaned then rested quietly with her eyes closed.

"Oh, Issah, please be okay. Don't die," Brianna pleaded. "I don't want to lose you when I've only just met you. Open your eyes. Issah. Please?"

As Tulia came to sit beside her, Issah's eyelids fluttered open.

"Oh, Issah, thank the Goddess," Brianna muttered.

"Ohhh, I have such a sore head and I'm cold — so cold." Issah chattered the words out between clacking teeth.

Together Tulia and Brianna carried Issah, like a saggy bag of grain, a few feet away from the water and laid her on a sun-warmed rock.

Tulia reached into her very soggy medicine bag and pulled out a small bottle. She held it to Issah's lips. "A drop of dizan liquid to warm your insides," she murmured.

Issah coughed and spluttered as she swallowed the fiery liquid. Tulia took a sip then offered it to Brianna. Brianna gulped the golden spirit, welcoming the burn all the way down to form a warm puddle in her stomach.

"Do you think the others...got out too?" Issah asked.

The stuttered question was the incentive Brianna needed to seek the others, but they were alone by the pool.

"I'm sure they did," she muttered as she returned to her sister's side. She refused to acknowledge the cold fear that fought with the sun's warmth for her heart and buried her face back in the crook of her arm.

"Brianna, Tulia, Issah, Conal," a gruff voice called.

Tulia jiggled Brianna's shoulder and squeaked, "Brianna, look. It's Amon and Dodi."

Both boys were bedraggled and bleeding from various scrapes and Amon had lost his bandages. The sight of his damaged face wrenched at her heart. It was a sickly gray color, still swollen and mottled from the Yabix poison, and his eyes wept yellow fluid as he peered sightlessly into the distance.

Brianna's heart leaped and, ignoring the shudder of her muscles and the groan in her bones, she climbed to her feet and flung herself at Amon. He wrapped her in a huge bear hug as the crippling storm of weeping she'd been holding back since this crisis began welled up and washed over her. Amon held her upright, clutched against his chest, his big hands stroking her hair in an ineffective attempt to calm the shudders that racked her body.

Dodi giggled, skipped over the rocks and tumbled into Tulia's waiting arms.

"Oh, Dodi. Oh, Dodi," Tulia murmured.

The boy planted big, sloppy kisses all over his sister's face and hands. He then slipped off Tulia's lap and went to sit by Issah as she lay with her eyes closed. He touched her forehead, stroking it gently until she opened her eyes. Then he smiled and kissed her as well. The joy of their reunion was overshadowed by the one lost companion and the menacing roar of the river as it hummed in the background. They stood in silence for many minutes, until finally Brianna found the courage to ask the dreaded question.

"Do you think Conal made it — over the falls?"

It was barely perceptible, the small negative movement of Amon's head, but it filled Brianna with so much pain and grief and ignited her smoldering anger. He tightened his hold around her shoulders and Brianna leaned against his side, taking what comfort she could. Curse the Tyban and their murderous ways, and twisted moonlights on the Abrogative Direktorate.

They had allowed this disaster. They had broken their promise and, despite their prestigious standing in the universe, she planned to have a word or two to say to her father when she finally met him. It was a dismal thing to break promises.

"Let's get away from here, away from the river," Brianna muttered.

She reached into her jacket pocket for the map that had guided them up to now, but when she pulled it out the paper turned into a misshapen ball of gray mush in the palm of her hand. "Oh no, the map has been destroyed by the river," she wailed.

What remained of her strength disintegrated with it—a forlorn emptiness crawled inside her and she would have sagged to her knees but for Amon's strong arm.

"Oh no you don't. You've brought us this far on a conviction only you believed, now's not the time to give in," he whispered in her ear.

"The map doesn't matter anymore, Brianna because we're here." Issah took Brianna's arm and slowly turned her around. "Look," Issah repeated.

Towering high over the lake was the Crystal Castle, its turrets rising like silent sentinels guarding a secret.

"We've made it, oh, fiery moons," Brianna breathed, transfixed by magnificence of the Abrasaxon stronghold.

"You see the castle?" Amon asked.

"Yes, Amon. We've made it."

"You've fought for this, Brianna. We can save them now, and Conal wouldn't want us to give up," Amon said.

Tulia tugged at her elbow. "We can do this, Brianna—all of us, together. We will find Hakon, he will help us."

Tears had dried in salty tracks down her pale face, now a pasty white with a sickly blue-green hue. Her teeth still chattered and goosebumps speckled the exposed parts of her arms among the rapidly drying blood from numerous shallow scrapes.

Brianna reached out and drew her into a hug. "You know because he helped you...that night?"

Tulia nodded. Seconds later Dodi pushed his way between them to be encased in a big four-way hug. They all trembled with grief, exhaustion and hope.

"We should go, Brianna. It's going to get dark soon. I know a safe place for us to rest." Issah's voice was a mere vibration in her ear, but it was enough.

Brianna pushed away, brushed her hair out of her eyes and studied each of her friends. The superficial damage wasn't too bad and the internal pain would not stop them from moving on.

"All right, let's go," she said.

Tulia had lost her crutch in the river and, with Amon still unable to see, it was slow going down the rocky path by the waterfall, climbing over boulders and slipping on smooth moss-covered rocks. The mist rose around them, a damp clinging cloud that choked their lungs like benevolent fumes. All around them the lush vegetation closed in, reducing the fading light to deep green gloom.

At last the ground leveled out and they crowded together, their soft gasps of pleasure echoed by the wind. After the black grimness of the underground river, the valley below where the river spilled into the lake seemed like a small piece of paradise. Curved white beaches sparkled in the soft green rays of the dying sun as though they were covered in precious jewels. The gently swaying fronds of gigantic sawas fanned the beach and formed a curtain that obscured the source of the twittering, whistling life that surrounded them in an orchestra of noise. Brightly colored shandinas with swirling tails and bright yellow beaks flitted everywhere. Their screeching was music to their ears after the roar of the river.

"It's beautiful," Tulia breathed as she gazed around in wonder.

The sun was dipping close to the distant peaks on the other side of the valley.

"Hurry. We need to reach the cave," Issah urged them. "I don't know what might be around these days with Saquin and Kybotek in control of the castle."

A light mist was rising above the water. At the other end of the lake a small waterfall tinkled over smooth, round rocks. Tiny orange qymaten with extraordinary bulging emerald eyes flicked in and out of the water, landing with tiny plops after each jump. The valley was shaded and cool, and even the shandinas had settled into the hushed silence of evening. The tight grip of tension eased its grip on Brianna's body as they walked. Even though she knew they weren't safe yet, it was hard to believe that this valley could harbor evil. As Issah hurried them along the edge of the lake, Brianna scanned the sand in a vain hope Conal had survived the falls.

Halfway around the first curve of the lake, she saw something on the beach — a rock, a patch of weed. She didn't dare hope. The dark patch appeared less and less like weed as she got closer.

"Conal," she yelled as alternate flushes of anticipation and dread shuddered through her. Could he have survived? Brianna began to run, exhausted muscles protesting at being forced to hurry through deep, soft sand.

Brianna flung herself onto the sand. Her hands scrabbled at the black, slimy strands of weed, pulling it away until she exposed Conal's battered body. Icy fear numbed her as she gingerly felt the cold, damp skin of his neck for a pulse. He slumped motionless and pale, eyes closed. His hair was plastered to his head.

Her fingers sought and sensed a feeble pulse beating. "He's alive," she croaked as the others crowded around.

"Is he really alive?" Tulia asked.

"Yes. He's a bit battered, but he's still breathing."

The rise and fall of Conal's chest was barely perceptible under the tatters of his shirt, which showed splashes of dark red. Blood still oozed from the cuts and grazes that marked his body.

Conal's eyes fluttered open. He groaned softly. "That was some swim," he mumbled. "I tried to hang on, Brianna. I tried."

Brianna patted his shoulder and grinned inanely. "You did well."

Suddenly a chill cloud of gloom crossed over them. Brianna shivered and looked up. The soft sunset hues of the sky had darkened as the sun dipped behind the snow-covered peaks.

Issah scanned the valley. "We need to go, Brianna. Can you carry him?"

"I think so. Help me get him on my shoulder."

* * * *

The cave was dark and dank with a small opening they had to crawl through. It was roomy once inside, with a clean sandy floor. Brianna laid Conal on the sand. He was ghostly white and so cold to the touch.

"Tulia, can you patch up this ratbag?" Brianna asked as she took off her jerkin and laid it over Conal's prone form.

"I'll manage," said Tulia, sorting through the soggy packets and jars of herbs she had refused to abandon, even when the weight of the bag threatened to drown her. She found the ones she wanted. "But what we need most is a fire. We need to dry him out. See, he's shivering. We all need to get dry and warm." She stared up at them, a frown puckering her brow almost into her bangs.

"Yes, Tulia, we all need to get dry before the night chill settles in. This time of moon cycle a damp mist rises from the lake. It's very bad for the lungs," Issah said as she dumped her small pack. "I will go get some wood if someone has a flint."

By the time Issah returned, they had determined that no one had a flint.

Tulia looked steadily up at Brianna. "You might have the gift of fire, Brianna. Try. The words go like this." She muttered several strange-sounding words.

Brianna nodded.

Tulia snatched up a few twigs and leaves, scraped them into an untidy pile then shuffled backward on her knees. Her big green eyes glowed, luminous with expectation.

Brianna stared at the pile of twigs as she drew a slow lingering breath into her lungs. She held it deep in her diaphragm and raised her arms, pointing her fingers at the pile. Slowly, on the outgoing breath, she chanted the magic words. With a thunderous crack a jagged flash poured from her fingers and hit the pile. Twigs and leaves bounced upward and fell, burning, back onto the untidy stack.

Brianna let her hand drop as Tulia grinned and began to feed the tiny blaze with bigger and bigger twigs. Finally she loaded on lumps of wood brought by Issah.

Issah hugged her. "Well done, sister."

"Less force next time—it's only a fire spell," Tulia censored with a smile.

Brianna giggled. "You have to remember, Tulia, I'm new at this."

Tulia gave her a sad smile and Brianna remembered what she had been meaning to ask Tulia before they fell into the river. But she kept silent now—the time had passed to ask such a question. Tulia didn't need it rubbed in that it was her little brother who had inherited the gift she wanted so badly.

As the others settled to sleep Amon sat slumped in the corner, his head hanging down while his hands turned his dagger incessantly around and around.

Brianna dropped to the sand beside him and laid her hand on his arm. "Amon?"

"I'm all right, Brianna, but I feel such burden now I'm blind. I can't hunt, fight or protect you, and I need a child to lead me around. I'm a bit of a waste of space."

She tightened her grip on his arm. "Amon, you were injured saving us. I'm sure your sight will come back— it might take time."

He laid his big hand over hers and gave it a squeeze. "No, Brianna, there is no cure. I suppose I should be grateful I'm alive, but I'm not. I have no life, no future..."

"But, Amon..."

"No, Brianna. We have no future either. Do you think your father would allow you to be tied to a broken-down, blind ex-soldier? You, his daughter, one of great magic power, deserves better than that. I would not even think to trap you by my side—the carer of a cripple."

"Amon, please don't say that," she begged, her voice cracking under unshed tears.

"You have to face it, Brianna. I'm sorry."

"So you don't care about me?"

"The reason I'm saying we have no future, Brianna, is because I do care about you."

"Then, if you care—"

"No, Brianna."

Desperate to hold her sobs in check, she got up and walked away. Deep down she knew he was right, but that was not what her heart craved.

Her new sister had been strangely quiet when she returned with the qymaten from the lake, and, unable to resolve the situation with Amon, she joined Issah by the fire.

"Issah, is something wrong?"

When Issah turned to face her, Brianna saw the shine of unshed tears in her eyes.

"I didn't want to alarm the others, but the castle is dying. I can see the black gangrene spreading up the turrets from here."

"Dying?" Brianna squeaked.

"Yes. Saquin is killing the heart of the Abrasaxon world. Without the Crystal Castle, our world as we know it will be extinguished. We have to get into the castle, overcome Saquin and release my mother, brothers and the other Abrasaxon held by Saquin. It is imperative we find the Abrogative Direktorate before it's too late," Issah said.

Brianna got up and went to sit beside Issah. "We will do it, Issah—you and I together, with help from the others. You say our father believes in us—then we must believe in ourselves." She hugged her sister close. "We'll win or die trying," she stated.

They sat together by the fire until it died into embers, listening to the mournful howl of the Sokomara.

Chapter Ten

"Issah, daughter of Hakon, show yourself. I know you are here. I can smell your magic."

Issah and Brianna both jumped up as the grating roar torpedoed across the lake and echoed into their cave. The others stirred behind them, but Issah was already gone, racing down the beach to the water's edge, her hunting knife held at the ready. Brianna came up beside her. They could see Saquin across the lake, perched on one of the walls that surrounded the castle.

"I'm coming to get you, Saquin," Issah bellowed back and pointed her blade in his direction.

Saquin laughed. "You can't defeat me, Issah, but you can save your family — your people. Come willingly, be my bride, and I will release all the Abrasaxon and allow them to live after I am ruler."

"And my father?"

Again Saquin chortled. "You ask far too much, my beautiful bride-to-be, far too much."

"Go shrivel in the moons' fire, Saquin," Issah swore in response.

"Tetchy, tetchy, my sweet one. Have it your way then." The big, ugly, muscle-bound brute disappeared. Moments later he reappeared with two young boys, one hanging from each of his beefy hands. He swung them out over the precipice. They hung suspended in the air like dead tunnel diggers at least one hundred feet above the lake. "So what do you say now, Issah? A simple 'yes' will save them."

Issah dropped to her knees in the sand. "Oh, Szymon, Hashnok. What am I to do?" she wailed.

Brianna touched her shoulders. "Issah, you know he's going to kill us all if we don't defeat him. He cannot let our father or any of his children live – they would be too powerful. You cannot give in."

"But they are my brothers, *our* little brothers, Brianna."

"Make up your mind, Issah. Will you come willingly?" Saquin bellowed.

Issah stood and faced her tormentor. She choked down her sobs of anguish. "No, Saquin. I will not be your bride."

Her reply had barely fallen silent when Saquin swung the bigger boy farther out over the precipice and released him. The child's tortured scream could be heard right across the lake as he hurtled head first toward the rocks below the castle wall.

Issah collapsed to her knees. "Szymon!"

Brianna grabbed her hand. "Help me, Issah. Help me," she begged as she held out her free hand and sent a stream of pink mist surging across the lake to retrieve the falling boy.

She struggled to reach the distance, but then Issah squeezed her hand tight and directed her untested power through Brianna. Suddenly Dodi was there, his arms clasped around Brianna's knees. The pink mist swirled and thickened. Szymon landed in the middle of the feathery cloud of pink, sinking so deep he disappeared for a moment. Brianna was terrified he was going to fall through, but then his head popped up. With the power of three, Brianna commanded her pink mist to return to them and bring Szymon with it.

Saquin's roar rattled around the lake. Disturbed by the noise, all the shandinas took to the sky in startled clouds of color. When they settled again Saquin had gone from the walls, taking Hashnok with him.

Szymon was still sobbing hysterically when the cloud tipped him onto the beach at Issah's feet. Realizing he wasn't going to die today, he choked back his sobs and threw himself down on the sand in front of Brianna. "Thank you. Thank you for saving me. My father will reward you handsomely for your deed."

Brianna smiled down at the boy on his knees in the sand. "There will be no need of a reward, Szymon — none at all. Please stand up, brother. It is not seemly that you grovel at my feet."

"You call me brother. Who are you?" Szymon demanded, first of Brianna then Issah.

Issah smiled. "Szymon, dearest brother, stand so that I can make proper introductions."

Szymon stood up, eyeing Brianna warily.

Issah touched Brianna's shoulder. "Szymon, meet your sister, Brianna. She is Father's first daughter."

Szymon reached out and took hold of Brianna's hands. "Oh by the Luna Goddess, at last we meet. Sister, thank you again for saving me —"

His words were cut off as Saquin reappeared and growled, "You will pay for that fancy trick, Issah, you and your unsavory gaggle of friends."

"Gaggle of friends... Curses of the moons on you, Tyban. It's time to teach you a lesson," Brianna snarled.

With Issah beside her, Dodi still clutching her knees and their newest addition, Szymon, holding his sister's arm, Brianna raised her hands, palms up. As she concentrated on the target of her wrath, she could feel her power building, fed with a fresh, tingling energy flooding through her from the others. Their joint energy felt so powerful she was suddenly afraid she might burst into flames herself. With a mental push, she sent a blazing ball of fire straight toward Saquin. It hit the wall at his feet in a spectacular explosion of flames, sparks and sparkling crystal rocks.

Saquin jumped back and roared ferociously. Ignoring Saquin's angry response, Brianna adjusted her aim. Saquin had no chance to dodge the second hurtling ball of fiery energy. It hit him squarely in the chest. He flew backward and disappeared from sight. They waited. He rose using the wall for support. It was impossible to tell the extent of his injuries, but his helmet was gone, releasing his black, flowing locks from confinement.

"So you win this round, Issah — you and your filthy Abrasaxon friends — but you will be mine in the end."

He waved his arms. The water of the lake sizzled and frothed. Qymaten, aqua taraqu, a mixture of green and brown firozts and weed rose to the surface to fizzle and disintegrate. "You will never get to the castle in time to save them. Give up, Issah."

"No. Moons' curses on you," she yelled back.

Saquin disappeared then and did not return.

"So that was another Tyban?" Tulia asked in a pitiful whisper.

"Yes, Tulia. Saquin is the strongest of the three Tyban we know have crossed back into Okana — he wants my power. He wants to rule the world and get revenge on the Direktorate for locking him in a crystal cube deep in the Black Mountains for eternity," Issah confirmed in a matter-of-fact voice.

"So we have three Tyban whitukas — firstly Zelig and the Gomahras, then that other one with the Yabix back there..." Tulia waved her hand in the air to vaguely indicate the location.

"Kybotek — Caller of the Dead," Issah said.

"Yes, and now this Saquin. How're we supposed to defeat them all?" Tulia mewed.

"Tulia, we'll defeat them or die trying, because if we don't succeed there will be no life for any of us," Brianna stated bluntly. "Now let's plan our next move."

"Szymon and I will try the boat on the beach. Maybe the water only affects living matter," Conal suggested. He seemed quite recovered from his run-in with the waterfall, except for the cuts and bruises all over his body.

"Good idea, boys. I can help lift it," Amon said eagerly.

"Be careful, don't touch the water," Brianna warned.

As the boys left, Issah's expression transformed into one of glum frustration. "If we can't cross the lake, we have to go around and that will take days and days. The castle will be dead by the time we get there," she moaned.

"Moons' curse. Look at that," Conal yelled.

The girls watched with despair as the boat disintegrated completely into a thick layer of brown froth.

"So, no boat. Moonlight and curses. I would do a travel spell but it's too unpredictable. We might end up in the lake or right in Saquin's hands," Issah said.

Amon touched Brianna lightly on the shoulder. "Brianna, why don't you part the water? You can move things — hold them back or bring them to you. I don't know much about magic, but I believe you could do it. We could all run across."

"But what if my power is not strong enough or peters out halfway across? We would all die."

Issah jumped up. "Come on, sister — don't doubt yourself. With all of us to supplement your power, you can do it, Brianna."

Brianna studied her friends. They trusted her. They had faith in her magic power — more faith than she had. She shuddered slightly. What if she failed? They would all die. Then again, if they failed to vanquish these Tyban, they would die anyway. "All right, let's do this."

With nothing to collect from the cave, they all lined up at the water's edge. Conal was ready to help Amon and Tulia, while the others reached out and attached themselves to Brianna.

Brianna demanded the water move. Nothing happened. She tried again. The water still didn't move. She dropped her hands. "It's no good."

"Try again, Brianna, only this time, repeat these words after me. It is a water commanding spell. It might help," Tulia said softly.

Brianna raised her hands and repeated the strange-sounding words Tulia spoke. She pushed the power she felt inside, out. With a sudden rush the waters slipped away to the left and right, leaving a dry path across the lakebed in front of them. The waters of the lake parted all the way to the opposite bank.

"Let's go," Brianna shouted.

But the others were already running ahead.

They heard Saquin give out a terrible roar, which rose to an ear-shattering screech over the sloshing of the walls of water on either side of them.

"I can smell Yabix. I can hear them. Brianna, tell me there are no Yabix. We are doomed," Amon grated out through swollen lips, pulling away from Conal's hold in an effort to retreat.

Brianna peered up and saw Saquin standing on the wall of the castle. She wanted to blast him, but couldn't afford to break her concentration. Then she heard another sound, the sound of metal on metal, of marching feet, slashing tails and the roars of Yabix. Their way was suddenly blocked. It was filled with Yabix. They poured down the waterless path on the lake bed led by Kybotek.

"I smell Yabix—I hear them. Tell me I'm hallucinating," Amon yelled.

"Go back, Tulia, Conal, take Amon back to the beach now. Run," Brianna bellowed. "Issah, help me hold the water until they are all in. We need to back up slowly, staying barely out of reach."

The Yabix pushed and shoved each other as they entered the narrow pathway. Kybotek charged forward, his sword waving over his head.

"Back up. Back up. Slowly. Hold the water. Hold the water," Brianna instructed.

They were almost back at the beach. Kybotek and the first Yabix were only feet away.

"Run. Everybody run!" Brianna hollered. She grabbed Dodi's hand as she turned and scampered back to the beach.

Moments later she paused, turned and waved. The water responded to her command, falling with a surge of sizzling froth. Roars and howls filled the air before they were cut off with gurgles and splashes. The water swished against itself, washed and flowed up the beach before it stilled.

Amon paced with jerky steps, his dagger clutched in his hand. "I smell Yabix. I smell them. I hear them. Can't fight them—can't see..."

Brianna touched his shoulder. He jumped.

"Amon, they're all dead. We drowned them in the acid lake. You don't have to fight them. We're safe—for the moment. Be calm, Amon," she croaked, barely able to hold tears of sympathy back as she watched his torment over his archenemy and his inability to see.

"Are you sure, Brianna? Are you sure you got all of them? I can still smell the stench..."

"The acid got all of them, and the Tyban, Kybotek. It's simply the flotsam on the top of the water you can smell."

Saquin roared again from the walls of the castle— only once, to express his fury at their victory.

"What now? Do we try again?" Conal asked.

"Yes, Conal, we try again—tomorrow. Brianna's exhausted," Issah replied.

Nobody said much as they returned to the cave. Everyone was feeling the weight of their failure to cross the lake. Brianna felt it most even though no one blamed her. While the others sat around the fire and talked, Brianna laid down at the back of the cave and closed her eyes.

As Brianna drifted in and out of sleep, she could hear Szymon relating his horrible experiences to Issah.

"He herded us all into caves way below the castle... Father isn't there... Kybotek came back to raise his brother from the dead... The castle is dying... Mother is all right... She is trying to summon resistance... They're afraid... No one knows where the members of the Abrogative Direktorate are... I'm afraid, Issah..."

At last Brianna slept.

* * * *

Brianna felt restored when she woke, and after a cup of tea brewed by Tulia she was ready to tackle the lake crossing.

In the pre-sun show gloom, they were already standing at the edge of the lake. The castle loomed above them. Even Brianna could see now that more than half the turrets were blackened with the creeping death.

She joined hands with Issah. They winked at each other and smiled.

"Let's do this, sister," she said.

Brianna felt kinship for the first time with the young woman who could have been her reflection — an awareness that she was family. It was more than the fact that they shared a father. It was something else Brianna couldn't define, something she hadn't felt before. They would always be there for each other. Sharing a bond that was more than friendship, and that was forever. Suddenly she was glad she'd come on this journey.

Brianna turned her sights back on the dying castle and let her power rise slowly before she drew on the others. As a precaution, she only opened up a pathway halfway across the lake this time. She figured this would stop any future surprise attacks by Saquin. The castle towered over them in brooding silence. As they reached the center of the lake, she opened up the path before them and closed the one behind to protect their rear. For the first time, she felt as though she was gaining control of her unruly, untamed power.

With the acid lake behind them, the only way up was a narrow rock path barely two feet wide, littered with jagged pebbles. It wound treacherously around the west cliff, under the full blast of the burning green sun that now rode high in the bleached sky.

Brianna's shivering soon turned to panting, and perspiration poured from her face as she helped Tulia struggle with the steep incline and rough ground.

Shadows from the turrets reached out across lake before they finally came to a huge wooden door. The icy wind that gusted down from the snow-capped peaks whistled and moaned around the walls. It tugged relentlessly at their hair and clothes like clutching fingers. Her sweat dried to a sticky chill, and Brianna pulled her jerkin more tightly over her breasts. Tulia's face was grim and white, but she had refused to rest on the protracted torturous climb.

The castle rose above them, made out of huge blocks of almost translucent crystal, shot with myriad colors. The crystal was warm to the touch and Brianna felt a vibration against her palm when she laid her hand on the nearest surface. The imposing arch that shrouded the gate and halfway up the ramparts glowed with a soft light. The gate was studded with suka spikes and held in place by huge zletic hinges. It was closed.

"Well, blessed be the moons, that's a welcoming gesture and all," Conal muttered as he examined the gate over.

"The gate is always closed, for protection. That, and the Sokamaras on the lampposts to warn intruders of dangers to come," Issah said quietly.

Conal frowned at Issah and tucked his hands on his hips. "So is that why it doesn't have a handle then?"

"No, Conal. It doesn't have a handle because Abrasaxon don't need handles to open gates. We use a simple opening spell." Issah's voice was tight and sharp.

"Do you think Saquin is still inside?" Brianna asked.

Issah glanced up at the impenetrable walls, her mouth turned down in a pout. "I know he is. The castle's still dying, see up there it is almost to turret windows now, and he would have to be in the castle itself to have that effect."

"So, what now?" Conal asked. A touch of impatience made his tone sharp.

Issah gave him a hard look. "You ask too many questions, Conal, like a child, with why, why, why."

"I'm not a child."

"Well, in that case, get your sword out and be ready to do battle. Tulia, you guide Amon. Szymon and Dodi, join hands with me and Brianna. I will open the gate and we will charge in and defeat Saquin." Issah laid her hands on the gate and whispered a strange concoction of words that meant nothing to Brianna. Nothing happened. She frowned and repeated the process. The gate vibrated but did not open.

"Issah?" Brianna hissed.

Issah held her hands wide in a gesture of defeat. "I don't know why it isn't working."

Brianna saw the glint of tears in Issah's eyes and the sharpness of panic in her expression.

She took her sister's hand in hers. "Try once more, Issah."

This time Issah spoke the words of the spell out loud. Again the gate vibrated, but did not open. "Saquin must have put a spell on the gate from inside," she muttered.

"And you can't break it? I thought the four of you were unbeatable." Conal's snide remark tightened the tension already surrounding them.

"Conal, enough of your criticism, Issah is doing her best," Amon growled.

"Yes, stop being mean. Spells are hard to break unless you know what has been used to bind them. Besides, Saquin is a very strong Tyban, and Issah and Brianna are untrained. Dodi and Szymon can't help much because they're only babies, not yet claimed by the gift," Tulia scolded.

"And what about you, Tulia? Haven't you been claimed yet? You always said you had magic," Conal spat out.

"Enough already." Brianna had seen tears appear in Tulia's eyes.

"No, Conal. The gift will not be claiming me—my destiny lies elsewhere..." Tulia's words faded into a breathy whisper.

"Enough, all of you. Join hands again. I am going to attempt a travel spell." Issah's sharp tone cut through the pain-filled silence that had followed Tulia's declaration.

The travel spell picked them up, whirled them around and over the castle walls. They clung to each other in the wild movement of the spell as they dropped with stomach-turning swiftness, hit something giving, bounced up into the air and back over the wall. With terrifying speed they hurtled toward the rocky path, landing with bone-jarring thuds as they tumbled out of the spell.

Tulia and Dodi burst into tears and Conal moaned as his head hit a rock and began to bleed. With a soldier's agility, Amon rolled a few clumsy somersaults and stood on his feet. Brianna clutched Issah as they spun into an untidy tangle.

Issah was almost crying by the time they'd all recovered. "I don't know what else to do. Saquin must have enormous power to put a barrier up like that and destroy the castle at the same time."

Brianna prowled along the walls and past the gate. "There has to be another way in." She poked, prodded and kicked at the gate with strength born of frustration. Refusing to admit defeat, she twisted and pulled each of the decorative spikes with determined tugs until her hands ached with the effort. Almost ready to quit her examination, she gave a particularly ornate spike one a final yank. It twisted in her fingers, loosened, and with an ear–splitting, tortured screech dropped down with a clunk, jamming her finger painfully against the crystal.

"Ouch!" she yelped as she dragged her finger free.

Directly below the loose spike a tiny hatch, barely more than two handspans wide, opened in the crystal wall. Brianna inspected it closely, her heart fluttering in excitement as she thrust her arm through up to the shoulder and felt around. The inside was smooth and flat. She managed to get her head through, but couldn't see anything so she tried to squeeze one arm through to feel around, but only succeeded in scraping skin off her shoulder and forehead.

She pulled back in disgust. "It's not much use. It's too small to get through, and I can't feel any handle on the inside."

Everybody gathered around.

"Maybe it's not too small," Tulia said, now hand in hand with Dodi. "Dodi's pretty small and he likes to squeeze into tight spaces and hide. It used to drive my mother to distraction."

Issah glanced from the door to Dodi. "I don't know, Tulia. It's pretty small."

"He could try."

Dodi smiled as he walked over to inspect the hatch.

"And if he gets stuck?" Brianna asked quietly.

They waited for Tulia to consider the risks. She gave Dodi a penetrating look and received a lopsided grin in return.

She shrugged. "He'll stop before that happens. Besides, he's never gotten stuck before."

Dodi nodded, his dark curls bobbing up and down on his forehead, angelic gray eyes dancing with real enthusiasm. He turned his back on them and silently began an elaborate process of measuring the fit of the hatch to his body. Nobody understood the calculations this silent child was going through, but at last Dodi indicated that the hole was big enough. Contorting his small body, he began to inch through the opening, head and shoulders first.

Issah helped Amon support his legs. Dodi had his head and one shoulder jammed through the gap. He whimpered as he eased the other shoulder through the tiny space, scraping skin from his arm and tearing his shirt.

They watched in silence. Brianna's breath collected in a painful lump under her diaphragm, her fists clenched at her sides. She glanced at Tulia. Her face was white and still, her fingers twisted her skirt gathers into tight spirals. Brianna stepped closer and laid her hand on the girl's shoulder. Tulia's shoulders were stiff and square, her spine straight, but even her rigid posture could not disguise the faint trembles that wracked her body. Brianna squeezed her shoulder gently. Tulia snuggled closer and rested her head against Brianna, her gaze riveted on Dodi, clamped in the clutches of the tiny hatch.

Dodi whimpered again and stopped moving.

"Are you all right, Dodi?" The boy gave no indication. "Dodi, are you stuck?" Issah's voice cracked with barely hidden fear.

Dodi whimpered and waved his feet.

"Push him," Conal said.

The others glared at him and he blushed.

"Shall I give you a push, Dodi?" Amon asked.

Dodi wriggled his feet again, vigorously this time.

"Hang on, Dodi," Issah said. "Amon's going to push you."

Carefully, Amon began to push on his feet.

Dodi didn't move. Amon applied more pressure and Dodi wriggled his hips.

"More pressure, Amon," Issah instructed.

Amon pushed harder. Dodi yelled in pain as he disappeared through the hole.

"You all right, Dodi? Where are you?" Issah stuck her head through the opening as far as she could.

Issah withdrew a fraction. "He's okay!"

Everybody smiled. The breath Brianna held *whooshed* out in a soft hiss, and she felt Tulia sag against her as tears flowed down her pale cheeks.

Issah peeked through the hole again and asked, "Can you see the handle, Dodi?"

There was a loud clunk. The gate shuddered, the hinges squeaked, and Issah barely had time to withdraw her head before the great gate swung open. Brianna and Issah charged through side by side, their arms ready to blast their foe. The courtyard was empty.

"Oh, it's beautiful!" Tulia whispered.

Brianna glanced around, and even with the tension surging through her as they waited for an attack by Saquin, she could appreciate the beauty before her.

The walls were shimmering with soft pastel lights inside the almost translucent crystal, and draped with a green and gold climbing plant. At the base, small shrubs were covered in delicate pink syniah.

In the middle of the heart-shaped courtyard, a white marble statue of a Sokomara towered over them. Water trickled from its eyes like crystal tears. Under their feet were smooth, polished tiles of crystal that were warm to the touch and all around brightly colored flemikos and shandinas fluttered.

"You have a nice home, Issah."

Issah nodded. "A home we'll share, sister, as soon as we reclaim it."

Issah smiled as she moved toward the robust wooden door in the back wall of the courtyard. It groaned softly as she pushed it open. Brianna was right behind her as she slipped through.

Saquin's grating voice vibrated through the air. "So you've come, daughter of Hakon, to give yourself to me in exchange for Abrasaxon lives?" The huge Tyban

seemed tired and weighed down by his heavy metal
armor with strutted wings folded together on his back.
Sweat beaded his forehead. He made no attempt to
instigate an attack.

"No, Saquin. I have come to kill you and reclaim the
Abrasaxon heart. I intend to restore my father as Grand
Archon of the Abrogative Direktorate, as it should be."

Saquin laughed, a harsh growling roll of amusement.
"You, Issah? All by yourself?"

"No, Saquin. She has not come alone. She has me —
her sister — by her side. I am Hakon's eldest daughter."

"You lie. Hakon has only one daughter," he roared.
"You're only a mortal — I can smell it on you." He
started to laugh, a gruff, grating noise in his chest that
made his shoulders shake back and forth.

"Wrong, Saquin," Brianna snarled.

Brianna and Issah stepped forward, shoulder to
shoulder. Brianna was vaguely aware of the two
younger boys hanging onto her belt as she and Issah
simultaneously blasted two fiery balls of energy at their
enemy.

Saquin laughed harder and fended the blasts off with
swipes from beefy, metal-armored hands, as if playing
a ball game. "Is that all you have, children? Go home,
before you get hurt," he sneered.

Rage speared through Brianna at his contempt. She
leaned toward Issah and twined an arm around hers,
their fingers clasped. This time they cast forward one
large ball. It whistled as it flew, leaving a trail of yellow
and white flames. It caught Saquin in the chest. The big
Tyban crumpled to his hands and knees as his metal
armor disintegrated around him. For a several minutes
he swayed back and forth, then he roared and forced
himself to his feet. With a wide swipe he ripped off the

metal mask that protected his face and stood there swaying, his once lustrous black locks falling in a tangled mass. The mask tumbled from his hand.

"Interfering Abrasaxon and mere mortals. How dare you challenge Saquin the Great," he roared as his arms began to windmill around his shoulder joints.

Without warning, the air was filled with whirling blades of steel and fire. Some carved great lumps out of the crystal while others flew over their heads. One decapitated the statue in the fountain while others pruned plants down to stocky stumps. Brianna yelped, ducked and dragged the two boys behind a low stone wall. Issah dropped and rolled behind what remained of the fountain. None of their chosen refuges were secure from the spinning blades. Amon, Conal and Tulia retreated as far as they could into a dark corner.

"Stupid children," Saquin screeched as he sent a line of whirling blades across the courtyard.

One hit the wall right by Brianna's head. She crouched down even farther as a shower of crystal struck her face and shoulders. Dodi whimpered.

"Fiery moons," Brianna cursed. "Stay here, boys."

As the last of the blades crunched into the crystal, Brianna gathered her body tightly and sprang from behind the wall. She ducked her head and rolled over and over until, with a thump, she crashed into Issah. They huddled together behind their inadequate shelter as another shower of blades whistled over their heads.

"What now, Brianna?" Issah asked. Her voice trembled with fear and anger.

"We blast him again then duck, then again and again, until we kill him," Brianna declared.

"Do you think we can kill him, I mean?" Issah sounded doubtful.

"I hope so, Issah. Ready?"

Each wrapped an arm around the other and clasped their free hands together. When the blades stopped coming, they rose as one and sent the full force of their combined power spearing across the courtyard. Their aim was excellent. The blast again caught Saquin in the chest. It spun him around and toppled him to the ground. He groaned as he rolled over, his chest smoking.

"Again, sister, again. While he's down."

The next blast caught the Tyban in the leg as he tried to rise, and he crumpled back to the ground. Even as he howled his fury and pain, he rolled over and sent another volley of blades flying across the courtyard. Brianna squawked as the blades dissected the remains of the statue that sheltered them and showered them with lumps of crystal and icy-cold water. It was only a matter of time before they would be exposed to the spinning fury of the blades. They would have to find a safer place. Lying on her stomach, Brianna peered around the corner. Saquin was standing now, both arms spinning to send a barrage of blades across the courtyard. There was no pause to retaliate in, and in moments, there would be nothing left of their shelter.

Chapter Eleven

A shadow washed over Brianna with an icy chill, then the turbulent suck and flow of air tore at her hair and clothes. She looked up. Huge blood-red, leathery wings moved lazily back and forth right over her head. The clink of metal hitting the ground was sharp. An icy blast froze the hairs on her arms as Brianna stared up and gulped. She tried to speak. Her throat moved convulsively and her chest heaved. When her words refused to form she tugged at Issah's shirt and pointed.

Issah obeyed her directions. Her face turned white as snow. "Sokomara," she breathed.

Brianna stared in fascinated horror at the legendary creature. The huge snout was square and solid with a fleshy horn sprouting out of the middle with lacy frills of flesh inside that vibrated and flapped as the creature breathed. It was as if they were alive and tasting the air. The wide mouth was filled with sharp white teeth – the front side ones long and pointed. Huge ears rose from the sides of the head like sails or deep-throated syniah.

Ribs of skin spiraled down from the tips to right inside the ear, and the whole ear swiveled continuously.

Strong hind legs held it in an upright position, while its muscular tail provided balance. The wings were semitransparent, and Brianna could see the bones that supported the webbing between each section. On the upper curve of the wings were small dexterous hands with sharp claws at the end of each digit. The whole Sokomara was covered in fluffy, bright orange fur.

The whole courtyard rumbled as Saquin discharged a stream of fire at the Sokomara. Loose rocks fell and shattered into tiny shards. Saquin roared. The Sokomara howled in answer. The courtyard trembled again as Saquin was hit with a blast of ice and snow. He retreated. Brianna peered around the corner. Saquin was covered in frost, with icicles hanging from his hair and beard. Another blast from the Sokomara showered him with icy debris. He turned and scrambled across the courtyard, his feet slipping and sliding in the slush.

He climbed the wall and stood for a moment on the top. "You might have won this round, Issah, with your heavyweight recruit, but you'll never find them. The Abrogative Direktorate is finished. You will come to me, Issah. In time, you'll come begging."

Before the next icy blast could reach him, Saquin launched himself off the wall, spread his mechanical wings and sailed into the night sky.

"Charlatan," grumbled a deep voice right in Brianna's ear.

She flinched as cold breath tickled her cheek, taken aback that the creature could speak.

"What brings you young ones to fight such an evil Tyban?"

The gentle tone gave Brianna the courage to meet the shrewd yellow eyes of the Sokomara with a direct stare despite the huge white teeth barely inches from her face.

"We have come to save the Abrogative Direktorate and the Crystal Castle from Saquin, Zelig and Kybotek."

"I see. So who are 'we'?" the creature asked.

"We are—"

The Sokomara hiccupped violently and the whole courtyard shuddered.

The creature shut its eyes for a moment as if in pain then opened them. "That charlatan promised to cure my hiccups. I took his pill and all I got was a sore throat and a massive headache from the incessant buzzing I can hear inside my head."

"Maybe we can help."

The Sokomara chuckled. "Maybe, little one, but first, tell me who you are."

"I am Brianna, first daughter of Grand Archon Hakon. This is Issah, his second daughter, and over there is Szymon, his first son. The others are mortals, Tulia and Dodi, grandchildren of Hildegarde, the Keeper of the Wisdom—"

"Ahhhh, my dearest Hildegarde. How is she?"

"We don't know. She has disappeared and so have all the Archons."

The Sokomara shook his head then hiccupped again, shaking everything violently. "Sorry... And the other two?"

"Conal, a mortal friend from home who escaped Zelig's spell when the evil Tyban took our families, and Amon. He is a brave soldier from the war. He lost his sight recently killing a Yabix to save us. We have come

to find my father, Hakon, to help us fight the evil."
Brianna spoke quickly, afraid of the Sokomara's next
move.

"Ahh, yes. It has been a sad—" He hiccupped again.

This time both Brianna and Issah were knocked off
their feet.

"Sorry, children. These hiccups are the bane of my
life. I have been exiled from home until they are cured,
but never mind me. This business of the Abrogative
Direktorate is a very sad tale. Dear old Donavon
passing without an heir caused a rift. Much evil has
passed back through the portal to wreak havoc on both
Abrasaxon and mortal. A sad day indeed."

"We need to fix it," Brianna stated emphatically.

"Indeed, but how, my esteemed magic one?" The
Sokomara hiccupped again.

"Maybe we should fix you first then you could help
us," Tulia whispered as she crept forward with her
medicine bag in her hands.

"Ahhh, I see you are a healer like your grandmother."

Tulia clutched her bag as she stared at the creature. "I
am only a child. My skills are limited, but I am willing
to try."

The Sokomara hiccupped again and Tulia flinched
away.

"Do not fear me, child, for despite our appearance,
Sokomaras are gentle creatures. We dine exclusively on
fruit and insects and live quiet lives in the caves of the
Sacred Mountains. We are usually creatures of the
night and love to go out and play in the moonlight."
The Sokomara lowered his head toward Tulia. "I would
be eternally grateful, child, if you can cure me of this
terrible affliction," he said softly. "My head aches

abominably, and it is hard to swallow my dinner with this sore throat."

Issah touched Brianna on the shoulder. "It seems safe enough. Szymon and I will take Conal and gather some food and blankets. I think we will be safer out here in case Saquin returns. We will also check that no one else is here."

Brianna hugged her sister. "Good idea. Be careful."

The Sokomara slowly lowered his enormous body to the ground. He carefully folded his wings into layers and settled them on his back and sides. He brought his hands forward and rested his chin on them. He hiccupped from time to time, the action shaking his whole body and the surrounding garden and crystal walls.

Tulia approached the Sokomara cautiously. He tried to smile, but all that did was draw the full lips back and expose the elongated teeth in the front, the huge grinding molars at the back and a wide, thick tongue of slimy yellow flesh.

"Do not fear me, tiny healer. I am Koshi, and I promise on my mother's life I will not deliberately harm you," the Sokomara said solemnly.

Brianna sat by Amon and watched Tulia measure out her herbs and seeds. She ground the mixture between two lumps of crystal.

"Tell me what is happening, Brianna. I feel so useless, unable to help or protect any of you," Amon said.

Brianna picked up his hand and squeezed it gently. "Don't worry, Amon. We have managed."

"I am glad you have Issah to help you."

Brianna caught the sadness in his voice and knew he was feeling left out and sorry for himself. "Without you, Amon, we would never have completed the first half of the journey or saved Issah, and without Issah, we couldn't have reached the castle. I do not have the power to fight Zelig, Kybotek and Saquin alone. She is my sister, Amon, and that has become very important and special to me, but it does not change how I feel about you. You're the one who has pushed me away, Amon, entirely because of your blindness."

He pulled his hand out of her grip now. "Yes, Brianna. It is as it must be, and it makes me doubly glad you will have Issah when I am gone."

"Gone!" she squeaked, making everyone start at the sudden desecration of the silence.

"Shhh, Brianna. I'm trying to work here," Tulia snapped.

"Sorry." The single word was choked out as she got up and moved away from Amon.

"Now, Koshi, I have made this elixir. I want you to drink it all immediately after the next hiccup." Tulia gave the Sokomara the cup, filled to the brim with smoking liquid. Moments later he hiccupped, the violence of the action almost spilling the contents, but Tulia steadied it with her tiny hands. As the hiccup faded Koshi poured the liquid down his throat and swallowed it in one gulp. They waited and waited. The others returned with food, blankets and a couple of lanterns. They waited. They ate, devouring the slightly stale bread, crumbly cheese, fruit and nuts. They sipped on jugs of fruit cordial found secreted in the pantry. Koshi watched them from yellow eyes, his head resting on his hands. He did not hiccup once while they ate or as they prepared their beds.

Tulia flicked her blanket out on the ground then stalked across to the Sokomara. "Well, Sokomara

Koshi, I believe I can officially declare you cured of your hiccups."

Koshi tried to smile, but quickly realized that his display of teeth was not comforting for any of them, so he changed his expression to sad again. "Tiny healer, I do believe you are correct, and I thank you for that. I wish to reward you for your kindness and assistance."

"There is no need for reward, Koshi," Tulia and Brianna chimed in unison.

"Maybe not, children, but I see a need in one of your companions, a need I can rectify. For you I will shed a tear, and give it as a gift to heal his eyesight."

"Oh, moons," Tulia whispered. "A Sokomara tear. Oh, my shining moonlights."

Brianna gaped at Tulia. She never used bad language — ever. Then she gaped at the Sokomara.

Szymon dropped the glass of cordial he'd just filled. "In the name of Diandon, he's giving you a tear. Oh, Abrasaxon hellfire — wait until Father hears about this."

Dodi jumped up and down and clapped while Conal slowly sat on the ground, his slingshot stones pouring unheeded from his hand.

"Now there is something to be impressed about," he spluttered as he flicked his bangs back out of his eyes and stared at the Sokomara.

Brianna looked from Tulia to the Sokomara, unable to make out the creature through the tears that blurred her vision. Her chest was so tight she could barely breathe.

Amon stood up. "Take me to him, Brianna, please."

"Come, child. Collect my gift. Bathe his eyes three times, one hour apart, and keep them covered in between. One hour after the third time, remove the covers and his sight shall be restored." The Sokomara's instructions were clear and simple.

Tulia reverently collected the single tear shed by Koshi in the carefully cleaned cup that had contained his medicine.

As Tulia stepped back with her precious gift, Amon sank to his knees in front of the Sokomara, his hands reaching out, seeking contact. With absolute gentleness, Koshi inserted the tip of his snout between Amon's hands.

Amon stroked the soft fur. "Dearest Koshi, how can I ever thank you for your gift? For one so great to honor a poor soldier in this way is... It is more than I can ever repay."

The Sokomara sighed. "Ah, my dear boy, you have more than earned my gift. I saw the horrors of the Yabix War, what the mortals went through to free their land from these alien invaders. Let us say no more."

"Thank you, Koshi. You have given me my life back. If you ever have a need, I will be there," Amon said as he struggled to stand up.

"I will also, Koshi," Brianna said.

"And a powerful friend I will have in you, Hakon's first daughter. Now go, begin the treatment."

Everyone watched in fascination as Tulia followed Koshi's instructions to the letter.

Issah leaned into Brianna. "This is so amazing. I never thought to see a Sokomara tear, let alone the miracle it can bring. I'm so happy for you, sister. Now you will not be parted from your Amon."

Brianna put an arm around her sister's shoulder. "Oh, Issah, I've been blessed by the Luna Goddess when I thought she had deserted me many times on this journey. All I can hope now is she also blesses us in our efforts to save our world," she said softly, "or there will be no future with Amon."

Issah returned her hug. "She will, Brianna, because we have good on our side. We'll find our father and, sister, we'll enjoy time together here in the Crystal Castle, you and I."

As they waited for the required hour to pass, Szymon and Conal huddled by a lantern, keeping themselves amused by playing a complex counting game with the slingshot stones. Tulia sat in front of Amon, watching the bandages she had placed over his eyes. Amon sat still as a statue, his back against the wall, legs crossed and hands twiddling restlessly with the beads hanging from his belt.

Brianna sat down next to Amon and took one of his hands in a desperate grip as she mumbled temple prayers under her breath. Issah pressed against Brianna's side, clutching her arm in a tight hug. Dodi crawled onto Issah's lap, and she covered him with a blanket. They waited. The Sokomara rested his huge head down on his hands and watched them wait. The second time Tulia tended to Amon, Brianna sat still and tense under the blanket Issah had thrown over her shoulders, listening, hoping and praying that the miraculous teardrop would heal his eyes. She never let go of Amon's hand.

Szymon and Conal had lost some of their interest during the second hour and crawled under their blankets. They were snoring gently.

Amon put his arm around Brianna's shoulder and pulled her close. Issah, Tulia and Dodi huddled together under the blankets. Dodi snored softly but Issah and Tulia were wide awake and counting off the time as it passed slowly.

The moons were almost touching the horizon when Tulia rose to apply the teardrop the third time. Brianna listened to Tulia and Amon discuss her ministrations in hushed tones, but another sound caught her attention. It was Koshi. He was whimpering and snuffling in his hands, trying to muffle his noise.

"Koshi is crying, Tulia," Brianna whispered. "I'll ask if he is okay. Be back in a moment."

"I'm nearly finished here if you need me," Tulia said as she began placing clean dressings on Amon's eyes.

Brianna eased out of Amon's embrace and out from under the blanket. She gasped at the icy chill in the air and the wind that whistled around the turrets of the castle.

She tiptoed close to the Sokomara. "Koshi, are you all right? Have the hiccups come back?"

Koshi lifted his snout and sniffed. "No, daughter of Hakon, the hiccups are truly cured, but the sore throat and the dreadful hum buzzing deep inside my head remain. It's driving me insane. I cannot sleep nor think for the noise, and I certainly cannot navigate my way home because this noise is interfering with my echolocation ability. If I cannot find food, I shall die."

"Oh, Koshi, perhaps when it is light, we can help you. Maybe Tulia has something to help, or I a magic spell."

"Ah, Hakon's daughter, I will be so indebted to you — all of you. Morning will come quickly enough. Go now, back to your companion's side. The wait will be over soon."

She slipped back under the blanket and cuddled into Amon. "Koshi has a headache. He is afraid the noise in his head will stop him from finding food. We need to help him in the morning."

"We'll do anything we can... Now rest, Brianna, Tulia." Amon lay his head back against the wall. "I am fine. It won't be long now."

She leaned against his shoulder and closed her eyes. Tulia nestled down by Dodi where he slept in the now-sleeping Issah's lap.

* * * *

Brianna started at the touch of a hand on her shoulder. She opened one eye, well prepared to glare at the guilty party, but it was Amon staring down at her with his smoky gray eyes. She twisted around so she could hug him. Issah was just waking and trying to push a very sleepy Dodi from her lap. Tulia was nowhere to be seen.

Amon returned Brianna's embrace, one hand touching her face, caressing the curves and angles. "Oh, Brianna, I've so missed seeing you — the sparkle in your eyes, the soft curve of your mouth when you begin to smile and…and everything."

"Oh, Amon — "

Koshi's soft moan cut her words off.

"The Sokomara is still not well," Amon said softly. "Tulia is already trying to figure out what ails him."

When they got to Koshi's side, Tulia already had him holding his gaping mouth open while she peered down the dark tunnel of his mouth and throat.

She pulled her head out from between the razor-sharp fangs. "I see something down there, but it's too dark to make out what it is, and it is too far down to reach from here."

"Why can't he just cough it up?" Conal asked, peering into the Sokomara's open mouth.

"Sokomaras do not cough, young man, we breathe through our specially designed nostrils."

"Well, that's a bit weird," Conal replied.

The Sokomara frowned. "Each to their own, young man. I've tried smelling herbs to make me sneeze, but it has not worked."

"We'll need light," Amon said.

Conal snatched up a fat stick from the fire, the end glowing red gold. "This will give enough light."

"Right, and cook the roof of poor Koshi's mouth, never mind about his throat," Amon said bluntly.

Conal's enthusiasm faded.

"I know. Glowworms—down in the dungeons—hundreds of them," Szymon announced loudly. "Come on, Conal. Let's go collect some."

Amon walked up to the Sokomara. He bowed slightly. "Sokomara Koshi, as you can see my sight has been restored. I owe you my life and pledge this day that I, Amon, will honor my debt and gift my strong sword arm and battle-honed skills to the protection of your person. I will forfeit my life if required to ensure your safety."

"Dear Amon, no pledge is required, but I would be honored in a time of need to have you watching my back," the Sokomara snuffled.

"Your time of need is here and now, Koshi, and I will do my utmost to free you of this irritation that makes you so miserable. All of us will."

"Well, let's begin, for I cannot bear it any longer," Koshi replied.

When the boys returned, Brianna stuck the small wriggling bodies of the glowworms onto a piece of sticky wekaza web Tulia used for dressings then hooked it onto a small stick. With the light ready, they all stood in silence, the unasked question like a heavy weight between them. Who was going into the Sokomara's mouth and halfway down his throat?

"You probably only need to go in a few steps. See that hanging bit, just at the back of the mouth? If you tickle that, it will bring on a cough. It should dislodge the obstruction," Tulia said as she pointed into Koshi's mouth.

Koshi screwed his face up into a wrinkled distorted mask. "You're going to make me *cough*?"

Tulia touched his face. "It will be all right, Koshi. It is the only way."

The Sokomara nodded, but appeared very unhappy.

"And the person doing the tickling?" Szymon asked.

"They... I, since I'm going to go in, will probably get dislodged too." Amon chuckled. "What do you have for a tickling instrument, Tulia?" Amon asked. "I owe this big boy."

Tulia pulled a large feather from her medicine bag. Amon took it and the light stick, climbed gingerly over Koshi's teeth and walked up his tongue. He tickled the hanging bits. Koshi coughed. Amon was knocked from his feet. He slid backward down the slimy tongue, bounced over the teeth and thudded onto the crystal tiles. The unknown object remained jammed in the Sokomara's throat. Koshi moaned. Amon tried again and moments later landed in the same spot with a grunt of discomfort.

"This isn't working. I think I'll have to go all the way in and dislodge it manually," Amon said as he stared into the dark tunnel of Koshi's throat.

Koshi's orange fur spiked up on end, his eyes wide and staring. "But I might swallow you. Oh, I couldn't bear it if I swallowed a mortal," he squealed.

He shut his mouth with a snap so loud it reverberated in Brianna's bones.

"Don't worry, Koshi. They can tie a rope around my waist and pull me back out if you swallow me," Amon said, grinning at Koshi's horrified expression.

It took some convincing but finally Koshi agreed and opened his mouth wide. Amon went first, accompanied by Conal holding the makeshift lamp high above his head, and Dodi, all three bound securely in a rope harness. Dodi held the end of another rope, and with Amon's guidance, squeezed past the object deep in Koshi's throat. He dragged the rope all the way around the object so Amon could tie it into a loop. Then Dodi dragged it out to the others.

"Okay, everyone, pull on three. One, two, three," Brianna yelled.

Amon and Conal worked together to loosen the object by wriggling it from side to side while the others hauled on the rope. There was a squelch, a glop and a slurp as the object broke free and flew out of Koshi's mouth. It clattered on his bottom teeth, rolled over them and dropped to the ground with a splat. Conal and Amon scurried as fast as they could out of Koshi's mouth and the Sokomara shut his jaws with a sigh.

Koshi cocked his head to the side. He appeared to be listening. He smiled. "Dearest children, I do believe the noise has gone." He yawned. "Thank you all. We will party later, but for now I'm going to have a nap... Oh, and by the way, you can chuck that wretched ball over the wall for all I care. I have no desire to see it ever again." With that, he dropped his head to his hands, shut his eyes, and began to snore.

Conal and Szymon were already making a wary examination of the offending object.

The multicolored hexagonal bubble was taller than Amon and just as wide. It hummed and vibrated.

Brianna moved closer. She could see disjointed shapes flapping and jumping inside the semitransparent casing. She leaned forward and put her ear to the surface. Angry voices emanated from the interior. "Issah, come and listen. Tell me what you think is inside."

Issah leaned close. "Oh, moons fire, I hear Father. He's yammering. He's angry — very angry." She looked up at Brianna. "I think the whole Abrogative Direktorate is trapped inside." Snatching up her knife, she tapped on the outer casing. "Father, can you hear me? Father, are you in there?"

The hum of angry voices stopped immediately.

Issah tapped again. "Father, it is Issah and Brianna. We've come to rescue you."

One of the shapes took on a deeper hue as it moved closer to the imprisoning skin. "Issah, it is I, your father. Brianna, my daughter, welcome. Use your knife to open the skin."

Issah stabbed the surface of the ball. Her dagger bounced back and flew from her hand.

"Father, I cannot cut it open."

"Brianna, is your gift manifest yet?"

"Yes, Hakon...Father, but I have limited control."

"Never mind your control, daughter, can you direct your power on the outside? We will blast from in here. Together we should be able to break the binding spell. It's very strong, so do not give up too soon," Hakon warned from inside the bubble.

Brianna called up her power and, pointing her fingers, she blasted the bubble. The skin glowed red and orange, but did not falter.

"More, Brianna, we need more power."

"Wait, Father, I have Issah here. She can help."

"But her gift is not manifest—it is dangerous…"

"Not if she channels through me, Father, and we have Szymon and a small boy called Dodi—he has magic before his time. They will help," Brianna yelled at the ball.

"Excellent. Let us begin." Hakon's voice was muffled.

* * * *

Brianna could feel her knees sagging with fatigue. It had been an hour already and there was nothing much to see for their efforts, but she would not give in. She so desperately wanted to make her father proud of her so she scraped up more power, chanted temple prayers and prayed to the Goddess as she worked side by side with Issah. Both Szymon and Dodi were doing their best to supplement their power.

Every bone ached, her head thumped and her hands burned and stung with the heat her power generated. A pair of strong arms encircled her waist. Amon was holding her up, had her pressed back against him as he mumbled encouragement in her ear. She felt herself rally and called forward more power.

With an agonizing screech, the bubble suddenly split open. Those inside were thrown about as the two sides of the ball rocked back and forth. In a flash, all seven prisoners leaped to their feet and began to straighten their clothes and hair in a desperate effort to keep their hard-won dignity and status intact. The tallest of them stepped out of the ball, long silver hair flowing free, velvet, heavily embroidered robes crumpled. He smiled and held his arms wide. "Come, children," he said.

Issah and Szymon bounded forward into his embrace. As Brianna hesitated he smiled. "Come, Brianna. I am Hakon, your father."

Brianna stepped into the circle of his arms and he tightly embraced his three children.

From tight in her father's embrace, Brianna heard Tulia and Dodi shriek.

"Grandmamma, Grandmamma."

Koshi lifted his head long enough to investigate his surroundings. "Well, I never, so much commotion..." he muttered. His eyes now opened wider as he took in the scene before him. "They were all in my throat? Oh my goodness. Ah, the world is saved, the Archons have returned. In that case, I will continue my nap. I need all the beauty sleep I can get for the celebrations ahead."

Amon patted Koshi's snout as the Sokomara laid his head down again. "We'll wake you, big fella, in time for the party."

Koshi began to snore.

Hakon kissed each of them in turn and set them from him. "We have much to talk about, Brianna, but first we must secure the land from the Tyban and close the portal through which evil is oozing." Hakon then looked over his shoulder. "Members of the Direktorate, I, Grand Archon Hakon, call you to order."

The five members of the Direktorate shuffled into a semicircle to the left of their leader. Hildegarde, with Tulia and Dodi clutched to her side, moved to the right. Brianna stood beside Issah and Szymon and faced her Abrasaxon father and his Archons. Amon and Conal stood quietly behind them. Across the courtyard Koshi snored on.

"Archons. Hildegarde, Keeper of the Wisdom. Before you stand our saviors in this terrible failure to protect the mortals of Okana and Okiyarra."

The five Archons and Hakon himself bowed to them. Hildegarde hugged her grandchildren as she nodded and smiled her beaming approval at Brianna. Brianna was unsure how to respond so she gave a small bow of acknowledgment to these proud and powerful Abrasaxon.

"Brianna, we are humbled by what you and your companions have done, and I and my fellow Archons" — Hakon paused then indicated each one as he introduced them — "Yosei, Orysat, Ruben, Shakur and Seidet" — he turned and nodded to Hildegarde — "and all Abrasaxon Archons who follow will forever be in your debt."

They may be proud, powerful Abrasaxon, but today they seemed somewhat confused and shamefaced.

Brianna stepped forward. "Thank you, Father. Archons, I am honored to be of service, but much has happened since your capture and I fear if we do not hurry, our world will be destroyed."

"Yes, daughter, I fear you're right. I can see the castle is dying and the absence of my wife and younger son fill me with fear. Come, all, to the Crescent Room. We must make plans to save Okana and Okiyarra."

* * * *

A short time later they were all seated around a circular table carved from green crystal. Hakon began to speak.

"Daughter, the Archons and I know nothing of what has happened since the fateful day Archon Donavon passed. Hildegarde had just paid her private respects to her dear friend when he took his last breath. In the next moment Donavon's nephew, Deinon, refused to take on the mantle of Archon and, without warning, a rift opened up between good and evil. Please tell us what has happened. What has brought you here?"

He indicated that she should stand. Brianna's legs trembled and she held onto the edge of the table for support. Her voice wavered in the beginning, not only from nervousness, but also from emotion. "Father, Archons and Hildegarde, I have come on a long journey only made possible by my companions" — she touched Amon on the shoulder — "Amon, a warrior from the Yabix War, Conal, the Mayor of Kenon's son and, of course, Tulia and Dodi..."

Her father glanced from her to Amon then pointedly at where her hand rested on his shoulder. She let her hand slide from Amon and fall to her side, nervous under her father's penetrating gaze.

"And later we came across Issah and saved Szymon. Anyway, the reason we came to find you was because terrible things have happened in Okana, magical things." She went on to tell of the day she found out the identity of her father and described Zelig's arrival, the kidnapping of the villagers and the journey they'd endured to get help from the Abrogative Direktorate.

"Father, we also need to find the Scorpion's Heart Syniah to save them — Mother, Da and all the villagers." Tears stung at the backs of her eyes as she finished speaking and sank into her seat.

Brianna's father's expression was grim and dark, Hildegarde whispered something in Tulia's ear and she tiptoed from the room. Brianna wondered where the crippled girl was going.

Issah then stood and told how she'd followed her father's instructions to find Brianna when the Direktorate had vanished and Saquin had captured the castle and its inhabitants, including her mother and brothers. She told of the rescue of Szymon and the destruction of Kybotek and the Yabix before they fought Saquin in the castle. Issah was crying openly by the time she sat down.

All the Archons had stayed silent while they spoke. Varying expressions flitted across their faces, and Brianna wondered what they were thinking.

Hakon stood. "Fellow Archons, not only have we failed in our sacred duty to keep the mortals of Okana and Okiyarra safe from evil, we have failed to keep our own house safe. It must never happen again, and the necessary procedures will be put in place in due course. First, though, gentlemen, we must secure and heal the Crystal Castle, the heart and soul of all Abrasaxon. Then we must free and heal the mortals caught up in this terror, and lastly, we must seal the rift between good and evil and drive out those who would destroy the balance."

When no one spoke in the silence that followed his speech, Hakon started issuing orders. Orysat and Yosei were to track down Saquin and destroy him if they could. Ruben and Shakur were tasked with the job of rounding up every Abrasaxon and bringing them to the castle, while Szymon and Conal were to find the missing castle inhabitants. Seidet and Hakon were going to seal the rift and Hildegarde, Tulia and Dodi were to begin the healing rituals for the castle.

Issah gave Brianna a quizzical glance then shrugged. Puzzled that she had not been assigned a task, Brianna waited in silence beside her sister. Amon stood just behind them, a hand on each of their shoulders.

At last Hakon finished issuing instructions and came toward them. "Children, come. There is not much time."

Brianna, Issah and Amon followed him out to the courtyard where Koshi still snoozed as he tried to catch up on his lost sleep. Tulia was snuggled down under one wing, deeply asleep, snoring in unison with the huge Sokomara. The three of them looked at one another, at the Sokomara, then back to Hakon. Brianna was not only puzzled as to why he had brought them out into the biting cold of the courtyard, but was beginning to get frustrated with the delay in finding the syniah.

Hakon pointed to the left of the castle. A majestic, snow-covered peak rose up to tower over the Crystal Castle. "Up there, children, is Donavon's retreat. He allowed no one to go there, but I do know he carefully cultivated and guarded the Scorpion's Heart Syniahs. This is where you must go to get the pollen you need to save your people."

Brianna's heart sank like a rock behind her breast. The task seemed impossible. "But Grand Archon... Father, time is of the essence."

He laid a heavy hand on her shoulder. "I know, daughter, I know, and I am loath to ask more of you after what you have been through, but I must heal the rift. Besides, you and Issah are my daughters. You are strong and smart, and you have at hand an impressive young man with a strong sword arm and a wealth of experience. You can do this."

"But how? Just to climb the mountain will take many days," Brianna protested.

Hakon started to laugh lightly. "It would, but I have organized a ride for you. Koshi will fly you almost to the retreat and bring you back."

At the sound of his name the Sokomara awoke, lifted his snout from his hands, and grunted. "Ready when you are, children. Well, as soon as the tiny healer who brought me word of my assignment wakes, of course."

Brianna promptly stepped forward and shook Tulia until she woke. "Koshi is ready to take us, Tulia, and you have work to do, healing the castle."

She yawned. "I wish I was going with you. I always wanted to ride a Sokomara."

"Next time, Tulia. You are needed here to help Hakon heal the castle."

Brianna's father appeared worried. "I don't know what you will find there or what difficulties you might encounter, but I have faith in you. You will endure and succeed."

Brianna wiped her tears of frustration away before they turned into icy droplets. This was not what she'd expected. Deep down she was disappointed that her father could not just cure the villagers of Kenon and Oroton.

He squeezed her shoulder. "Be brave, Brianna. When you return with the pollen, I will come with you to free them. I wish also to speak to your mother about your future. Go with my love, daughter. All three of you return soon, and good luck."

Szymon shoved heavy coats into their hands and secured a three-person saddle to Koshi's back. As soon as they were settled Koshi launched, and moments later the castle was left behind.

The air was icy and the wind caused by their momentum whistled past their ears. Brianna held on with a white-knuckled grip as the undulating movement of Koshi's flight bounced her up and down in the saddle. Below, the crags of the mountains were stark and rugged, with jagged caps of glistening white snow. They kept rising. Behind and below them the Crystal Castle grew smaller and smaller. The air was thin and so cold it burnt her lungs as she dragged it in. She could feel Koshi now struggling for each breath. He was slowing down and losing altitude as his breath became more labored.

Finally he thudded to a clumsy landing between two angular outcroppings of rock. "I can't go farther — the retreat is just on that next ridge. I'll await your return. Go safely."

The path Koshi indicated was relatively free from snow, but it was narrow, rough and strewn with small boulders.

"I'll do a travel spell." Issah reached for their hands, already chanting her spell.

Brianna had come to hate the swirling, chaotic motion of Issah's traveling spells but she said nothing, just held hands tightly with Amon and her sister as she gave herself up to the twirling motion.

With a grunt she hit the ground, rolled and sat up, her head spinning. Amon was lying flat on his back a few feet away. There was no sign of Issah.

"Issah," she yelled, but her cry was muffled by the snow that blanketed everything. "Issah, where are you?"

"I'm here, Brianna — I can see you, but I can't get through Donavan's protective spell."

Brianna peered around at the unchanging white. She heard her sister yelling. She stared harder, shielding her eyes from the brightness. Then she saw her, a mere gray blemish on the other side of an icy curtain. Brianna jumped up and ran toward the curtain. She passed right through and came to a halt beside her sister. She could see Amon walking warily toward the curtain from the other side.

"Come through, Amon," she instructed.

He joined them. "What now?" he asked.

Issah gave a lopsided smile. "I suspect Donavon's spell prevents those of magic intruding on his retreat. I cannot cross the barrier and my traveling spell will not work either. Sorry, but I'm unable to take you any closer. I'll have to wait here while you two go alone to get the syniahs."

"But I have magic…"

"You do, sister, but you are also mortal. Now go. I will be fine here with a shielding spell, a warm fire and the food in my bag."

Just before they crossed the hazy curtain, Brianna looked back. Her sister seemed so small and young in the vastness of the mountain. She hated leaving her alone, but Issah waved them on. Brianna watched until Issah began spinning a shielding spell in the form of a small, triangular shelter to protect her from the weather then turned away, hoping Issah would be okay until they returned. Amon took Brianna's cold hand in his warm one as they turned their backs on Issah and walked through Donavon's shield.

After an hour of hard slogging through knee-deep snow, they came upon a small clearing and a sturdy stone structure set way back against the rising cliffs. They went through the door and found themselves in a comfortable cottage that extended right back into the cave behind it. It was comfortably furnished and the walls were lined with shelves filled with bottles of ingredients — each one carefully labeled. Together they searched every shelf. There was no bottle labeled with the word 'scorpion' or illustrated with a representation of the deadly creature.

"If the pollen's not here then Donavon must have the syniahs growing somewhere outside," Brianna said, heading for the door.

Amon obediently followed her out into the snow. They searched until it was too dark to see and they were forced to retreat to the cottage. Amon lit a fire while Brianna sent a mind message to Issah. Her sister assured them she was fine for the night. It troubled Brianna to leave her sister out on the mountain alone, but there was nothing she could do about it.

* * * *

She woke in the early hours with Amon's arms around her as they snuggled close in the narrow cot used by Donavon. Not sure what had woken her, she listened with acute concentration, but there was only heavy silence all around. Outside, the sky was just beginning to lighten. The fire was still a glow of orange in the corner of the room, and she was cocooned in warmth. She stretched, sighed, and went to settle again when suddenly she sneezed. As she took another breath, she sneezed again.

Amon lifted his head. "Are you all right?"

"Can you smell it, Amon, the perfume? It's the perfume of the Scorpion's Heart Syniah. I can smell it. The syniahs are here in the cottage."

Amon sniffed. "I can smell a sweet perfume, but we thoroughly searched the cottage last night, Brianna."

But even as he spoke she scrambled out of bed, snatched up the lanterns they used earlier, and lit them both. "They have to be inside this cottage, Amon. The smell is so strong."

She circled the compact space twice before she discovered the small, darkened indentation in the back wall and the heavy wooden door blocking it. The door squeaked as she opened it and stepped onto a narrow landing leading to steep stairs carved into the rock. It was freezing. She shivered and sneezed again. The perfume was cloying now. She descended with tentative steps, Amon right behind her. The scent of the syniahs became stronger the farther down she went, and now she could hear scraping and scratching. There was something alive here in the silent darkness. Something that knew they were coming, because as they drew closer, the rattle and scraping grew more agitated.

With her heart a cold lump in her chest and her stomach churning, Brianna stepped off the bottom step onto the sandy floor of a huge cavern. The arched roof loomed above them. In the center was a large skylight constructed of transparent material. The morning light radiated down and cast a luminous glow into the center of the cavern, illuminating what appeared to be a pit. The noise she had heard was coming from the pit and increased to a frenzied crescendo as she neared the edge. She gasped. The lantern fell from her nerveless fingers as she backed away from the edge with unsteady steps. "Oh, fiery moons! Huge scorpions!" she squawked.

The rattling increased when Amon peered over the side, and now Brianna could hear scrabbling on the rock walls. They were trying to get out. Deadly killers with forward pincers for holding their prey, beady eyes and flexible jointed tails, each tipped with an enormous, slightly curved spike that with one stab could deliver enough venom to kill a creature as big as a Sokomara.

Amon backed away from the pit. "I saw the red syniahs."

Brianna nodded. "Donavon could not have chosen better guardians for the syniahs—four huge scorpions. I didn't know they grew that big," she muttered, her mind already tussling with the problem of retrieving the syniahs from their savage, alien guardians.

"Well, there will be no problem getting down into the pit," Amon announced as he dragged a sturdy wooden ladder from its hook on the back wall.

Brianna managed a smile. "What would I do without you, Amon?"

He leaned in toward her, and for a brief moment his lips caressed hers, sending a tingling warmth through her veins.

"So what is our next move? Surely a couple of your fiery blasts would knock them over."

Brianna walked slowly and deliberately toward the pit. The rattling increased. She drew in her breath and summoned her power, pleased to find that it was getting easier each time she tried to command it. Staring unblinking into the five sets of eyes on the nearest scorpion, she raised her hand and fired off a ball of white heat—enough to stun, but not enough to kill. She felt deep down that the syniahs needed their guardians and she felt no animosity toward the scorpions, even though they would kill her without compunction if they could.

The blast hit the scorpion, cracked and sizzled, then dissipated into harmless blue sparks. The scorpion swept its tail up over its sharp bony face and stabbed the spike into the soft earth floor. Brianna tried again and again, but her efforts only made the scorpions more agitated. They scrabbled around the enclosure, climbing over one another, swiping at the air with their tails. Their hard shells crunched and cracked as they sought access to their tormentor above. Finally, as all four stumbled into a tangled heap in one corner, Brianna quickly switched to a shielding spell, hoping to hold them in place while Amon picked the syniahs. By the time Amon had dragged the ladder to the precipice, the scorpions had untangled themselves and scurried through the shield toward where Amon stood, just out of reach.

"Wretched creatures, just like the Yabix. Why come here?"

Amon chuckled. "Well, I don't think the scorpions had a choice, they were hiding in crevices on a meteor that crashed here hundreds of years ago. As for the Yabix, well, they wanted to invade our lush green planet."

"Regardless, moons' curses on Donavon. Magic does not work here at all. What was he thinking?" Brianna brushed stray strands of hair off her face as she paced up and down.

"No magic includes the Tyban..."

"I know, but it doesn't help us. How can we, mere mortals, fight four alien creatures three times our size and armed with toxic venom that would kill Koshi with one drop?"

"One at a time, Brianna, in the old-fashioned, mortal way. Let's lure them out, one by one, and kill them. Then we can get the syniahs."

"But then..." She snapped her mouth shut on her words of protest. There would be time enough after they had saved her people to worry about the protection of the syniahs. "Let's do it."

Together they propped the ladder against the wall of the pit. Immediately one of the scorpions began to scramble up the wooden structure, clinging precariously to the rungs with clawed feet. With the use of its tail and the huge front pincers, it managed to heave its armor-plated body over the edge of the pit. It pinioned Amon with a beady glare from its five pairs of eyes and snapped its huge pincers together with a loud clacking noise. Amon immediately went in hard with his sword and shield aloft. He sought a soft spot between the solid plates that covered the segmented body. Brianna struggled to remove the ladder, as the second scorpion was already clinging to the bottom rungs. She twisted the ladder and shook it. The scorpion fell, hissing and snapping, back onto its companions. She laid the ladder down then pulled out her sword and charged the scorpion from the rear. One savage thrust buried her sword up to the hilt in the first gap between the body and the tail. The scorpion hissed and writhed. She withdrew the sword just as Amon scored his second hit — right between the ten beady eyes. The scorpion wavered, stumbled and toppled heavily to the ground. It slumped on its back, all eight legs twitching spasmodically as it died.

"One down, three to go," Brianna yelled, ecstatic at their easy victory.

Amon was already hefting the ladder back to the edge of the pit.

Brianna inspected their foe. It was a magnificent creature. Thick black shell plates tinged with edges of green made up the creature's natural armor. Brianna remembered Da saying they wore their skeleton on the outside, and Brianna was fascinated by their cold, primitive beauty. As she stepped away, ready to do battle again, a leg twitched and a pincer fell open. A shadow loomed over her. A light breeze whistled past her ear and she felt the sprinkle of liquid. She looked up, froze for a second, then dropped and rolled. A poison-laden spike slammed into the dirt right beside her shoulder. Sand sprayed and splattered from the impact.

Brianna lost her grip on her sword as she scuttled backward on her bottom. "Oh, raving hojaks, Amon, it's still alive," she bellowed.

A second spike slammed into the ground beside her. Ten sets of eyes glared down at her as the alien creature completed its division into two complete scorpions.

Amon bellowed from beside the pit. One of the scorpions turned and lumbered toward him, pincers opening and closing. Brianna rolled to the right as a pincer cut the air where she'd been lying. She scrambled to her feet, searching for her fallen weapon as she rose.

"Got to get them back in the pit," Amon yelled from where he was jumping up and down on the very edge of the cavity. As the first scorpion charged him, he leaped to the left and rolled away. The scorpion, intent on its charge, tried to halt, but despite using all legs as brakes, it slid forward and nosedived into the abyss, its viciously armed tail flailing in the air as it went.

Brianna darted across the cavern toward the pit with the second scorpion in pursuit. She could feel the air being displaced behind her as the pincers snapped open and closed inches from the back of her neck. The edge loomed close. She turned to face her foe before she threw herself to the ground right under its armored body. As the pincers swung down to reach her, the changing weight unbalanced the scorpion head over heels and back into the pit. Brianna reclined, gasping and trembling until Amon reached down and took her hand to pull her up.

"I've never seen anything like that. It split in two when it died. We now have five scorpions to get past," Amon growled.

Brianna glowered at the pit. "I can't believe Donavon would weave such an unbreakable spell. The syniahs must be so powerful they can never fall into the wrong hands, but, with Donavon gone, how are we ever going to get the pollen and save my family?" Tears welled up and she wiped them away with an angry swipe of her sleeve. "Moons' curse, moons' curse, moons' curse," she muttered savagely, plonking herself down on the nearest rock.

She ignored Amon as he paced back and forth, poking and prodding various items stored in the cavern. Finally he exhausted things to explore and came to sit beside her. He was absently plucking the strings of a small instrument, adjusting them to suit his ear. Then he began to play, hesitantly at first then more fluently. Brianna recognized the tune as a love song often sung by passing entertainers. He smiled then began to sing. She smiled despite her frustration and despair. Amon was serenading her. Her heart melted at his spontaneous gesture of romance and comfort. As the last note floated into the darkness, she registered how silent it was. There was no rattle from the pit. She got up and tiptoed to the edge. All five scorpions had relaxed into a jumbled pile, peacefully sleeping. She walked slowly away.

"Amon, play and sing again. The scorpions have been lulled to sleep. I can go and get the syniahs if you continue to play."

He smiled and began to play the same tune again. Brianna snatched Conal's dagger out of her boot and climbed down the ladder into the pit. With soft footfalls she skirted the sleeping creatures and crept up to the blossom-laden vines. With delicate movements she sliced the stem of the first syniah, breathing in the heady perfume as she went to place it in her bag. In that moment the perfume faded and the syniah began to die. It wilted, turned brown and rotted right in front of her. Her heart pounded and a wave of nausea washed over her. She wanted to rage and curse, but she strangled it down to a tiny whimper.

For a long time she stared at the dead syniah in her hand. There had to be an answer — something she was missing, some essential key to collecting the pollen. Hildegarde had come to see Donavon before he died. Did she know Donavon's shields against magic entities? Could Hildegarde be the key? She searched her mind for memories, but the idea was too far-fetched, even for her imaginative mind, and it wouldn't help anyway because Hildegarde wasn't there. But the thought persisted. She rolled it around in her head, trying to get a purchase on the elusive seed inherent in the idea.

Then it came to her — the dagger that had come to her in Hildegarde's cave. It had felt right to have it, like it belonged. She reached into her other boot and pulled out the intricate zletic dagger. The rich black metal glowed almost silver in the muted daylight drifting down from the opening in the cavern roof. It vibrated as she closed her hand around it and stepped forward to slice the second syniah. She waited, syniah in one hand, the dagger in the other. The syniah stayed luscious and dewy, its perfume strong and sweet. In a frenzy of action, Brianna sliced every open bloom from the sturdy vines that wound in between the rocks. With her bag full, she escaped the pit, remembering to pull up the ladder after her.

When Amon saw her, he stopped playing. "You were gone so long, Brianna. I was afraid for you, but more afraid to stop playing."

"I have the syniahs. We must hurry back to the castle."

* * * *

As Koshi came in to land, Brianna could see her father and Hildegarde waiting for them. All around them other people — strangers — scurried to and fro. She could also see that the castle was no longer black halfway down the turrets, but myriad beautiful glowing colors refracted in all directions by the crystal.

As they slipped from Koshi's back, Hildegarde hurried forward.

A deep frown furrowed her brow. "Did you get the syniahs? Did you get them?"

Brianna opened her bag. "Yes, Hildegarde, we got the syniahs. I used your zletic dagger to cut them. I'm sorry, but I took it from your cave. It was like it chose me. I always intended to return it."

Hildegarde grabbed her shoulders and pulled her into a rib-crunching hug. "I always knew you were smart, young lady. Too smart for those priestesses who would've locked you up. I always knew you would handle your gift when it claimed you. You keep the dagger, Brianna, it's my gift to you. I have another one — it was Donavon's."

As soon as Hildegarde released her, Hakon hauled her into his arms.

"My daughter. I'm so proud of you — both of you, in fact," he said loudly as he also drew Issah into his embrace. He held out his hand to Amon. "I am a very blessed Archon, as are my daughters, young man, to have such a trustworthy guardian as you, with your strong sword arm. I have something to offer you for the future, Amon, a small token of my gratitude, but for now time is of the essence. We must go…"

A huge wind rushed over them and his next words were swept away on the draughts of two pairs of Sokomara wings. Not quite as big as Koshi, but just as ugly, Koshi's companions landed with grace beside their fellow Sokomara.

A short time later, armed with pollen carefully extracted from the red blooms, they zoomed down the mountain and low over the land of Okana. The landscape was almost identicalto the map Brianna had stolen and destroyed. She was going home to her day of reckoning, but she wasn't afraid anymore. She could feel her father's strong arms encircling her waist as he held her against his broad chest, and she knew her sister was just behind him. On the other Sokomara, guided by Szymon, were Amon and Conal. Hashnok guided the third with Tulia and Dodi clinging to Hildegarde. Hildegarde sat up straight with both hands gripping the saddle. Behind her Tulia shrilled in delight.

In that moment Brianna knew she was not alone — she was part of a family.

Chapter Twelve

Then they were skimming over the black turrets of Zelig's castle. They circled once then came back for another swoop. The flesh rippers squawked and fluttered off in clouds of black feathers. The villagers seemed oblivious to their arrival and continued to stumble and carry the huge lumps of black zletic from the hole in the ground in front of the castle. They moved slowly, their bodies wasted, hair matted and clothes in tatters that barely covered them in places and provided no protection against the cold wind that swept across the valley.

As they swooped again, each passenger on the three Sokomaras pulled out the pouches of carefully prepared pollen from the Scorpion's Heart Syniahs and began scattering it. The pollen fell like red rain, drifting down and covering everybody in the courtyard. It stuck to the moist castle walls. The people raised their eyes. Brianna could see the confusion and pain that flitted across their faces before the grains of pollen touched them and realization came. As it did life returned and they helped one another to gather in a protective group. Where the pollen touched the dying earth, red flames burst into life, and as they died away tiny green vines sprouted.

Zelig rode out of the castle on his smoke-breathing whituka. He glared at the people huddling together, then scanned the sky. Red pollen floated down and he screeched and tried to withdraw into the castle, but it was too late. On Zelig, the grains flashed red and black. His howls rose up and stabbed at their ears as they glided past. He jumped from the lumbering whituka and ran, his long robes streaming out behind him, through the wall, down the hill and along the creek. His gaunt, bony face contorted into a grotesque mask, long-nailed fingers clawed at his straggling locks. With huge slaps and shakes of his head and clothes, Zelig frantically tried to brush the pollen from his body as he fled the castle. Unfortunately for him, the glowing red powder stuck like glue.

Koshi swept around again and, as they hovered over Zelig, Hakon, Issah and Brianna joined hands and blasted him to smithereens with an enormous, swirling blast of fiery magic. When the blast faded, the only indication that Zelig had ever existed was a small sprinkle of black ash that floated away on the wind.

The Gomahras dashed back and forth, grunting in panic. With their leader gone, they were confused and angry. The pollen smoked when it touched their slimy skins. They didn't even hesitate at the dark mark on the ground that had been Zelig. With clumsy bounds they hurried along toward the bridge. Without pausing they scurried across, with flat feet slapping noisily on the graying planks.

It was then that Hakon pulled out of his robes several of the small green stones Conal had found for him on the shore of the lake. They glowed softly cradled in the palm of his hand.

Slowly Hakon closed his hand into a fist. "I will make a multiplying spell—enough for every Gomahra to have some."

When he opened it, the stones were dust. As they skimmed low over the Gomahras, Hakon scattered the green powder liberally on their heads. Moments later there was nothing but gooey puddles contaminating the bridge. Assured no Gomahras remained, they turned back to the castle, the Sokomaras landing gracefully side by side. At first the villagers backed away with joint cries of awe and fear, but when they saw who had arrived with Sokomaras everyone surged forward to greet them.

Brianna searched the faces, backing away from the crush. "She's not here, Amon. She's not here! None of the priestesses are here," she screeched, her mind collapsing into an incoherent jumble of fear and grief.

Amon peered over the milling crowd. "Maybe we missed them."

She tapped his shoulder. "No, there's Da, alone! We have to find them." Her heart pounded with the memory of her mother being carted off by Zelig that fateful night. Panic tightened her stomach as she ran with a stumbling gait toward her da. Amon was right behind her.

Lek met her halfway, still trying to shake off the last remnants of confusion.

"Where?" Brianna blurted out.

Her da shook his head. "I haven't seen her since we were captured. I tried to stop her from fighting Zelig, but she refused to go peacefully." His eyes were filled with pain and guilt. "I think they took her and the priestesses to the dungeons because they didn't succumb to the spell." He moaned, already turning toward the castle.

Brianna pulled him back. "Stay here, we'll go."

At first he resisted her restraint, but, weakened by his days under the spell, he gave up quickly and sank onto a rock nearby.

"I'm coming," Conal cried as he leaped up behind Amon.

"Oh no!" gasped Amon. "The castle is dissolving!"

"The castle must have been an extension of Zelig's evil person." Hakon groaned as he swept his outer robe off. "With him destroyed, the castle can no longer be sustained. Go, children. Issah and I will hold the castle from destruction until you emerge if we can," Hakon shouted as he waved his hands in the direction of the castle.

"Come on then, we don't have much time!" Brianna grabbed Amon's hand and together they charged inside the dark castle.

Conal thudded up behind them as they entered the door.

"Mother!" Echoes mocked her. "Mother!"

Deeper and deeper they plunged into the dark bowels of the building.

Conal grabbed Brianna's arm. "Shh! Something's coming!"

Three Gomahras shuffled around the corner, already screwing their pug noses up, ready to spit.

Brianna gagged at the stench but lifted her sword and charged side by side with Amon.

"Die!" he yelled.

Together they slashed at the Gomahras and dodged globs of spittle flying their way. Amon managed to inflict a fatal gash to the chest of one creature. It screeched its death throes as it bled goo all over the floor, but the second one managed to elude their slashing blades.

"Stand back!" Conal ordered as he twirled his slingshot carefully in the confined space.

As they backed away, Conal released the first green stone. It thumped into the Gomahra's head. A puff of orange smoke filled the enclosed space as the Gomahra exploded, and all that was left was a splotchy puddle of muck.

The remaining Gomahra spat a stream of muck before turning to run, but Conal had already reloaded. A green stone whizzed by. Conal's aim was deadly and the last Gomahra dissolved before it hit the floor.

Above them the castle creaked and groaned as parts of it collapsed. Huge blocks of stone crashed from overhead, partially blocking the corridors.

Sidestepping the puddles of dead Gomahra, the three of them raced down the narrow steps leading to the dungeons.

In the distance, a faint voice cried out.

"Mother?" Brianna yelled in answer.

"Down here, child. The end door."

Her mother stood stooped at the bars of a cramped cell lined with smelly straw. Congealed blood formed dark bracelets where the chains that bound her hands and feet had rubbed. Her delicate features were white and strained, her long blonde hair matted, but a fiery light lit her eyes as she fastened her gaze on her daughter.

Above them, the blocks of stone that made the castle grated together. Showers of pebbles and dust descended on them. Amon ignored it all as he picked at the lock with his sword. At last the lock clicked and the door swung open.

"Oh, Mam, I'm sorry!" Tears flowed down Brianna's cheeks as she felt the weakness of her mother's embrace.

Above the rattle of chains the castle screeched again.

"We haven't got much time!" Amon raised his sword and, with one well-aimed swipe, severed the chains holding the priestesses prisoner.

All around, the walls were sagging and contorting. Doorways crumbled as stones ground together and bulged out of line. Blocks of black rock swayed inward, narrowing the corridors.

"Hurry! It's going!" Amon yelled.

Everything shimmered, sharp edges softened, supports buckled. The rocks moaned and crunched all around them.

"It's caving in on us," Conal cried, but his footsteps only faltered briefly as he helped Tennille and another woman stagger along the narrow corridor.

Amon's voice steadied him. "Keep going, Conal. We're nearly there. Keep it up, Brianna," he said and smiled at her.

Her breath came in gasps as fear crawled over her skin. She tightened her hold around her mother's waist. "Hurry, Mam! Hurry."

In obvious pain, her mother tried to move faster. She clung to Brianna as they staggered up the steps, jumping over fissures that opened up in front of them without warning and dodging lumps of rock that tumbled from above.

Behind them great blocks of stone began to fill the corridor. In front of them the doorway distorted and narrowed. Amon pushed the women through one by one, and Conal followed.

Her da was waiting on the other side to help them through. Hakon and Issah stood beside him, their hands held high, faces pale and glistening with sweat at the strain of holding the castle together. Lek lifted Katrina into his arms and carried her out of danger before they embraced.

The stench was almost overwhelming as the black rock tumbled into an untidy heap. A cloud of dust filled the air as the grinding and moaning died into heavy silence. It didn't take ages for the dust to settle, and all that remained of Zelig's castle was a blackened patch at the center of a newly sprouting meadow. Brianna stared at the remains with a sense of disbelief. It was finally over.

Issah almost knocked Brianna over as she pounced on her and wrapped her in a bear hug. "You're safe, sister. We were just barely holding the castle, but you're safe. Everyone is safe. It's over."

Dirty and haggard, his clothes torn and grubby, the mayor straightened his back and walked regally forward. With Amon's help, he climbed onto a large boulder.

He held his hands out to the people of the two villages with tears tumbling down his ruddy cheeks. "Conal, my son," he boomed, grabbing his startled boy and pulling him roughly against his chest, "and his friends have saved us from the horrors of an evil no good citizen could imagine. We are now free to return home."

"Oh, Father!" Conal choked out between sobs.

Brianna turned and saw her mother clutched to Hakon's chest. Katrina sobbed as Hakon gently stroked her hair. Her stepfather stood silently beside them. Brianna watched the scene, suddenly swamped by confusion overlapped by a layer of sympathy for the man who was her da. He smiled at her and beckoned her over. She went reluctantly to her stepfather's side, feeling totally out of her depth seeing her mother in her biological father's arms for the first time. She wanted to hug them both together — if however briefly to be united as a family — but she felt a heavy weight of guilt about her stepfather's displacement.

Her stepfather placed his arm around her shoulders. "It's all right, Brianna. It's a family hug that is many cycles overdue." He pushed her forward and her parents opened their arms to include her in their embrace.

* * * *

With the balance between good and evil restored, it was time to celebrate, and Kenon Village did it in style. Nothing was said about Brianna's violation of the Destiny Books, even though she confessed all to her mother. Over the next few moons, she spent time with her Mam, Da and her life force-father, and was allowed to participate in the discussions about her future. Amon was welcomed into the family and their relationship sanctioned by all three adults — on one condition. She had to complete her training at the Crystal Castle before she and Amon made any serious commitment to each other. Brianna tried to argue against it, but she didn't have the heart for it really, because she thought it was sensible.

Besides, she had a sister, two brothers, a covenant mother *and* a father to get to know — a whole new family, in addition to perfecting squillions of magic spells, potions and powers in the next couple of moon cycles, not to mention capturing, killing or otherwise making harmless any evil Tyban that may have crossed unnoticed through the rift before it was sealed.

All too soon it was time to return to the Crystal Castle, and she bade a tearful goodbye to her mother and stepfather before she mounted Koshi behind her father. She waved frantically as they soared over the village, a mixture of emotions twisting around inside her as this new chapter in her life began. After the freeze cycle she would return for the birth of her new sibling, and to celebrate her own birth event with her mother, and perhaps her father, but in the meantime she had more than enough to keep her busy. The terrifying journey had brought her more than a father. It had shown her who she was, what she was capable of, and brought out an inner strength she'd never known she had. She was Brianna.

Glossary

Abrasaxon — good humanoids with magic (guardians of mortals)
Abrogative Direktorate — ruling council made up of six Archons
anjoa fruit — watermelon
Archon — Ruling Abrasaxon (royalty)
Black Mountains — Mountains where Tyban are banished to when they hurt mortals
breket — bacon
celinda trees — palm tree
chirum — male deer
Circle of Fledglings — Initiate priestesses
cycle rotation — a year
Destiny Books — ancient texts similar to a bible to guide mortals through life
dizan liquid — brandy
doffer brambles — blackberry bushes
domnak — donkey
elsuda — insects

firozt — frog
flemiko — butterfly
flesh scavengers — vultures
flick-tongues — lizards
forum — town decision-making council made up of priestesses, and educated citizens to make decision about the town
fruition moon cycle — summer
gark tree — oak tree
gezz — bees
Gomahra — goblins
gort — cow
hojack — crows
ice cycle — winter
kachine — mosquitoes
Keeper of the Wisdom — a wise woman of magic who, records legends, heals people and usually has some Abrasaxon blood.
Latidon — Hakon's older brother
leperatic disease — disease caught fromallows Gomahras to t. Transforms victims into a Gomahras.
moon cycle — a season
night hoots — owls
Nixets — pixies
Okana — Twin land with Okiyarra - Brianna's home
Okiyarra — Twin land with Okana
ozina — water lily
qymaten — fish
Reaping moon cycle — autumn
red moon's eclipse — a curse, "for goodness' sake"
Retreat — a nunnery
Sacred Mountains — mountains dividing Okana and Okiyarra where the Abrasaxon reside
Saquin — humanoid tyban

Scorpion's Heart Syniah — large white flower with great healing and magical powers

shandina — birds

skerry rats — rats

Sokomara — large dragon-like creature

sonats — bats

suka — silver

Sun cycle — a day

sun show — sunrise

syniah — flower

tahua — hare

taraqu — snake

teklicks — crickets

ternot — willy wag tail (bird)

terrates — chooks

tolufa fruit — coconut

Tomatite — green stone that kill Gomahras

tunnel diggers — moles

Tyban — evil humanoids with black magic

Watchers — mortals who work with Abrasaxon to monitor Tyban activity

weeper — corn

wekaza — spider

Wet moon cycle — spring

Whituka — monsters of varying types

Yabix — alien monster

zeppler — squirrel

zletic — gold

About the Author

Dionie was a closet writer for several years before she got brave enough to share her work with anyone until she joined Eyre Writers Inc, a creative writing group in the seaside town of Port Lincoln and really began to improve.

Her first book was a 100,000 words family saga novel, but after studying children's literature at university she embarked on a new direction—writing a young adult fantasy novel.

After being made redundant from the job she loved in 2011 she became a carer for her frail, vision-impaired mother and turned to fulfilling her dream of becoming a writer.

When Dionie is not writing she enjoys spending time with family and friends, especially her mother, and three wonderful adult children and adorable grandchildren. She also enjoys egg decorating and carving, reading of course, painting, gardening and cooking.

Dionie currently lives in the beautiful 'city of churches', Adelaide South Australia.

Dionie loves to hear from readers. You can find her contact information, website details author profile page at http://www.finch-books.com.